FOUR DAYS

FOUR DAYS

A SIX-YEAR-OLD'S WORST NIGHTMARE

Original Manuscript by

Robert Schick

ISBN:	Hardcover	978-1-4257-6991-8
	Softcover	978-1-4257-6980-2

This book was printed in the United States of America.

To order additional copies of this book, contact:
Xlibris Corporation
1-888-795-4274
www.Xlibris.com
Orders@Xlibris.com
41844

This book (with the exception of the swear words which are way below her dignity and which certainly must have been inserted by a ghost writer, as I certainly should have known better!) is dedicated to my mother whom I lovingly and genuinely regard as 'The Fountain of All Wisdom' in my life and who has the grace to attribute those swears most likely to a typographical error rather than her son's bad manners. The reader can only imagine how lucky I have been to have her guidance.

Chapter 1

3:20 PM, Day 1

The 40-knot gale wind exploded the wave over the bow. The blinding sheet of salt spray felt like glass shards on the exposed skin of the two men, as the Coast Guard rigid inflatable crashed down the back of the roller and was wrenched violently to starboard. Seawater poured over the pontoon as the craft bucked then rose nose up into the next roller.

Arms cramping with strain and fatigue, Commander Lewis fought to control the helm as the ocean pounded them, relentless in her power to challenge anyone stupid enough to be out in these conditions. It was a contest, man against Nature, and man wasn't winning. The next wave hit them nearly broadside, tipping the craft dangerously close to capsizing, the extra water inside the inflatable now hampering maneuverability.

"Jesus, Tony, even a boxer gets a freakin' rest between rounds," he yelled, the words thrown back in his face by the gale. Lewis was strapped into place with the four-point safety harness, which was the only reason he was still at the helm. Gloucester Police Detective Tony Fiori nodded as he strained to look through the spray for the other boat. He hung on to the overhead steel roll bar, both arms vertical allowing the rain and sea spray to run down inside the sleeves of his Mustang survival suit before pooling in his boots. Nothing was dry. He had long since lost his hat to the wind; his eyes smarted from the salt water, his footing getting more treacherous.

They were positioned in the lee of Ten Pound Island, theoretically for protection from the full fury of the weather. Even so, the waves rolled in ceaselessly in five-foot patterns, the wind was increasing, and the light was rapidly disappearing. What wasn't concealed by the spray was beginning to be hidden by the fog. Visibility now measured in feet. And still no sign of the other boat.

This was one shitty place to wait for a drug bust.

"Can you believe I volunteered for this crap?" Lewis screamed. "Should have pulled rank and sent you out with Mallory."

"You would have missed all this fun, Commander. Gloucester weather can turn from miserable to deadly in a heartbeat, especially when the fog rolls in."

"I can believe it after seeing this shit. How long you want to hang out here?" yelled Lewis, still fighting the helm to keep the bow into the wind.

Fiori shook his head. "Drug dealers don't exactly call and make reservations. Could be any time now, if I make my guess. They might be assholes, but they won't risk the delivery if this storm worsens. Any more coffee?"

"Check in the foredeck locker. Should be some near the life jackets."

Fiori unclipped his safety line and went forward on all fours. As he reached the locker, a roller broke over the bow, drenching him, adding more seawater inside his boots. Fiori found the thermos and was working his way astern when the howling wind swung the inflatable broadside to the waves. The boat suddenly flipped up, throwing Fiori backwards across the hard flooring, onto the leeward pontoon, and over into the ocean.

Fiori grabbed frantically for anything near his hands, but found nothing. He went under, tried to kick to the surface and came up, only to hit his head on the under side of the inflatable. The boat had drifted over him. He was kicking with the waves but the boat was drifting right with him.

Lewis left the helm, released his own safety harness and reached over the pontoon, stabbing his hand blindly into the water to find Fiori while the inflatable swung wildly in the seas. Lewis knew Fiori had little time before the weight of the boat over him would mean certain death. That is, if he wasn't already gone! He thrust his hand under water again and again, finally touching something that felt like a gloved hand. He grabbed hold and hung on as his arm threatened to pull out of its socket.

The two men were joined in a death struggle: Lewis pulling in one direction, the tide and surf pulling Fiori in another. Finally, Fiori's head broke the surface. He gasped for air, but took in a face full of seawater, coughed violently, and went back under.

But Mother Nature was merciful this time. The waves took a brief rest; the inflatable came down the backside of the trough and Fiori floated out from under. At least his head was above water, but Lewis couldn't tell if Fiori was breathing or not. He was no longer coughing, or was he no longer breathing?

Lewis used the lull in the surf to haul Fiori over the side. Both men landed roughly before Lewis recovered his own balance enough to flip Fiori over on his back to begin CPR. Blood gushed from a gash in Fiori's forehead. Lewis tried frantically to get air in Fiori's lungs but time and again he had to break the rhythm to hold onto the gunwale so as not to be thrown overboard. Somehow he had the sense of mind to tie Fiori's still lifeless body to the roll bar.

"Damn it; breathe!" Lewis yelled, desperately pumping Fiori's chest. Seawater poured over the side as the boat was hit by a new wave pattern. Lewis looked up and saw they were out of the protective lee of Ten Pound Island and now drifting in the active shipping channel.

Lewis pressed again, frantic in his effort to get the man to breathe. Then, without any warning, Fiori threw up seawater and bile like nothing Lewis had ever seen. Coughing, thrashing, Fiori fought to free himself from the line he thought had trapped him under the craft.

"Easy, easy!" Lewis said. "I got you. You're back on board. Just breathe."

Fiori coughed more seawater up, rolled over on his side gasping and gasping. "Didn't think . . . I'd see . . . you again," he sputtered between gulps of air.

Fiori grabbed hold of the roll bar and pushed up on his knees, his chest heaving. The water was now several inches deep in the bottom of the boat and rising. Back at the helm, Lewis tried to power them into the wind. Too late, the propeller had snagged something, which was rapidly winding around the shaft.

Lewis heard the racing engines, but felt no forward movement. Fiori yelled back to him: "Cut the throttle fast! Your shaft is wound."

"Wound with what?" Lewis screamed back into the wind.

"Lobster trap line. It's dragging your stern under. Give me your Bowie. Quick!"

"You're crazy! You're bleeding."

"No time to argue. Give me your knife."

Lewis handed over the knife and cut power to the engines before he ground Fiori into hamburger with the twin props. Seconds seemed like days to Lewis who tried but couldn't see any part of Fiori's bright orange survival suit.

Just then, Lewis saw the knife break the water followed by the rest of the detective. This time Fiori and the boat were being carried in the same direction so dragging him over the pontoon was easier. Like saying wrestling a gorilla was easier than wrestling an elephant. Dead weight was dead weight, but Fiori was back on board and the propeller was free.

Lewis pressed the ignition button and the twin Evinrude 250's roared with power as he reached for the Ship to Shore. "Command, this is 338. Come in. damn it . . ."

Chapter 2

4:47 PM, Day 1

The CABA bus sprayed through the puddle and skidded to a stop on the gravel. The windshield wipers were barely able to handle the downpour, and Reggie Martin nearly missed seeing the figure at the unlit bus stop.

Carrie lurched forward, bumped her knee on the metal seat back and dropped her Scooby-Doo lunch box on the floor. She was the only passenger and was sitting with her little legs crossed in the same seat she always used, right by the door. As she reached for her lunch box, the bus door hissed open and smacked back against the guardrail by Carrie's book bag.

The wind-driven rain came through the open door like a fire hose; both Carrie and Reggie ducked away to avoid being showered. Both shouldn't have bothered. The front of the bus was instantly drenched. Hostile was too kind a description for the man who boarded. Carrie shrank down in her seat at the terrifying sight of those eyes, hooded, darting, angry, and the ugly scowl that came with them. Carrie pinched her nose closed over the stench of the man.

"Yuck!" she said out loud.

Reggie knew immediately he should have kept going. Belatedly, he hit the hydraulic button to close the door. Mistake number one. The man had anticipated the move and was already wedged against the door.

"Shit, man! You trying to keep me out in the rain, Mister?"

Reggie said nothing as the man took the final step up into the bus.

"My mommy said swearing isn't very nice," Carrie said, still holding her nose.

"Be quiet, Carrie," Reggie shushed. He was wheezing more noticeably.

"Well, now isn't this sweet, Miss Manners in the pink raincoat." The man pulled a dog-eared photo out of his jacket pocket, smiled and put it back. "Let me guess; you must be MacKenzey's little girl. Have I got that right?"

Carrie stared at him, not realizing that her silence confirmed what the man wanted to know.

Twisting slightly to hide what he was doing, Reggie slid his left hand towards the red button to send an emergency signal back to the terminal on Pond Road. Mistake number two. The man saw what he was doing in the ceiling mirror near the open door, whirled, and gave Reggie a vicious backhand to his jaw, sending blood, spit and a chipped tooth against the windshield. Without thinking, Reggie grabbed for the cleaning cloth to stop the bleeding. Mistake number three. The cloth was stuffed in the dashboard right next to the emergency button.

"Are you stupid enough not to have understood the first time?" the man asked, yanking the Scooby lunch pail out of the girl's hand and smashing it down on Reggie's fingers.

"Mister, that's my lunch pa . . ."

"I told you: Don't do nothin' stupid," the man said to Martin, interrupting Carrie mid sentence. "Should have listened."

"I didn't do nothin' stupid; I was reaching for the cloth."

"Yeah, sure, and I don't got eyes!" The man moved towards the girl.

"Listen, kid: you are coming with me and you ain't going to need that lunch pail where we're going, so forget about it."

As the man reached for her, Carrie skidded further down in the seat, just out of his reach. "Who says I won't need my lunch pail anymore? I need it everyday."

"Shut up, kid. I don't need your sass. Come here! Now!" Carrie held her book bag closer to her chest.

"Leave the girl alone. I'm just taking her home." Reggie's voice was close to a whisper. The pain in his arm was spreading up his shoulder.

"You ain't doing nothin' of the sort, man. She is going where I say, and it ain't home."

The man dropped the lunch box and went for the girl. Carrie hit the stranger with all the fury of a six-year old. She tried to get under the seat, but he pulled her up. She threw her arms at him, arching her back and twisting away. She reached for the safety railing and tried to kick him away.

It was no match. She scratched him, but the man simply overpowered her. He put her under his arm, but as he started down the stairs, Carrie swung her book bag at the man's face, connected with his ear and knocked him off balance into the mirror, which broke and cut his forehead. Her effort was to no avail. The man fled into the rain carrying Carrie under his arm and threw her hard into the backseat of the car waiting on the corner. No one saw them drive off.

Reggie's gasping became louder as he made one final effort to get the button. He was dizzy; the edges of his eyesight were black, out of focus. His chest felt like it had exploded, because it had. Reggie never felt his lifeless finger fall on the emergency button.

Chapter 3

4:05 PM, Day 1

"Roger 338; command here," Master Chief Jones answered.

"On my way back," Lewis yelled into the mouthpiece. "Fiori has a head wound that's going to need immediate attention. He will need an ambulance."

"Roger that, Sir. What's your ETA?"

"Should be there within six to seven minutes. Have your crew at the wharf."

"We'll be there, Sir. Over."

Jones hit the station emergency alert button. He was putting on his foul weather gear as the on-call men ran into the Command Center.

"Commander Lewis is en route back from the outer harbor with a passenger with an unspecified head wound. Must be serious as he requested an ambulance. Grab your gear and meet me at the wharf ten minutes ago. Their ETA is less than five minutes so move your asses."

Jones was pulling his headset on as he reached the door. "Billy: get an ambulance here then call the hospital. Tell them to expect a serious head injury within the next twenty to thirty minutes. Got that?"

"Roger that, Master Chief".

But Jones never heard the reply; he was already out the door running down the ramp to the wharf.

He realized immediately that the tide, having been driven into the inner harbor by a full moon and the fury of the storm, was higher than he would have expected. The wharf, sturdily constructed with steel support beams, still seemed to rise and fall with the surges as the angry water pulsed up through the planks, washing the wharf in foam, seaweed and flotsam, coating it with the head of a good malt ale. Like being on the deck of a submerging submarine, Jones thought, half expecting the call to clear the deck: Diving now! Diving now!

The medic team and three on-duty sailors reached the wharf seconds after their Master Chief. The two medics, struggling with the metal gurney and the blankets blowing in the gale, tried to muscle the stretcher into the wind to make it easier to handle. The other three were well drilled in emergency landings and positioned themselves with throwing lines whose ends had been cleated off to prevent them from falling in the water if Lewis missed the toss. Danger hung in the air like wet laundry. The wharf was awash, the tide rolling along the planks meant this was going to be no easy drill. Bad footing could mean injury, maybe even death if someone slipped and got crushed between the inflatable and the pylons. Timing would be critical: either rescue or more disaster.

Tense with expectation, Jones began barking orders into the wind: "Ready stern and bow lines and two mid-ship spring lines. Here's the sequence: stern line first; port mid-ship spring line second. Soon as its secure, throw the bowline. Don't under throw in this wind. Make fast the 6-ounce weight on the free ends so Commander Lewis can grab them.

"Medics: ready your APRAB. Tie off the free ends to those two cleats so you don't lose the patient." Jones pointed to the iron cleats on the edge of the wharf. "We are going to have to secure Fiori tightly before we off-load him. For Christ's sake, watch your step in this mess."

"Aye, Master Chief," the men snapped in unison.

Jones knew his team was skilled, but, nevertheless, he ran through the training sequence of the All Purpose Rescue Bag in his mind to make sure he hadn't missed anything. The medics were going to have to jump aboard the pitching inflatable, tear apart the heavy Velcro straps, load the patient in between the two layers of mesh, re-close the Velcro, and manhandle the results back onto the wharf. Jones knew that even though the APRAB was designed like an Oreo cookie with the patient sandwiched between the woven nylon mesh that was secured with wide strips of Velcro, he easily could still lose the patient if anything went wrong. After all, this was a government design.

One of the medics asked: "Master Chief, should I load a back board?"

"Not a good idea in this wind," Jones answered. "Could sail and throw you off balance. We'll have to risk not using one." Immediately he heard the roar of the twin 250's He shouted, "Heads up; she's coming in. Ready all lines. Make your first throw your best one, men. There will be no time for second chances. Stern line first! Brace your feet. Give me all loose coil on the throw. Ready?"

Commander Lewis came into view around the edge of the wharf, working both throttles deftly, trying to match boat speed, surf roll and the closing distance to avoid a crash. Forward port throttle; back starboard; forward both. Lewis was coming in too fast and throttled back hard on the port side engine to swing the bow to the left. The boat, slammed by a trailing roller, raised, tilted dangerously as the whole side was exposed to the rising gale. Fiori was thrown against the bow locker. Lewis swung the helm to port in a final attempt to control-crash the wharf and pin the inflatable to the pylons long enough to grab the first line.

"Loose the stern line NOW!" yelled Jones just as Lewis hit the pylons, but the wind took the stern line out of Lewis's reach. He let go the helm to grab the line, but slipped as the bow swung out and away from the wharf. He had to make an instant choice: line or helm? Jones made it for him. "Spin your helm hard to port, Sir, then grab the line. NOW!"

Lewis obeyed, threw the helm over, came close enough to be boarded, brought the bow back in tight and left the throttles engaged as he grabbed the line and secured the stern. For the moment, anyway, he had made land.

Jones jumped aboard, followed instantly by his mate who skidded into the roll bar, lost his footing and pulled Jones with him as they slid across the wet flooring of the inflatable. Recovering, both men moved towards the unconscious man as a gust of wind swung the nose of the craft away from the wharf.

"Grab your helm, Sir. Port full rudder; half forward starboard throttle. HURRY! Nose in. Grab the bow line!"

As the nose of the inflatable inched back into the wind and towards the wharf, the third seaman tossed over the final line, which Jones caught, brought up the slack smartly, made it fast and went back to the helm. Lewis threw the throttles into neutral, left them in idle until everything was tied off and went back to the stern line to snug it up. The tide pushed him away and the turbulence of the waves gave him no secure footing for leverage. His muscles strained as he propped his feet against the gunwale and threw his whole back into each pull. Timing his effort with the receding wave, Lewis finally brought the stern in, cleating it quickly before the incoming wave could pull him away again.

The medics and Jones had slid Fiori into the mesh sandwich and were flattening the Velcro closures as Lewis jumped to the wharf to help with the transfer. The two men on board got Fiori up on their knees as Lewis and the others reached out to catch the leading edge of the APRAB. There was too much fabric for a good hold and only Jones had any control. The unconscious detective slid towards them on a rising wave and the bag slid out of their hands. Fiori smacked down on the gunwale just as Jones and Lewis pulled back hard, barely managing to keep Fiori on board.

"Christ" yelled the corpsman. "Watch his neck!"

"Roll the edges into a tube so we have something to hold onto" shouted Lewis. "Are the safety lines secured?"

"Aye, Sir."

"Then let's try again. Get him on your knees. Steady. Steady. Watch the wave. Now. Pass him now! Grab the tube. Jones: follow him on. Now. Come NOW!"

As the wave raised the inflatable, with three men pulling and two pushing, the team stepped onto the gunwale, quickly onto the wharf and placed the bag, with Fiori still safely in it, down hard on the gurney and made for the shelter of the station. The up hill grade was taxing; the men were breathing hard as the medic ran along side trying to get a pulse on Fiori.

Jones ripped open the Velcro tab then the collar of the survival suit and put his fingers on Fiori's neck. "There's a pulse, weak, but there. He needs the hospital."

The team reached the large, swinging doors of the station and pushed through into the protection of the garage. Inside, out of the howling wind and the driving rain, the tension seemed to instantly ease as the men no longer had to fight the weather and the gurney. The tension for everyone except the medics, that is. They swung into well-rehearsed action.

The top half of the APRAB mesh was pulled off and cast aside. Not daring to move Fiori any more than necessary, the medic opened the jacket put his stethoscope under his shirt and listened to the heartbeat. The other medic put a neck splint on the sergeant, checked again to make sure the airway was clear and put on an oxygen mask. Fiori was still out.

"90 over 60 and not steady. We've got shock here. This head wound has bleed like hell."

"Any other wounds?" Jones asked.

The medic moved his hands under Fiori's torso to the back of his neck. "Nothing sticky," he announced.

In quick succession, the two medics worked to stabilize Fiori; they started an IV drip and elevated the patient's legs to prevent further shock.

"We won't lose him, Jonesie, but I'd be happier if a real doc took over before his signs drop any further."

"Roger that. The ambulance is en route. It will be here by the time we wheel him out front."

They reached the entrance just as the ambulance was backing in, its red light flashing against the building. Jones succinctly summarized the patient's conditions and treatment then backed out of the way as the ambulance crew took over, slamming the doors and speeding out towards the hospital.

4:27 PM, Day 1

Meanwhile, on the other side of the harbor, within hailing distance of where Lewis and Fiori had been moored minutes earlier, the sleek cigarette boat rafted alongside the beat-up lobster boat, off loaded five heavy bails, and, in less than three minutes, turned to head out of the harbor. The lobsterman threw nets over the bails, then lashed lobster traps down on top of his new cargo. The driving rain and early darkness were good cover as he turned his stern to the heavy rollers, motoring downwind towards the protection of Smith Cove.

4:58 PM, Day 1

Back at the CABA terminal, the day shift was ending. Most of the telephone operators had put their headsets down and were in varying stages of fixing their hair, putting on lipstick or gabbing loudly about the errands they had to do before dinner.

The only thing Dan wanted to gab about was where the new trainee would meet him for dinner and for whatever afterwards. The tight sweater she wore was . . . distracting. How the hell could she hold those things in place without a bra? *Wish my buses had such structural integrity*, he mused.

But that was a problem for another day. Right now, Dan wanted to go home but couldn't, because there was one bus still out on route. Where the hell were old man Reggie Martin and bus number 39? He was ten minutes late and showing no sign of coming in.

Just then, the piercing siren of the emergency alarm went off. That had to be Martin! Dan ran to the desk to get to the phone "Reggie, come in", Dan yelled. "MARTIN? ARE YOU THERE? PICK UP THE PHONE!" No answer. Why didn't Martin pick up?

On the run through the garage, Dan grabbed his rain slicker and patted the pocket to check for his cell phone. As the door opened, he was hit in the face by the driving rain.

Ten years of running this small transportation company on Cape Ann, 30-plus miles up the coast from Boston. Mostly keeping 48 buses one-step away from the bus graveyard was a full time nightmare: make-do was his lead mechanic. But for all that, Dan still loved the one machine he'd never begin to understand: the ocean. Just as soon as she seemed predictable, she'd throw a wave pattern at you that would hurl a ten-pound gear housing at you or fill your fishing nets so full of cod that you'd strain those same gears trying to haul in the load. And the next day? She'd leave you with nothing but seaweed and broken urchins in your nets and bills in your pockets. Go figure. Typical female, he thought.

But that was exactly why he'd settled back in this New England seacoast town. The smell of salt air. The rolling of the ocean. The sand squishing between your toes. The softness of the fog on your face. Nothing like it. But the smell: no one from Kansas could understand the smell of the sea: one part salt, one part fish, one part mystery, one part freedom. Put them together with a quartering breeze off the beam and you could understand the lure of the ocean. Maybe then you also could understand the mystery that was strong enough to take a perfectly sane man from the warmth of home (and the tight sweater he was just musing about) and toss him out in the cold, angry surf where a wrong step could kill.

There's an enigma for you, Dan thought as the garage door lifted into the overhead tracks. He turned on the yellow blinkers on the roof of the truck and sped out to find Martin. The old rumor surfaced in his mind, the one that claimed his buses were used to move heroin around the Cape. It was nothing that he had been able to confirm, but the tightness in his stomach warned him that he might find proof tonight.

Chapter 4

4:48 PM, Day 1

Laurie MacKenzey told herself she was beyond stress. Working two jobs since getting a divorce kept her barely above breakdown level. Barely in control of her anger, she had no patience, no time for her daughter, no time for herself. Her schedule had schedules and free time wasn't even on the list. Living wasn't on there either. Existing had taken over. Managing the small insurance office was simple, predictable and boring, but at least the money was steady. Even so, though, she was constantly running out of money before the month ran out of days.

So about four months ago, Laurie had started working on the side as an associate for one of the smaller realtors while she studied for her own real estate license. In fact, she had her first closing in about twenty minutes.

Her cell phone rang. "Hi," she said with professional cheeriness, "this is Laurie MacKenzey."

"Laurie: Janet. Where's the payoff summary from the bank?"

"I left it by my printer."

"Well, unless your printer has teeth and ate it, it isn't here and we can't close without it."

Janet was Laurie's mentor, a senior broker who for the fifth straight year was the only female member of the President's Round Table for selling over $3,000,000 of property in the previous twelve months. "Listen, Laurie: this is too big a deal to screw up with fifteen minutes to go. You get here and find it. Now."

"Janet, Carrie's bus was due ten minutes ago. I'm at the stop now and only three minutes from the office. I'll be there before Blanchford even shows up."

"You can't; he's here now and he's leaving right away for Europe. He has to be out of here no later than 5:20. No mortgage summary, no completed documents. No completed documents, no closing. No closing, no commission. Do you see where this is going?"

"I'll be there as fast as I can; this isn't my fault." Janet's good, thought Laurie, but Queen Bitch had a new contender when it came time to getting her commission. "I can do the form over if I have to. Can you call the bank to get the figures faxed over?"

"Laurie, have you lost it? The mortgage office closed at 3:30." Janet slammed down the phone.

Laurie said "I'm sorry, Janet" to a dial tone and threw the cell onto the passenger seat. "Where the hell is the bus? Of all days . . . I don't need this right now." The windshield wipers swished, swished, squeaking with an annoying screech on the down stroke as Laurie drummed the steering wheel and checked her watch. Ten seconds later than the last time she looked.

Times had really changed in the last 18 months, she thought, going from no need for a job and plenty of free time to two jobs and no free time. *I flunked wife and now I'm flunking Mom, and probably just flunked a future in real estate.*

"Where's this stinking bus?" Laurie asked the front windshield. Not able to wait any longer, Laurie put the car in gear, turned the wipers to high, and set out to drive the bus route in reverse, praying she wouldn't miss the bus in this rain.

Chapter 5

5:05 PM, Day 1

"Jeeze, Rocker, what the hell took you so long?"

"Ran into a little delay. Stupid bus driver thought he was a hero. Fixed his ass. Shit, it's wet out there." Rocker shook the rain off his cammie jacket, splattering water over the dashboard and the front seat. As he pulled open the snaps to get at his cigarettes, he sprayed more water over the map that was on the seat and on the driver, who started to swat Rocker's arm away, saw the look on his friend's face and kept quiet.

"Ah, look what you done, man," Rick moaned. "The ink's already running. That's our only directions, Rocker; you get that paper too wet, we ain't never going to find the cabin."

"You're always worrin', Rick! I know where we're going. Been there once anyway just to make sure," Rocker paused to light his cigarette. "Besides, when's the last time I ever got you lost? Huh? Tell me! Who pulled your butt outta trouble how many times? Huh? Shit, there's like a compass in my head, man. Point my nose at it and I'll find anything."

Rocker, whose real name was Paul Connor, let his thoughts drift back to why he was there. He'd been a drifter, broken family, lots of short term jobs of no particular substance: waiter, bartender, even worked changing oil at a national franchise. While there, he had noticed a leak in a head gasket, pointed it out to the owner, and saved the guy a bundle in engine repair.

Turned out the customer ran his own business, was looking for a mechanic, and hired him. Rocker was a good mechanic, intuitive, clever and had a knack for sensing when equipment was about to fail. It didn't take long before the machinists, who competed for his time, recognized his talent. Rocker went from mechanic to lead mechanic, to section chief, to shift supervisor, and was in line for plant foreman when problems started happening. The boss, MacKenzey, called Connor into his office at the end of a shift.

Leaning back in the seat and taking a deep drag on the cigarette, Rocker replayed that conversation for, what, the millionth time . . . ?

"Close the door, Paul. You want coffee?"

"No thanks, Mr. Mac. Been a long day."

"Actually that's why I wanted to talk with you: It seems we're having too many long days. I'm getting too many complaints, Paul, and they're all in your area. What's going on?"

"I can't explain it, Mr. Mac. Seems like no matter what I do, the next day it goes to shit."

"Let me tell you, Paul; I got machinists who don't want you touching their machines, griping that it's costing them money every time you work on them. So guess what, Paul: it costs them money, it costs me money. How the hell am I supposed to keep machinists when their gear goes down the shit hole? You tell me."

"You can't, Mr. Mac; I know that."

"Well, why the hell aren't you doing something about it?"

"Are you sayin' I'm not doin' anything?"

"I'm saying that what you're doing isn't working and it's beginning to cost me where it hurts. Whatever is happening with your work, Paul, has got to be fixed. And fixed right now. You understand?"

"Mac, are you accusing me of doin' bad work? Cuz if you are, you're fulla shit!" Connor leaned over the front of the desk, eyes flaming.

"Hold on, Connor; let's . . ."

"Hold on yourself. I don' gotta take this shit from no one!"

MacKenzey bolted out from behind his desk, grabbed Connor by the shirt and pulled the man towards him. "You're not on thin ice any more, Connor; you just fell through. You're fired! Get outa here. You're finished." Pushing Connor away, MacKenzy shouted, GUARD!" through the glass door. "Take this man to the door and make damn sure he stops nowhere between here and there."

"Yes, Mr. MacKenzey. Let's go, Paul."

The security guard went to grab Connor's arm but the smaller man pushed him away and started towards MacKenzey yelling "You bastard. You can't fire me. I ain't done nothin' wrong. You're blamin' the wrong person."

He swung a fist at MacKenzey. Ducking under the punch, MacKenzey came up fast, head-butted Connor on the chin, spun him around and threw him to the floor.

"Cuff him," MacKenzey said to the guard.

"Fuck off, man." Connor yelled at the guard. Turning back to MacKenzey, he spat, "Fuck you, too, MacKenzey. You shit. You got no idea who you're dealing with. You ain't finished with me yet, Not by a fuckin' mile, you ain't!"

#

And it hadn't been his fault. "It's been a long time, Rick," Rocker said. "I bet that bastard MacKenzey thought I had forgotten."

Chapter 6

5:10 PM, Day 1

Carpenter had the wipers on top speed, the defroster blasting on high, but he still had to wipe the windshield with his hat to be able to see out. Could miss an aircraft carrier in this weather, he thought as he turned off Blackburn Circle onto the extension of 128. The light at the bottom of the hill was in his favor but he still slowed, turning to see if one of Gloucester's other drivers was going to run the red light. The street was narrow and twisted around street lights and a house or two that had been built a hundred years ago close to the dirt road for the horses, but much too close to the road that had long since been paved.

Just past the variety store, where the road widened enough to allow a bus to squeeze in by the curb, Dan saw the taillights of the CABA bus blinking orange as he pulled in behind it. He slammed the shift into park and put his own emergency lights on. Dan couldn't see any passengers on the bus as he walked down to the front door. Why was the engine racing so? Strange, he thought. And why was the door open in this weather?

As Dan reached for the handle to pull himself up onto the steps, the answer was obvious. Broken glass covered the steps, and his driver was slumped over, his boot jamming the accelerator to the floor. Reggie's right hand was mangled, dripping blood on the rubber gasket of the gearshift. Dan felt for a pulse but knew immediately that the man was dead. The disgusting smell of urine and feces confirmed that.

Dan grabbed his phone, dialed 911 and turned to see if anyone was in the bus, when he was startled by a shriek behind him.

"Is he dead?"

He twisted back towards the door to see a woman holding her hands over her mouth, her eyes wide with fright. She backed into the dark and repeated her question:

"Oh, my God, is the driver dead?"

"911.Gloucesterpolicestation,sergeantIacona.You'reonarecordedline. Goahead."

"This is Dan Car . . ."

"Is who dead? Who is that speaking?" the cop on the switchboard demanded.

"Don't come up here, Ma'am. We have a problem here. Sergeant, I'm Dan Carpenter owner of CABA and I'm at stop 18 on East Main and . . ."

"Where is my daughter?" the woman demanded, pushing to get by Carpenter. She shoved hard against the man standing in her way.

"Give me a minute, lady! I'm talking to the police. Get back. Now!" he commanded. "Sergeant, send a car here. It's too late for an ambulance but you're going to need one. My cell phone number is . . . ."

The woman pushed, more weakly this time; her shoulders shuddered with her sobbing.

"978 . . ."

"I got it, Carpenter. You're on caller ID. Squad car's en route. Keep the woman out of that bus and get out yourself. Don't touch a damn thing. Nothing!"

"Yes, I got it." He switched off and held out his arms to block the woman from climbing further onto the steps. "We can't go in there. Police orders. Come with me to the truck."

"I have to see if my daughter is in there." Just as Dan thought this couldn't get any worse, the woman stuck her head around his arms and screamed again.

"That's her Scooby lunch box!"

She went limp in Dan's arms. He hadn't seen it before but there, just behind the driver's seat, on the floor was a smashed child's lunch box, dry blood visible on the corner. All of a sudden, Dan knew he had more than the death of his driver on his hands. His mind flipped into high speed, working through what could have happened. It was enough of a disaster with Reggie being dead, a total nightmare if the woman's child were dead also. Who else could be hurt? How many other passengers were there? Were they alive? Did anyone see what happened?

Still carrying the half-conscious woman, Dan awkwardly kicked open the passenger door and placed her on the seat of his truck. The siren of the arriving squad car shrilled as Dan turned to meet them.

5:21 PM, Day 1

Three people jumped out of the police car, their trained eyes taking in the condition of the woman in the truck and the man backing out of the side door.

"Hey, Dan" said the driver, Peter Amero. He and Carpenter played basketball together at the Y in the Over 40 league. "You know officer Santinello and Detective Fiori?" motioning to the man and woman in turn. "What've you got here?"

Detective Naomi Little Bird Fiori listened intently as Dan quickly summarized what he had found not four minutes earlier.

"Santinello," Amero directed, "put cones and flares in front and behind the bus, and move the woman's car out of the way." Meanwhile, he phoned for another squad car.

Her trained eyes taking in all the details of the crime scene, Naomi made her own call to the station to report in:

"We've got a problem out here, Chief: one driver dead, maybe murdered; one school girl missing, maybe kidnapped, but maybe just missing in the area; and one hysterical mother on scene, no maybe about hysterical."

"Who is she?" Chief Marren asked.

"Laurie MacKenzey, missing girl's mother. You better send the crime scene unit out, Chief, and the coroner as soon as he can get here. It may already be too late, but we should have the two major roads off-island blocked and the other patrol cars alerted to a possible kidnapping."

"Will do, Naomi, but "If we are facing a kidnapping, the man or men have a 15-25 minute lead and in 25 minutes, the child could be nearly in New Hampshire, way beyond a local roadblock."

"You're probably right, Chief, but I still think you better order it anyway. Oh, and, Chief, you need to be out here."

"On my way

Naomi slipped latex gloves on as she carefully stepped around the glass on the stairs and moved over to push the driver's foot off the accelerator pedal. She turned off the engine and began to go over what had happened. She could see the injury on the driver's head, the broken fingers on the right hand and what could be blood on the frame of the broken mirror. Returning to the maintenance truck, Naomi found the woman slumped over in the front seat, head in hands, tears running through her fingers.

"Ms. MacKenzey?"

The woman looked up. "I'm Detective Naomi Fiori. I need to speak with you," Naomi said in a gentle voice. "I know you are upset, but I need your help."

"Of course. Anything. Oh, God, I can't lose her."

"Please tell me about her . . . your daughter?

"Carrie. She's only six. Carrie is supposed to be on the bus and she isn't and I don't know where she is and what if she's missing . . . ?" Laurie MacKenzey started to cry again and Naomi put her hands on the woman's shoulders and waited.

"Ms. MacKenzey, is this Carrie's normal stop?"

"No, I was waiting at the stop and she didn't come. I'm needed back at the office and rather than waiting, I thought I could drive the route backwards to school to see if I could find the bus . . . and I got this far . . . and . . . oh, I can't lose her."

"How old is Carrie" May I call you Laurie?"

"Of course; she's six. A cute little six-year old and my whole life."

"Do you know for certain she was on this bus and that she didn't go home with a friend?

Laurie started to cry again. "I saw her lunch box. It's all smashed in on the floor of the bus."

Naomi hadn't met Laurie MacKenzey before, but learned that she worked at a local insurance company, found out she was recently divorced and liked Laurie even more as soon as she had put two and two together and realized who her ex was. She got a very thorough description of little Carrie and what she had worn to school that day just as Chief Marren arrived.

"Hate to tell you this, Naomi," announced Marren before she could start. "Tony isn't coming. He is on the way to the hospital with his head cut up."

"What happened?" she gasped.

"You know he was out with the Coasties looking for the drug delivery we heard was going down today. Guess he got knocked overboard. Tried to lower the harbor by drinking most of it. Lost some blood and is at the ER as we speak. So the case is yours, until he is back."

"Is his wound serious?"

"Commander Lewis didn't know, but thought he only needed some stitches. You know how hard his head is anyway!"

She nodded with a tight smile. Naomi and Tony were the best detective team Gloucester had ever had. Between the two of them, she outside and he inside, they could read a crime scene as if they had scripted it.

But right now, no crime scene was as important as her husband. She stepped aside, dialed the Emergency Room number from memory, reached the intake clerk and instructed her to wait until she got there before any final treatment was given to her husband. Most ER staff would have ignored such a call outright, but Naomi's training as a Passamaquoddy Shaman was well respected in this hospital.

Satisfied for the moment, she hurried to finish in order to get to the hospital.

"Are you going to call in the Feds?" she asked Marren.

"Already did when Peter told me we had a possible kidnapping. They're just waiting for me to confirm it. What's your take?"

"The driver's dead, Chief, but there is not enough evidence to tell me he was murdered. The wound on his forehead might have dazed him but I don't think the blow was hard enough to kill him. I mean, he was hit with a tin lunch pail, not something heavy. I don't think he was shot but I won't pull him off the wheel until the coroner gets here."

"Reggie Martin, wasn't it?" asked Marren.

"According to Carpenter."

"Last I saw of Martin he was pushing his luck and 3-400 pounds at the same time. Could have died of an overload on his ticker."

"Could be. Doc Mathison will tell us soon enough. Listen, I'll check again with the ER to see if I can stay until he gets here. As soon as I can get away, I need to be at the hospital."

"Go to it."

She nodded. "Thanks. Maybe Amero can find out about Martin. Feels like he's just a victim, but we should check to see if there're any problems at CABA that we don't know about. Anyone out for him personally. Any threats. He knows the drill, anything he can dig up that might help. By the way, have you got the state Blue's on the roadblocks?"

"Done, and our guys on Blyman and 128. Completely shut down. I told DPW to raise the Blyman drawbridge so no one could get by. We're searching every car, period. Right now, only way they're getting off this island is by boat. And I've told the Coast Guard to close off the mouth of the harbor at the breakwater and board anything that attempts to leave the harbor."

"So you mean the good news is that we only have to search 29,000 homes and 33 square miles between here and Rockport?" Naomi asked with a grimace.

"Yup, and do it before anything happens to the girl."

"Amen." Naomi stripped off the gloves as she strode back to the squad car.

Chapter 7

5:10 PM, Day 1

"Let's haul ass, Rick," Carpenter instructed as he jumped into the passenger seat. The car was moving before he slammed the door and turned to check the girl in the back seat. "We've got maybe five minutes to get off island before shit hits the fan."

Pinto nodded, took a quick look at the kid in the rearview mirror, and stomped on the accelerator. After leaving the bus behind, Pinto handled the old Plymouth through the rain and the increasingly deeper puddles without incident. Without incident outside the car, that is. Inside was another story. Initially quiet in the back seat, the little girl seemed to regain her temper after a couple of minutes. Pinto watched her toss her head, her mouth pinched to one side. Carrie kept cutting her eyes towards the door. She looked up to see Pinto in the rear view mirror and raised her eyebrow, as if to say 'are you going to stop me?'

Seconds later, as Pinto slowed for a stop sign on Bass Avenue, Carrie reached for the door handle and was halfway out the door before Rocker reacted. He reached over the seat, just catching the collar of her raincoat, and hauled her back inside.

"Listen girl, try that again and I'm gonna cuff you one. Now sit still, you hear me?"

Carrie didn't answer, but Pinto could see her glance moving around the back seat, probably judging her situation when she didn't think he noticed. Pretty cool for a little kid, Pinto thought. Seemed like she was older than second grade but that could be just the way she sat so straight, determined almost.

"OK, Rocker. Where to?"

"We need to get to the cabin, but if that damn bus driver hit the alarm without me seeing him, we could have cops all over the place any minute. See if we can get over the bridge."

Pinto made it through the first traffic rotary and headed down the hill to Grant Circle. He calculated the time since they left the bus and figured there was time for the cops to react, but just barely enough. They had a pretty good chance of making it without being stopped.

But he hadn't counted on cops being at the hospital. Alerted to a possible kidnapping, the patrol car had left the ER and in less than a minute was parked across the middle of the two outbound lanes of 128, blue flashers on high. Pinto could see two cops flagging down cars on the opposite side of the circle.

"They got us blocked, Rocker. I can't run it. If we get stopped, there ain't no way we're getting by with the kid in the back."

Rocker had seen the cop car at the same time. "Hang a right here before we reach the cops. Head toward the hospital. Be cool. Nothin' fast."

Pinto was in the left lane, but to get onto Washington Street he had to cross in front of the stopped car on the right. Just as he started up, Carrie made another dash to the door and had it half-opened as Pinto hit the breaks. "Get the kid!" he yelled to Rocker.

Rocker turned to hit the lock, but Carrie was too quick. She had her head out the door and was swinging her feet out by the time Rocker could jam his fingers into the space between the glass and the door, getting just enough of a purchase to pull the door back. Carrie yelped, pulled her feet up and just barely missed having them caught in the door. Rocker backhanded the girl across the cheek. She let out a scared wail. Swerving to avoid the car on the right, Pinto swore: "Rocker, you promised me not to hurt the kid."

"I didn't hurt her; she's faking. Just drive!"

"She almost got outta the car, man. You get in the back and watch her. Sure as shit hope those people in the car didn't see her."

"No way they saw anything. Just get us outta here. I'll worry about the kid." Leaning over the seat, Rocker said, "Try that again, kid, an' I'm really gonna hit you."

Pinto power slid around the car on the right, heading north down Washington away from the traffic circle and the flashing blue lights.

5:11 PM, Day 1

The driver of the car on the right, Harold Granger, jammed his breaks on as the gray Plymouth cut him off. His wife, Nellie, who had never driven a car in her life but who never let that small detail ever stop her from giving her husband instructions, thrust her hands against the dashboard, breaking a nail before she was jerked back by her seat belt.

"Harold, watch out! Didn't you see that driver?" she demanded.

"Yes, dear." Harold rolled his eyes like he always did. Nellie saw him like she always did. "Don't you roll your eyes at me, Harold Granger!

"Yes, dear. Wasn't my fault that man drove in front of me." After 41 years of marriage, Harold knew he wasn't going to win this argument. Hadn't won one yet, certainly wasn't going to happen today either. "Nellie, did you see that car?"

"Of course I saw that car, Harold. You nearly hit it."

"What I mean was, did you see the back door open? Looked like someone was getting out of the car: a little girl, I think.

"Don't be silly, Harold. What child in her right mind would get out of a moving car?"

"I don't know, my Nellie, but that's what I saw."

By now, Harold and Nellie Granger were nearly through Grant Circle, where a patrolman stopped the car. The officer motioned for Granger to roll down his window as he played his flashlight on the older couple and then on the back seat. His right hand floated just over his holster.

"Good evening officer," Harold politely said. "Is something wrong up ahead?

"Just checking every car. Please open your trunk; I need to look in there, too."

The patrolman came back to the window. "OK, keep going. Move along."

5:20 PM, Day 1

Addison Gilbert Hospital was only a couple of hundred yards off Grant Circle and less than two miles from the Coast Guard Station. Two ER technicians were waiting just inside the sliding glass doors as the ambulance backed into the loading dock under cover from the storm. The two techs helped slide the ambulance stretcher out of its locked position, dropped open the collapsible legs and quickly wheeled the patient into the examining room.

"Who've we got here?" the one tech called back over his shoulder.

"Fiori. Tony Fiori," the ambulance driver responded. But he knew full well from several other trips in the past few years that saying anything more than Fiori was redundant. In his line of work, he was a regular guest of the ER. The staff knew him well, liked him even more, but they adored his wife. Fiori was a patient from another era, often apologizing for inconveniencing the ER crew. Self-help was his treatment of record.

"Surprised he didn't insist on driving himself in tonight," the tech said to no one in particular.

The corpsmen wheeled Fiori into a cubicle as the head nurse, Gertrude Palazolla, who ran the ER like a medical drill team (and, for that effort, was called Commander) barked out her orders. She saw the head wound and took Fiori's vital signs herself. She was aware from his many previous visits that Tony was tough. More importantly, Palazolla knew to call Naomi Little Bird, Tony's wife, before final treatment was rendered. She hadn't done that a couple of years ago when Tony was brought in for something or other, and when Naomi found out her husband had been discharged before she had been consulted, a new definition of "chewing out" had been established.

As tough as she was, the Commander had met her match. Truth be known, had there been a vote at the time as to who won, most of the ER staff would have voted for Naomi . . . secretly, of course!

Naomi was a pure-breed Passamaquoddy Indian, as close to a Shaman as a woman could be in her culture. Her father, Henry Eagle Feather, was a Shaman as was his father and grandfather before him. Henry had no son so Naomi had learned many things normally passed through bloodlines to the firstborn male. She was respectful of Western medicine, but she knew her ancestor's healing remedies, natural tree bark, roots, herbs, plants and the like. Naomi Little Bird had her own ideas of the proper mix of both traditions.

Henry Eagle Feather was considered a modern Shaman in that he shared the healing methods with Naomi's mother with whom Naomi spent hours while she administered her husband's potions to all in the Pleasant Point Passamaquoddy community in Maine. Naomi had healing hands and practiced the natural ways of her father.

Tony was a fighter. His pulse strengthened, his body temp rose and his breathing deepened as the IV drip replaced lost fluids and his body pulled back from shock. The triage doctor examined, flushed, and stitched the wound, temporarily bandaging it before sending him down to radiology for x-rays of the wrist.

Half an hour later Tony was wheeled back to the Emergency Room where Naomi was waiting. Alert, he smiled as he held out his hand to his wife. "Want to play doctor, Little Bird?" he teased.

"Always, my warrior, but it doesn't look like you're, ah, up for it right now. What did you go and do to yourself?"

He told her briefly about being out on the harbor and what he remembered about going over board. As he spoke, she rested her fingers on his temple then on the sides of his neck, getting her own reading on his life energy. She clucked her tongue, a sign that she was displeased about something. Tony didn't wait long for confirmation.

Naomi had her own medicine kit. Before treating her husband, she followed another tradition of the Shamans and smudged her forehead with ash from burnt

River Birch logs. The Shaman knew the healing powers of the tall River Birch: its head grew towards the Spirit of the Sky while its feet, anchored in the wet soil, absorbed the nutriment of the Earth Mother and passed Her lifeblood through its trunk as it reached for the wisdom of the Sky Spirit. Naomi raised her arms in supplication, allowing the healing lifeblood of the ash to flow to her out-stretched fingers. Finishing her silent petition to the Healing Spirit, she unwound the gauze covering her husband's head wound. She clucked her tongue again.

His stitches were neat and close, Naomi noticed. The wound looked clean, but not properly dressed. Reaching into her carry bag, she pulled out several small cloth bags tied close with string. She sprinkled a brownish powder on her hand before rubbing her palms lightly together. She pressed them gently onto the wound itself. She was careful not to tug on the knots of the nylon stitches. She traced her fingers in circles around each stitch on both sides of the cut, adding more of the mixture as it was absorbed into the skin.

She cinched the first bag closed and pulled a small vial out of the second bag, screwed open the cap and dripped the contents over the entire wound. From the third pouch she removed several sprigs of herbs, crumpled them over the wound, brushed off her hands and put the first gauze pad back in place. Naomi placed four leaves over the pad, put a second pad on top of them, and then rewound the ace bandage around Tony's head. She secured it with the two metal clips as the doctor swept into the room carrying the x-ray films. He raised an eyebrow at the woman who had clearly just done something to his bandage and started to challenge her when she spoke first.

"You closed my husband's wound nicely, doctor. Thank you for your care. You may not have read in my husband's chart that I expect to be called before treatment is rendered."

Not accustomed to being challenged, the physician raised and eyebrow, grabbing for the medical records lying by his patient's feet.

Naomi went on. "My people also have a tradition of healing to accompany your treatment; I have just finished my work while you were occupied elsewhere."

Still reading, the doctor said: "and what exactly had I failed to finish?"

"Certain techniques with which Western medicine is not familiar. Adding ground bark from the red cedar for release and purification; sage for cleansing and increased blood flow; lanolin from the deer fern to open the pores, aloe to soothe nerve endings that were severed by the cut; then bay leaves to draw out any infection and, finally, green tea leaves to absorb it. I reapplied your bandage as you had done. Oh, and I added a pinch of dried apple," Naomi concluded in a tone that indicated she had no intention of being challenged.

The doctor finished reading Fiori's medical file, including the note inside the front jacket, and decided he need not question her added treatment. Lanolin and aloe he knew about, but he made a note to look into deer fern; that was new to him.

"And the apple? What is that for?" the physician chuckled. "To keep me away?"

"No," Naomi responded. "Apple is for sexual strength."

Making a note to stop on the way home for a basket of apples, the doctor turned on the light behind the Plexiglas and snapped the x-ray films into the clips. In a tone that was almost collegial, he explained what he saw.

While swollen, the left wrist was intact.

"What do your people use for swelling?" the doctor inquired.

"Black tea, Swiss Pine needles, dried apple and bee balm which we apply in a paste mixed with garlic root."

"More dried apple, I see," he commented with a smile.

"We believe when the skin is broken, some Life Forces like Truth and Balance and even sexual desire are lost. We add apple, the Original Fruit, to replace them".

"What about the smell of the garlic?" he asked.

"There is no odor. The tea neutralizes the sulfur in the garlic, while the pine needles increase stimulation."

The doctor shrugged. She had such a healing air about her, he figured the mix couldn't hurt and might even teach him something.

In less than an hour, Fiori was ready to go home. The ER doctor thought he was wasting his time but offered nonetheless to admit the patient and keep him over night. Naomi declined, Fiori winked at the doctor, and with an understanding smile, the Commander wheeled him out to the car.

"Be careful not to pop any stitches, Tony. I heard Naomi might have added some extra dried apple to the treatment mix."

5:12 PM, Day 1

Pinto let out a long sigh as he put the cops behind him. He had been so focused on the danger of being stopped that he was clenching the wheel. He relaxed his grip and shook his fingers loose to reach for a cigarette. Rocker was quiet, deep in thought, and it made Pinto nervous when his partner drifted off like that. Like he was on another planet.

"Hey, Rocker. You here?"

"Yeah, I'm here. Just thinking of our options. We gotta get off this stinking island. Circle around and take the drawbridge off the Boulevard. Head over there."

"You nuts? If the cops were just there on 128, you think they forgot about the bridge? No way, man. I bet they got the bridge up, for Crissake."

Rocker was silent. The girl in the back seat was whimpering and rubbing her cheek where she had hit it on the armrest when he'd backhanded her. Her check was bright red from being hit and tears were running down her face but at least she was quiet.

Carrie pulled her arms even more closely around herself "I want my mommy."

"You'll get your mommy, kid. Later. Now shut up!"

"I want my mommy!"

Rocker twisted about in his seat, fist raised, but Pinto grabbed him. "She ain't goin' nowhere; leave her alone."

"Leggo of me, Pinto!" Rocker pulled his arm away. "You drive; I'll take care of the kid! Just drive!"

"I want to go home, now, Mister." Carrie said to the back of Rocker's head. "My mommy is going to be worried. And it's all because of you. You're not a nice man."

"Listen, Carrie," Pinto said quickly before Rocker could answer. "You're goin' home. You're goin' to see your mommy, all right? Just wait. We got things to do first. Then you see your mommy. So sit down and be quiet."

Carrie obeyed. Pinto could see her lower lip was still quivering and tears were still running down her cheeks, but she settled down. Not a single car was on the road, which was good, Pinto thought. No one to see the kid. Problem was they would be in downtown Rockport before too long, where the narrow, one lane roads would make it easy for the girl to jump out again. As they passed the sign to Halibut Point State Park, he started to speak when the other man slapped his thigh.

"We ain't going through Rockport. Too dangerous. I got an idea. Halibut Park. They got a museum building we can hang in."

""If it's closed for the season, maybe there's no one there."

"Ain't gonna be no one there in this weather, shit-head! That's why I thought of it in the first place. Park ranger probably left after Labor Day so the place is all ours."

At the turn of the last century, Halibut Point had been a thriving quarry, providing Cape Ann granite that had been used as far away as the Holland Tunnel connecting New York and New Jersey. Now, in spite of the museum, mostly picnickers, over-sexed teenagers, or locals casting for striped bass off the granite ledges down by the water used the park. Pinto followed the path as it twisted under the overhanging vines and tree limbs. The rain was lighter under the canopy, but the going was slippery because of the leaves that had fallen on the path. The grassy area curved behind the museum and ended in front of a maintenance shed where wheelbarrows and old tools were propped against the wall next to a tractor with a blue tarp lashed down over the engine. Pinto untied the tarp, cursed as pooled water splashed over his jacket and pants, and placed it over the hood of the car.

"Gimme the light, Rick. Need to figure out how we're getting in."

As the flashlight played over the near side of the building, both men could see the first floor windows, a back door, and what looked to be a pull-up metal door probably going down to a basement. Rocker held the beam on the handle.

"Go yank it open," he told Pinto.

The hinges, nearly rusted through and bent near the corner, gave off a loud screech. Rocker snapped off the flashlight.

"God damn, Pinto. Why not get a loudspeaker and jus' tell everyone we're here! Shit!"

"Don't go blaming me. Anybody knows rusty metal ain't quiet. Besides, no one's out in this rain anyway."

"You better hope your sorry ass you're right."

Rocker stepped down the stairs first, cursing as the cobwebs caught his face. The smell of mildew was thick in the air. Pinto followed with the girl and pulled the bulkhead door closed over his head. They found themselves in a damp, musty room that must at one point have been part of an active quarry. The walls were granite, stepped down where slabs of rock had been cut away. Tiny flecks of mica sparkled in the flashlight's beam. Huge tree trunk timbers supported overhead floorboards. Carrie started to cough as their movement through the basement stirred the granite dust that covered everything.

Rocker played the light beam further and found stairs that led to the first floor and the main part of the museum. A wooden trap door covered the stairwell but when Rocker pushed against it, the door gave way easily. A kerosene lamp hung by the stairwell. Rocker smelled it, then shook it to see if fuel was in the basin. Pinto picked a matchbook out of his pocket, struck a match, lit the wick and adjusted the height to get an even flame before switching off the flashlight to save the battery.

The first floor was a large, open room with tools and implements similar to those down in the basement. The office had an old leather couch, a metal desk, two other padded chairs, and a small, Formica-covered table. There were no windows so Rocker risked throwing on the light switch even though he expected the electricity to have been cut off. Surprisingly, the ceiling lights flickered on. In a cheap aluminum cabinet, Pinto found packages of instant coffee, dried soup, plastic milk for the coffee, several packages of trail mix, crackers and a partially used jar of peanut butter.

"Least we won't starve," Pinto exclaimed.

"We're not going to be here long enough for you to worry about starving. It's early, but we might as well get some sleep. Find us a way to keep the kid under control. I don't want her trying nothin' funny. I'm gonna sack out on the couch. Put the chair against the door so she can't go anywhere while we're sleeping."

"He gets the couch while I get the padded chair. Sonofabitch always thinks of himself first," Pinto mumbled

The girl had sunk down in the corner. Feeling a little sorry for the kid, Pinto took a coat off the rack, spreading it on the floor near her to make her more comfortable. Rocker was already snoring.

"He doesn't treat you very nicely, does he?" Carrie whispered, more as a statement than a question. "I wouldn't be his friend if he treated me like that. How come he is your friend?"

"Well, we're not exactly friends, more partners, though sometimes I wonder about that."

"If you're partners, why does he boss you around?"

Pinto shrugged. *Kid's right; seems like I get the crap jobs more frequently now.*

"I bet you don't get the same as he does, do you?" the girl asked, settling herself under the coat.

"No, not exactly."

"Then why do you stay his friend, I mean his partner?"

"Cuz there's a lot of money I'm getting . . . if everything goes."

"You must get a lot of money to let him talk to you like he does. My daddy makes a lot of money but when he yelled at my mommy, she made him get out of our house. And now she doesn't get much money. Will that happen to you, too?"

God, this kid sees thing pretty good, Pinto thought. "Don't know for sure. Rocker's got all the connections. Without him, I'd be nowhere, really."

"Are you somewhere now?" she asked.

Pinto couldn't answer. The little girl asked the same question that had been running through his mind for days now. *Truth is, I ain't nowhere at all. If Rocker cuts me out, then what? What have I got? I've got shit, that's what. He can't double me out now, though; I know too much, but when I get my cut, I'm history. Won't need to take any more crap from him then.*

He forced a smile. "You ask pretty tough questions for a little kid. Look, you better sleep now. Don't want him thinkin' you and me is plotting anything."

"Good night." Carrie turned to the wall then quickly rolled back. "Will you say my prayers with me?"

Chapter 8

6:20 PM, Day 1

Naomi was backing out of the parking lot when Fiori's cell phone rang.

"Fiori."

"Tony! Chief Marren. How're you feeling?" Since it was the Chief, Tony held the phone so Naomi could hear.

""Hey, Chief. Not as bad as it could have been. Next time we have a drug bust in the middle of a monsoon, you better send a younger man. My head got cut up a bit and my wrist is swollen, but nothing's broken. The Doc said I should be good to go in a day or two." Tony could hear his wife clucking her tongue and caught her shaking her head in disapproval.

"Well, I got bad news, Tony. You're goin' to have to put the two days on hold. We've had a possible kidnapping and need you two back over here."

"Back where?" Tony asked, confused.

"Naomi was here but left to check on you." Tony looked at his wife who was nodding, her forefinger up in a signal to wait a minute.

"Kidnapping of whom?"

"Laurie MacKenzey's little girl."

"Carrie? Ah, shit!"

"Yeah, Carrie it is. The CABA bus she was on never made it to her stop and never made it back to the garage. So when Carpenter couldn't raise the driver on the phone, he drove the route, found the bus, the driver dead and—"

Tony cut him off. "Who's dead?" he demanded as Naomi looked over.

"Old man Reggie Martin."

"How do you know Carrie was even on the bus? Couldn't she have gone home with a friend?"

"I'm afraid we found her lunch box lying all bashed in on the floor of the bus. Laurie said it was her daughter's."

"So how do you know it's a kidnapping? Maybe Carrie just bolted. She's a savvy little kid for as young as she is."

"Well, we don't know for sure, but she's missing. That we do know. And we've got a possible murder scene so I can't rule out kidnapping. Need you and Naomi to take a good look at the bus, Tony."

Over louder clucking from his wife, Tony agreed and rang off, promising to be at the bus within the next ten minutes.

"OK, Naomi, what else haven't you told me?" Tony asked with an edge.

"Tony, before you get all worked up, there just wasn't a good time to tell you what was going on. I needed to make sure you got proper treatment first."

"Right, right, thank you. Well, I got the treatment so bring me up to speed."

Naomi gave him a quick summary of what she had seen at the bus and the steps she had instructed Chief Marren to take. Tony nodded.

"You did well, Little Bird, very well. Let's get over to the scene so I can see for myself."

Naomi slowed and pulled to the side of the road. "Listen carefully, my warrior husband. We will go to the bus so you can see on the very slight chance if you find something that I missed, but we are going on one condition. And there will be no argument. We will stay as long as I say and we will leave the second I think you are overdoing it."

In no position to argue, Tony accepted, smiling to himself, knowing that the chances of his finding something she missed were close to zero.

Chapter 9

6:28 PM, Day 1

The Fioris pulled in behind the bus just as the coroner, Walter Matheson, arrived. Tony and he had worked together too many times.

"Another sunny day in paradise, Walter," Tony said, shaking the coroner's hand. "You know my wife, Naomi."

"Of course! Good to see you again, Naomi." Matheson grinned. "But paradise I'm not so sure, Tony. Got rain enough for a new ark."

"Got that right," Tony laughed. "So before we all wash into the harbor . . ." Let's see what we've got here," the coroner concluded, stopping at the stairs to the bus. Taking in the scene, Matheson opened his crime scene bag, grabbed some latex gloves and activated a tape recorder, which he strapped to his belt. He put the headset on, tested the sound level, then began to describe what he was finding, breaking the scene into grids, recording what he saw in each block of space. As the coroner recorded his observations, Tony made quick drawings in his own spiral notebook of the details he knew would be critical to determining what had happened.

Matheson was methodical. He photographed the dead driver from various angles, including close-up shots of his broken fingers, scraped under the nails of the driver's right hand and put the debris from each finger in a separate evidence bag, labeling each before putting them back in his kit. He probed in the driver's mouth, examined his right ear and the cap that had fallen on the floor.

He then took more shots of the child's lunch box. Holding the lunch pail by the corner so as not to smudge any prints, he compared the indentations on the lunch box to the size and shape of the wounds on the driver, dictating more details into the recorder before putting the lunch box in a larger evidence bag.

Tony, meanwhile, examined the broken mirror. "Take a look at this, Walt. There's blood up here."

"Definitely blood. Doesn't appear to have come from Martin, though; it's too isolated and too far away. And what little gift have we here?" he added, pointing at a brown hair that had been caught in the frame. "Just waiting for us to find you, weren't you?" Matheson fished tweezers out of his bag.

"This isn't Martin's," Tony said. "Hair is brown and too straight. And, besides, there's no spray pattern to connect it to Martin. It must have come from someone else when the mirror was broken. You have a tape measure, Walt?"

"Sure, here. What are you thinking?"

Tony measured the height from the mirror to the step. "69 inches. Well, almost 69 and a half. Whoever broke the mirror must be, what? If it's from the top of his head, a little under 6 feet tall. Right?"

"If it came from the side of his head," Matheson posed," could be several inches from the crown in which case he could be over 6 feet."

As Tony turned back towards the front seat, he noticed a dirty smudge on the hand railing and bent down to smell it. "Mud, Walter?"

"Probably the same as the mud by the front seat there," Matheson said nodding to the floor.

Tony knelt to look more closely where Matheson had indicated. He stood up and looked thoughtfully at the smudge on the handrail. Tony raised his right arm and cupped it around an imaginary object and moved closer to the steps.

"Let's say the guy was carrying the girl under his arm. Let's say she was struggling and kicked against the railing. Threw him off balance and he hit his head on the mirror when he got cut like this." Fiori pantomimed what he had described. "The smudge is about the right height to have come from her boot if she was being carried." Matheson asked: "Is there any glass behind the door?"

"No, none. There's a tiny shard caught on the rubber gasket here," Tony said pointing at the glass panel in the front of the door. "Nothing behind it at all, so the door was definitely open before the mirror was broken."

"That leads credence to your theory, Tony."

Tony opened the fare box and recorded the time and amount of the last transaction. "The last fare was $1.25 and the time 4:38. That's the cost of a child's fare. Judging by the time on the tape, I would say that it was paid at the school. The after-school program gets out at 4:30. Kids walk to the bus, load up and the bus pulls out 8 minutes later. Seems about right."

"What's the amount of the toll before that?" Matheson asked.

Tony unrolled the paper spool. "Nothing; that was the only fare. The recorder resets at the beginning of each run. So if no one else got on the bus, Carrie and Reggie were the only ones on it when the kidnapper showed up. So I don't seem to have a witness."

"What if someone were already on the bus before it got to the school?"

"Not possible: school is the first stop. No, the girl was the only passenger."

Matheson switched off the recording, labeled it with crime scene info, date and time and put it into his kit with the other information they had collected. "We're finished here, Tony. I'm gong to take a quick look outside, but in this rain, there's a small chance I will find something useful. You can tell the ambulance crew they can take the body."

As Fiori left to find the ambulance driver, Matheson went to the patrol car to tell Chief Marren he was finished and that Tony would brief him, as he wanted to get back to the lab and get to work without further delay. A minute later, Fiori rapped on the window, opened the door and plopped down in the back seat glad to be out of the rain. He had been so absorbed in the scene inside the bus that he had forgotten about his head. The throbbing hadn't forgotten, however.

"Here's what it looks like, Chief. Judging by the position of the bus, it was a routine stop, not an emergency. Bus was pulled over close enough to the curb for someone to get on. The driver was in his seat, no rain on his uniform and his boots were dry, so I don't think he left his seat to check on anything outside. I saw no puddles of water anywhere in the rear seats either; nothing to suggest anyone had an umbrella dripping water, boots dripping water, etc. All the footprints were up front.

"I believe only one man got on. There were only two sets of footprints on the steps, one made before the mirror broke (because there was water and residue underneath pieces of glass) and one after it broke. So someone got on before the mirror was broken. Whoever got on didn't pay, however, as the last transaction (and the only transaction) was at Fuller School. And it was a child's fare. So maybe whoever got on when the bus stopped had no intention of riding, or at least had no intention of paying for the ride! Can't say for sure which it was, but something happened after the guy got on that caused Martin to get in trouble."

"Maybe the guy just didn't want to leave a witness behind," the Chief interrupted.

"I don't think, in a technical sense, Martin was murdered. There is not enough trauma either to his head or hands to have caused death. The guy clearly grabbed the lunch pail and swung it down hard on Martin's fingers, since the dent on the pail nearly matches exactly the shape of his broken fingers. Why did the perp go for Martin's hand? Probably to keep him from getting to the call button. But at this point, I think a heart attack killed Martin.

"Let's assume for the moment that the guy grabbed Carrie, she struggled, pushed her foot against the railing, had enough power to push the man into the mirror causing it to break and him to get cut. Walt will match Martin's to the blood type on the mirror frame to see if that theory holds."

Chief Marren interrupted. "Naomi was talking with the child's mother who said that the girl was very headstrong, determined about getting her own way. Any good prints?"

"The lunch box will be our best bet. At this point, all we know is that the perp is about 6' with brown hair and strong enough to carry a feisty 6 year old.'

With that, there was a knock on the window and one upset woman outside in the rain. "Listen Chief, you've had enough of my husband. He's officially off duty as of now. I'm taking him home before he gets in any more trouble."

"He's not in trouble, Naomi. He's in charge of this investigation."

"Maybe he's not in trouble with you, Chief Marren, but he is with me. If you want him to be any good for you, then you have to give him up to me at least for the rest of the night. After that, I will let you know in the morning if he is ready for you. Are we in agreement, Chief?"

Marren was about to say something, thought better of it, and nodded instead. Tony stifled a grin, said good night to his boss, and caught up with his wife. "Before we go, take a quick look at the steps and the ground just outside the bus doors and tell me what you see. You might find something useful."

"Tony Fiori, I won't raise my voice out of respect for you, but you will get in the car right now so that I can drive you home to bed where you belong!"

Startled, he only now accepted that his head was throbbing and decided to obey. In their car, Naomi in the driver's seat, she added, "Besides, my warrior, I already examined the ground outside."

Tony settled back in the passenger seat, smiling. *This is why I married this woman*, he said to himself. He shut his eyes.

7:07 PM, Day 1

Michael Valchon was soaked by the time he offloaded the bails onto his pickup on the Maritime Wharf at the end of Rocky Neck. Five bails, a minor fortune in heroin and the blue "O's": OxyContin. One of the bails had been torn, the corner seam separated, so Valchon wrapped it in a tarp and put it underneath the others before throwing lobster traps on top of everything. He thought there was little chance a beat-up pickup loaded with lobster gear was going to attract any attention, even assuming anyone was insane enough to be out in this downpour to begin with.

Valchon's truck bounced over the iron ties and coils of rusty chain of the marine railway, then out onto the narrow road. After winding through the one-way, single lane roads of Rocky Neck, he drove cautiously over the causeway to the stop sign at East Main. There he stopped short, staring.

A CABA bus was all lit up, with yellow police line tape wrapped around the perimeter of the bus stop. Two patrol cars had their lights flashing blue probes constantly into the rain. A third car, which Valchon knew was the unmarked driven by the Chief, had just pulled in. A patrolman stood in the middle of the intersection, controlling what little traffic there was. There was no way Valchon could get by without driving close to the cop. He held his breath and rolled down his window.

"Hey, office . . . . Oh, Santinello! I see you got the shit duty. Why's the brass inside outta the rain while you get drenched out here?"

Santinello walked over to the truck and rested his arm on the mirror. "Jesus, Mike; my ass is so wet, it's got wrinkles. What are you doin' out in this shit?" He looked back at the load and cocked his head.

"Doesn't look like your traps are very secure, Mike. You hit a bump and they're gone. Here, let me help you put these on better."

As the cop reached for the end trap, Valchon threw the shift into park and jumped out. *Jesus, if he sees what I've got . . .*

Frantically, Valchon reached for a coil of rope, loosened it and shouted too loudly to the cop, "Here, Jimmy; catch!" and threw him the line. *Anything to keep his hands off my cargo,* he thought quickly. "This should be good enough. You hold this end, while I push the traps. There. Now toss it back over." Valchon ran to the other side of the truck. He looped the line around the hook, snug it up and threw it back over the top again.

"Coming back to you, Jimmy." Valchon ran back around the rear of the truck, got the line from the cop and nudged himself between the traps and the policeman, hoping to block the view of his truck bed.

Santinello stopped, looked closely at Valchon, then reached out and put his arm on Valchon's shoulder and spun him around.

"You Okay, Mike?"

"Yeah, why? 'Course I'm Okay."

"You seem kind of frantic. It's like you got stinger ants, man."

"Nah, it's cool. I'm sick of this rain, that's all. Need to get going, get dry. Say, you want to meet at the Nest for a beer after you get off?"

Santinello motioned with his head towards the bus. "Can't tonight, Mike. This is going to be a long one. Catch you later."

Valchon lifted himself up into the cab and spun his wheels to get away. "Don't forget the Nest, Jim," he shouted out the window. In his hurry to leave, Valchon drove off without even closing his window, his heart racing with the panic still surging through him.

Chapter 10

7:09 PM, Day 1

Eyes closed, Tony had been thinking about what had happened in the bus and the implication of what they didn't know.

"Let's face it, Little Bird," he said, "all we really know is that Martin got into some sort of an altercation with an unknown man and died. We have a bashed-up lunch box, a missing child, and a near-hysterical mother. Except for some mud on a railing, we don't have any proof that these things are connected."

"How else would the mud have gotten on the railing?" Naomi asked. "I thought your guess was a good one."

"Not sure. We didn't see mud splattered anywhere else but there was dirt on the floor below the first seat by the door. Walt is running that down now, but we've got other things to set in motion first before we go assuming the worst. What's your read on the mother? Anything out of sync?"

"Think she's straight, my Warrior. A friend knows her from work. Thinks the world of her. Says she's damn near super mom how much she does for her daughter. My take on her reaction to her kid being missing and all was genuine. Those tears were real. She did wonder if her ex had anything to do with the girl being missing. I guess he's been pushing her hard to get custody of the girl."

"Hard enough to kidnap?"

"Don't know. Dave MacKenzey is not known to have a long fuse if he doesn't get what he wants, but kidnapping? I don't think he'd go that far. You'll want to meet him tomorrow so you can make your own judgment."

Tony continued. "You know, I don't think Matheson or I missed much on the bus, but there wasn't a whole lot to see. At least it seemed that way to me. There was no weapon, I mean other than the lunch box and I don't know if you could call that a weapon."

"That sort of means the guy didn't get on the bus to get even with Martin. If he had, wouldn't he have brought something with him to do Martin in with?"

"Good point. Maybe Martin just got in the way. Maybe he was attempting to keep the guy from harming the girl?"

"I don't know. You know what's bothering me about the kidnapping idea? Why leave the lunch box behind? If Martin is out of the picture and there is no one else around, why take the kid and not the lunch box too?"

They wrestled with these thoughts in silence. The car was warm and Tony closed his eyes again.

"You know, there's another reality," Tony said. "What if we have a child molester on our hands?"

"Don't want to think about that option, my Warrior."

"Me neither, but if we have a kidnapping, at some point we will have to think about that."

"I can't imagine what condition Laurie MacKenzey will be in if that plays out."

"I don't think we should even raise the possibility with her," Tony stated.

"I agree. But what if we don't have control of how she hears?"

7:18 PM, Day 1

Voices filled the hall as the off duty patrolmen on teams two and three reported in.

"Grab a chair, guys. We have us a real one, I'm afraid." With the men crammed into his office, the last two standing in the doorway for lack of room in the office, Chief Marren paused. He knew without needing to see a mirror that he looked as tired as he felt. And he was afraid.

"We've got several possible scenarios. One is the perp had it out for Martin and evened whatever score he had. Two is the perp was high on something, got on the bus, had words with the driver, hit him, thought he had killed him, freaked, then split. Three is the guy wanted the girl for some reason that we don't know, somehow knew she was on the bus, grabbed her, then ran off. Based on what little we know, option three seems to float the best, but we have too much to run down before we can say for sure. So here's what I want to happen:

"Artie, call Mrs. MacKenzey and tell her to bring a good picture of the girl with her and get it here as soon as possible. We need to get it in the paper. Call the GDT, find out who's on the night desk and see if he can get us on tomorrow's front page. Might as well see if the Globe's possible, too. Go get on that.

"Peter, I want you to get with Carpenter. You run with option one and see if Martin pissed off anyone at CABA enough to get whacked. I want you to prove option one wasn't the live one here. Understand? Questions? Good, then go to it.

"OK, here's the plan for the rest of you. You guys on team two got the street. Split up however you want but I want one of you to go to Fuller School and talk with the chaperone that loaded that bus this afternoon. Make certain that Carrie MacKenzey was on the bus and if anyone else got on with her. Make sure no one else is missing. Find out if anyone was seen hanging out at the bus stop that didn't belong there. Someone else follow the bus route. Talk to anyone who lives near all the previous bus stops and see if they remember anyone getting on or off.

"The last one of you .... Actually, I want you, George. You live on Rocky Neck. You work the scene itself. Knock on every door within eyesight of that stop, every door of anybody who catches the bus there, anyone who even smells the bus. Somebody must have something to tell us."

"Chief, do we know how the guy got out of Dodge?" George asked.

"Could be he parked a car there. Could be he lives nearby and took the child home. Could be culprit number two was waiting in a car. That's why you get the big bucks, George. Good thinking. Go find him.

"Now, team three. You guys go home."

The last two men from team two turned and loudly booed. "Shit, Chief. You got the assignment wrong. That hard duty belongs to team two."

"Get your asses out of here!" the Chief yelled good-naturedly. "These guys are going home ..." He paused ... "to change," a pronouncement that was met with boos from the three members. They knew what was coming. "I want you three to work the bars, the card games, Dunkin Doughnuts, the wharf. Any place that's open. Any place you see someone hanging. I want to know what's being said. Who's bragging. Who's threatening. Who's beefed about Martin, CABA, the potholes in East Main, anything you can think of that could be related to this shit. Clear?"

There were no questions and the last team filed out. Artie stuck his head in the door. "The MacKenzeys are here, Chief. Want them to wait?"

"No. Bring them in." Damn, I'm tired, he thought, and the night hasn't even started. The Chief rose and stuck out his hand to introduce himself.

7:32 PM, Day 1

Naomi turned into the driveway of their cottage and switched off the headlights. Their home was a small, dark-shingled saltbox typical of the houses on the way to Lanesville. Naomi had loved it from the beginning, as it was nestled into a small clearing that abutted Dog Town Common, a chunk of forested granite that would never be developed. The house had white trim that mimicked the stands of clump birch trees around which Naomi had planted mountain laurel, small evergreen hemlocks and azaleas.

In the back in the one sunny spot behind their kitchen window, she had an herb and vegetable garden, which contained the traditional kitchen herbs plus non-traditional plants given to her by her Shaman father: Bee balm, Wintergreen, Wild Plum, Elderberry, Goldenrod, Milkweed, Raspberry and others. This part of her garden Naomi Little Bird held in reverence, entering it only after acknowledging the Sky Spirit and the Earth Mother from both of whom came Life and Nurturing Energy. The garden was laid out in a circle, plants carefully placed in the quadrant where tradition required. In the Eastern quadrant were those plants that spoke of dignity and respect for the environment; in the North were plants useful to mental health and the balancing of mind and spirit; to the West were those that brought introspection, mental and physical awareness; and to the South were the plants of peace, respect and understanding. All were placed as generations of Shamans had done before and would no doubt for generations to come. It was the way of her People to honor the generations that had come before and the Life Blood they had passed down.

Tony didn't know the names of all the plants, nor had he been given the Shaman traditions, but when the two of them had cleared the scrub that had preceded the garden, Tony was required to leave as Naomi prayed for guidance as she placed the plants. The process took her three days and nights of fasting and meditation, after which there was a small empty space centered within the larger circle of the garden. She instructed Tony to go into the woods and bring back the sitting stone. She gave him no instructions, except to open his mind for guidance that he would be led to the proper stone.

For hours Tony had wandered, and without realizing it had circled back several times, resting and thinking how foolish he must have looked if anyone was watching. The third time he had entered the same clearing and had rested on the same rock, it finally dawned on him that he must have been sitting on the granite he was supposed to bring back. Problem was it was too heavy for him to lift, which he was embarrassed to report back to Naomi, thinking that he had failed her assignment.

The two of them returned to the clearing and constructed a skid from several juvenile oak trees that had fallen near by onto which they had lashed several cross sections before prying the granite block up and onto the sled. Hours later after hauling it back to the garden and placing it where Naomi had instructed, did she proclaim that that was the stone he was to find.

Tony always had wondered if he was just being humored by his wife, except for the fact that whenever he sat there, he went away renewed. It was because Harmony and Balance were centered there, she told him.

"Let's get you to bed, my Warrior."

The two of them ran through the rain to the back door and into the dark and, thankfully, dry kitchen. The only light was from the blinking on the phone, which Tony went to retrieve before Naomi could object. It was Lois calling for Chief Marren to ask if Naomi would call the station.

"He's buttering me up, isn't he?" she asked Tony. "Thinks by being nice to me I will give you back to him sooner."

"He's in a hard place, Little Bird. He needs us but doesn't want to cross you. Before you call him, tell me what you saw back at the bus."

"The rain covered a lot of the message from the ground and so did the footprints of all the people who went before me. I saw the presence of at least five or six people, one that was definitely female and one that was definitely made by someone who was having trouble walking straight. Several were similar and probably belonged to the policemen wearing uniform boots, all walking back and forth from the back of the bus to the patrol cars.

"The one that spoke the loudest was the wobbly one. I first saw the print on the first stair of the bus. It was clearer than the others because a large piece of the broken mirror protected it and was made by a man walking up the stairs. It was his right shoe and it had a definite ridge on the ball of his foot near the outside edge. The glass seemed to magnify it, which made it clearer to see. There is about a one-inch indentation in his sole that has a sharp line at about 2 o'clock on the hole. I would guess he stepped on a piece of metal that tore the leather and left the ridge."

"Did you see it again?" Tony asked.

"Twice. It was easy to see because he was walking away from the front of the bus, while every other print goes towards the back. But after two more prints I lost him totally. The sidewalk was clear of anything useful."

"What did you mean by wobbly?"

"The print going up the stairs had weight evenly distributed on the sole. There were two more prints on the sidewalk made by the same shoe. The first of the two left more debris on the outside of the sole. The second had more debris on the inside sole. Some of that would be normal because there was no new material being picked up so there would be a decreasing amount left behind with each subsequent step. But what was left showed more of the weight on the inside of the imprint. That's what I meant. The man must have been swaying from side to side between the two prints."

"You mean like he was drunk?"

"No, not at all. The prints were deliberate and in line. It was a weight change between the two times he put his right foot down. I would say he was carrying something that either he shifted in his hands or was moving if he kept it in the same hand. I couldn't tell."

"How about the smudge of mud on the hand rail to the left of the stairs." Tony didn't want to say more for fear he would influence her opinion.

"Yes. It was mud, but not from the bus stop. It had more clay in it. It was put there on the way out of the bus and also by a shoe, a smaller shoe that also left a few pieces of sand in the smudge. They were collected elsewhere because they were on top of the clay, which would have been deposited first."

"The smudge on the railing was the same material that was on the floor by the first seat on the right. It was also near where the man left a trail of dirt and water before he left. Walt sampled both deposits but I agree; they came from different sources. Walt and I guessed that the man picked up the girl under his right arm and carried her like this." Tony repeated the motion he used to show Walt on the bus. "He then got to the second step on the way out when the girl kicked against the railing and threw the man off balance causing him to hit his head on the mirror. We found a hair in the frame along with dried blood."

Naomi, deep in thought, began to nod

"Then we have a definite kidnapping. I need to call Marren."

Naomi nodded, reluctantly, and went to the kitchen to get them something light to eat before she put her warrior down for the night. Fiori called the station.

"Chief? Tony here. After we left you, Naomi told me about the footprints she found outside the bus. Both of us think we have a kidnapping on our hands."

"How certain are you of that?" Marren asked.

"You know Naomi, Chief; I'd hate to bet against her, but to be on the safe side, I don't think you should cancel anything you have set in motion."

"Agreed. Anything else?"

"Tony paused, thinking. "Well, I hate to bring this up, but if we have a child molester here, things could get ugly."

"Oh, shit, Tony. Don't even think that."

"Well, thinking doesn't will it. All I'm saying is we need to be prepared for that."

"And do you mind telling me how you prepare for a child molester?" The men talked longer as Marren recounted his meeting with Carrie's parents. Something Marren said caused Tony to interrupt.

"Say that again, Chief."

"MacKenzey said if he put up the reward money, he would want the kid to live with him."

"No before that. Did he say a million dollars?'

"Yes."

"That's a pile of money."

"I think he was trying to convey he could afford it and his ex wife couldn't."

"Well, we already know that. What struck me was how quickly he came out with the million dollar figure."

"Hit me the same way."

"Maybe we've got something else going on, Chief. If you and I reached the same conclusion that quickly, that he could easily afford that kind of reward, then there might be others who think he's loaded too. Maybe this isn't something against CABA or Martin at all. Maybe this is a shake down of Dan MacKenzey."

There was silence as the men thought about that possibility.

"Look, Chief; do me a favor, Naomi will kill me unless I get off the phone. Will you call Dan MacKenzey now; ask him to make a list of people who may be mad enough at him to extort him and . . ."

"From what I hear, Tony, he hasn't got enough paper for that list."

". . . and a list of anyone he has fired recently. Anyone he does business with that he has pissed off lately."

"The list just got longer."

"One more thing, Chief; tell him I will be in his office at 8 tomorrow morning to go over his list. I don't think he was behind this, but I want to see his reaction when I ask him."

8:47 PM, Day 1

Somehow, the car found the garage and she got out. The only detail Laurie remembered about the drive home from the police station was thinking she needed wipers on her eyes to clear the tears. This whole scene was worse than a bad afternoon soap opera. The woulda, shoulda, coulda's paralyzed her with guilt.

After filling the teapot and putting it on to boil, she took her favorite picture of her with Carrie at the beach, slumped down at the kitchen table, her shoulders shaking with her sobs. She kissed the picture, willing hard to hear the laughter that was pictured on her daughter's face, willing to feel the squeeze of her little hand. But the picture was quiet; grief has a silence all its own and the only squeeze she felt was a steel wire that had lassoed her heart and dragged it to the pit of her stomach.

She was so deep in her grief that she thought she heard Carrie whistle and jumped up to find her, before realizing it was the teapot and not her little girl. She got her mug and somehow made it up the stairs and into Carrie's bedroom, where she found her daughter's favorite white teddy bear and hugged it to her breast. Still in her raincoat, she sat in the rocking chair, stroking the bear's head, and cried herself to sleep.

Chapter 11

2:49 AM, Day 2

Fiori reached for the rope. He couldn't quite grab it. Just as he touched it, the wave crashed on him and forced him down deeper. He could just barely see the rope and tried frantically again to kick for it. His feet didn't kick. He couldn't move his left leg at all. He struggled, nearly out of breath, his lungs painful. He tried to exhale, to get more time, but instead of letting air out, somehow he was breathing water, choking, gasping, Out of air. Couldn't reach the rope. And the wave crashed again. He took more water in. There was no air, only water. *I can't breathe*, he screamed: *My leg, my leg!*

Fiori bolted upright, sweat running off his face. He couldn't move his leg, looked down and realized the sheet was twisted around it. He fell back on the pillow. The case was soaked. His heart was pounding. He realized he'd been dreaming and closed his eyes. He reached over for Naomi but touched nothing. He reached again and sat back up, just as she walked in the bedroom door.

"You had a nightmare, my warrior. You kept kicking me and yelling for the rope. I'm afraid you have opened some stitches thrashing around. There's blood on your pillow. Lie back down and let me see."

She put her hands on his forehead and began lightly rubbing her fingers over his temples. Her fingers were soothing; Tony's heartbeat slowed and his breathing became normal. Naomi unwrapped the bandage.

"Ah. The two stitches nearest your ear have broken loose."

She cut small strips of tape to pull the edges of the cut back together, reapplied fresh gauze pads and bay leaves, and rewrapped his head.

"Drink this. It's sandalwood and honey clover tea to calm you." She handed him the hot tea and snuggled behind him as he drank. She resumed rubbing his forehead, gently back and forth, from his eyebrows to his hairline, back and forth, humming a song her grandmother had taught her.

He reached up for her hand and slid it down over his chest. "Let me show you where your fingers can calm me even more."

She giggled, kissed him on his good ear and withdrew her hand. "Can't go popping any more stitches, warrior." She kissed him again, leaving her lips on his for a few warm moments. "We can see how well the stitches hold tomorrow. You need sleep now." She took his cup, leaned over to kiss each of his eyelids and turned out the light.

She could tell he was asleep before she reached the door. She looked at him, bowed her head and raised her hands towards her sleeping husband. She closed her eyes and her mind went far away, away to where her father had taught her to put the restless Spirit. Satisfied and centered herself, she quietly said her thank you and went to bed.

6:15 AM, Day 2

The rain had stopped during the night. The air, still waterlogged, was heavy. The chirping of the early rising birds signaled work to do, bugs to find. The pulse of the day was beginning to pump, as the ferns around her were shaking off the rain and uncurling in the warmth of the sun.

Tony came downstairs to join Naomi in her garden, meditating on the sitting rock they had struggled long ago to put in place. She sensed him before he spoke. She could tell he was refreshed; she felt his Spirit was at peace even if his thoughts weren't.

As if knowing what he would ask, she said: "I have spoken with Chief Marren. Matheson has verified that the blow to Reggie's head was not fatal; he died of a heart attack. He definitely was not murdered. Matheson is running DNA tests on the hair you found and should have the results by noon. Still no word of the girl, I'm afraid. It's been over 12 hours now."

"I kick myself for sleeping instead of looking for her. Too much to do for me to be in bed, but I was so tired. Think I slept in the car before we got home even."

"Be at peace about your guilt, detective warrior. You were in no shape to look for anything but your pillow. Besides, others were out. The Chief had teams all over town most of the night. Everyone is meeting in his office again at 7. I have been here since before the sun showed, listening to my Spirit. There is a strangeness that I feel. There is evil around the girl that should scare me, but yet it doesn't, and I don't know why."

6:58 AM, Day 2

Fiori dressed and drove the two of them to the parking lot on Rogers Street behind the station. The lot was crowded so he knew there would be a full meeting room. No one showed any mercy on him as he walked into the conference room on the second floor.

"Nice of you to get out of bed for us, Fiori."

"Had sweet dreams did you? Some of us had our asses in the street all night, sugar plum."

"Wish I could be a fuckin' detective. Sleep all night and take the credit all morning. Shit!"

Tony took it all in the good nature in which it was given, but still he was glad when Chief Marren came in. The room quieted except for the scraping of chairs as the people took their seats. Others refilled their coffee cups. The chief looked drained already, still in yesterday's clothes. He kept pushing his hand through his hair, a nervous tick that Tony always associated with the chief trying to clear his thoughts by rubbing away the confusion. Looked like he had been doing it all night . . . and without any success, judging by how he slumped in his chair.

"OK, whadda we got? Peter: you lead off."

"Right, Chief." Amero paused to take his notebook out of his pocket. "Spent a couple of hours at CABA, but I don't have much to show. We went through every personnel jacket in the place, every roster, every locker, every desk. Dan even called in the various supervisors and the maintenance guy who turned the bus over to Martin. Nothin' at all. Everyone loved Martin. Couple of the other drivers had been planning a secret farewell party over at the Rum Line for Martin next week. They seemed kicked in the ass to learn he was dead.

"I've got one loose end. Martin had just had a physical, part of the company's normal routine. I called the doctor's office to see what I could find but only got an answering service at that time of night. Doctors spend more time in bed than detectives, I think!" That drew a laugh even from Tony, who held up his hand like a gun and pulled his finger back.

"Any drugs in Martin's locker, Peter?" Tony asked.

"No, nothing. Well, a spare oxygen tank. Martin had severe asthma. An inhaler was there, but it was a prescription. Ordered by the same doc I tried to call."

Tony hadn't expected anything to show up at CABA but at least it had been thoroughly run down. Dan wouldn't hide anything. Hell, he couldn't even fake a good move on the basketball court! Lois was next to report.

"Chief and I met with Dan and Laurie MacKenzey last evening. The mother's pretty shook up; half a step below hysteria would be more accurate. She is blaming herself for letting Carrie ride the bus to begin with. Can't really fault her for that, though: kids all over town, even two or three of your kids, take public transportation home after daycare every day. Let's face it: it isn't exactly Baghdad here. Both Chief and I think Laurie's totally clear." Lois paused for a drink of water.

"What about the father, Lois?" Tony asked. "What's your take on him?"

"Mixed vibes on him. His reputation is, he usually gets what he wants. I've heard from my cousin who works with Laurie MacKenzey that he has been pushing real hard for custody of the girl. Mostly sexist bullshit about a working mother not being able to take care of children properly, but don't get me started on that! Guess she was pretty upset about it and couldn't afford her own attorney to fight back."

"Why now? I mean, why is he leaning on his ex now?"

"I didn't ask that. My guess? It's because he has such a hard on to get even with her for beating him. She got the girl. He lost the girl. That simple. He doesn't like losing and this one cost him some face with his yacht club crowd."

"Enough embarrassment to kidnap? Why spend the money for a high-spread lawyer if you plan to heist your own kid? Besides, when he gets his daughter, what's he going to do with her? Lock her in the house all day so no one knows he has her? Not likely. No disrespect intended, Lois, but we're barking at the wrong fox on this hunt."

Lois snapped back: "Well excuse me, Detective Holmes."

"No, no, Lois. Shit. That came out wrong, No offense intended. Guess I'm feeling guilty I bagged it on you guys last night and I was just trying to help sort through this."

"Did you get that on tape, Chief?" Lois asked with a grin. "Closest thing to a public apology I've heard from Fiori since I've been here."

Tony knew he hadn't totally blown it, but he stood up, opened his hands in mock supplication and sat back down with the best impression of regret he could muster.

"One last thing," Lois continued. "We sent a recent picture of Carrie over to the *GD Times* for today's paper. It's the first possible kidnapping Gloucester has had that anyone can recall, so they held up the press and gave us above the fold coverage."

She tossed a copy of the morning paper on the table where everyone could see the headline that screamed: DRIVER DEAD. LOCAL GIRL MISSING across the top. The subheading was ominous: BASHED LUNCH BOX SUGGESTS KIDNAPPING. "Hard to miss that headline! Sure hope it makes someone call in for a change, but you know how helpful our locals are," she added. Her sarcasm was greeted with grunts of agreement.

The chief rapped his knuckles on the table to redirect everyone's attention. It was Jenkins' turn. His team had been responsible for checking the school. "We spoke with the Principal, the Assistant Principal, Carrie's teacher, even her teacher's aide, the maintenance crew and the bus monitor. The long and short of it: No, no one saw anything out of the ordinary; no, there were no suspicious cars that they remembered; and yes, unfortunately, Carrie had been helped into the bus by the 14 year old daycare Intern, who promptly fainted when she realized she might have sent Carrie away to be kidnapped."

The verification that Carrie had actually been on the bus silenced the room. Two patrolmen crossed themselves, grateful that their own kids had been on a different bus yesterday.

The chief resumed rubbing one hand through his hair and nodded to team Three to begin. The two patrolmen had started on either end of Rogers street, methodically working every bar and hangout. Other than getting soaked and greeted with more silence than cooperation, they had learned precious little. There hadn't been much activity because of the rain. They found one usually reliable snitch who had heard a major drug delivery was supposed to be coming into town, but he had been unable to verify specifics.

Jimmy Santinello interrupted. "Sorry to butt in and I don't know if there is anything to this. But you know the chief was thoughtful enough to invite me to hang out in the rain at the bus last night. Mostly nothing happened, you know, just waving through cars, telling people I had no idea what was going on and so forth."

"That part must have been hard!" someone joked from the back.

"Yeah, well screw you, too. Sorry, Naomi. Anyway, I'm standing at the head of Rocky Neck and Mike Valchon pulls up. He's a small-time lobsterman, pretty much a loner. So he drives up, makes small talk and starts to pull away when I see that his traps are piled pretty high and I'm afraid they might fall off. So I stop him and start to rearrange them and Valchon blasts outta the cab like he's got a Stinger up his ass, throws me a rope and generally rushes around like he's never loaded traps before. Keeps standing between me and the load. So he ties things off, jumps back in the cab and tries to act the king of casual and invites me to have a beer at the Rum Line when I get off duty.

"Now how likely is that? I mean, you'd think we were asshole drinking buddies, or something. So as he's driving off, I catch his face in the outside mirror. Man, he was as scared as a broken condom, you know what I mean?"

"Maybe he was scared you'd accept," the earlier jokester suggested to more laughter.

"And maybe he was connected to that delivery I was out with the Coasties for, Jimmy," Tony said. "Let me talk to you after the meeting."

"George," the chief said. "You're last. I need some good news. What have you got?"

"Not much either, Chief. I went door to door down the Neck to Sailor Stan's and then the same for a hundred yards on East Main on either side of the bus. I guess the rain kept people pretty holed up. Old lady van Hawkin next to the parking lot heard a car horn honking away. Only reason she noticed it was it interrupted her Oprah show. Forced her to miss part of a book review she wanted to hear. Not much from the variety store, either. They had fewer walk-ins than normal because of the rain. Seems like they knew most everyone who came in, or at least recognized them by face anyway. I didn't get much of anything helpful, I'm afraid."

"What about the honking, George? Any theory?" Tony asked.

"Not really, Tony. She was the only one who heard it. Or at least the only one who mentioned it. She said it was near the end of the show which she said was over at 5."

"When she said 'a while,' got any idea how long?"

"Sounds like it went on for ten or fifteen seconds. Made her miss a description of some love scene. Hope I'm that interested in love scenes when I hit 83!"

"Sounds like one of yours, George: you know 10 or 15 seconds of lovin' and you're over!" The jokester was willing to risk the chief's glare for that one. Even Marren stopped running his hand through his hair and smiled.

Tony, though, was running some options through his mind, trying to explain the honking. Some driver could have been irritated that he was being held up. But by what? Another car in front of him? Maybe the car the kidnapper used? Maybe the guy pulled in front of the bus, forced it over, got out to go inside to get the girl . . . ? Could have been 20-30 seconds? Maybe a minute? That would have been enough time to piss off someone behind the abandoned car.

Or was there another explanation? Could the honking have been a warning to the man inside, maybe someone waiting in a getaway car? Maybe he was trying to hurry up the guy inside the bus. In either case, maybe the driver was losing his nerve, getting scared, afraid of being seen. New to kidnapping? Maybe someone with a conscience getting cold feet?

"My take on the honking is that it's related to the kidnapping," Tony said. "If you compare the time of departure from the school, which we know from the collection machine, and the time of the honking, a little before 5, which we know from the woman, that would place the honking spot on when the take down happened. So why the honking?

"Two thoughts. One, the perp abandoned his car in the middle of the street to run inside the bus to get the girl. In this case the honking could have come from someone who was pissed that he couldn't get by. Two, the honking was an accomplice getting nervous for some reason and trying to hurry up the guy inside."

"What's your take on how long the guy was inside the bus?" Chief Marren asked.

"Hard to know exactly, but . . . 30 seconds minimum, minute and a half max, I would estimate."

"Personally, I'd go for the second choice, Tony," Lois cut in. No driver in Gloucester is going to wait 30 to 90 seconds before honking. I got flipped off after 5 seconds on the way in here this morning, and that was at the beginning of the day when tempers are longer fused. At the end of the day, anxious to get home and out of the rain: no way would they have waited that long. Besides, the bus was pulled over to the curb, so even if the perp had left his car in front of the bus so the driver couldn't get away, there was still plenty of room to get by. I go for your second choice."

"In that case, we're looking for at least two people. Be nice to find the driver. If he was nervous, maybe we could sweat him to get the goods on the other guy. Got to find him first, though. I'm going back to van Hawken's and see if we can dig anything up. Then I'm going to take Jimmy's suggestion and find Valchon. After that? MacKenzey is next."

"You want me to make the appointment?"

"Thanks, Chief. No, I'll drop in unannounced. I don't want to give him any time to work up a story."

"Your call, Tony. You've got the ball now. Naomi, are you going to let him run with it?"

She nodded, deadpan. "He'll sneak out if I don't. Anyway, I know Laura, Chief, but even if I didn't, my people rank harming children above murder so I want the perps more than anyone."

Tony added, "Naomi gave me a read last night on the man who grabbed Carrie. She thinks him to be an inch either side of 6 feet with a hole in his right boot. Hate to bet against her; she's better than a blood hound . . . and a lot more fun to sleep with!"

More laughter.

Chapter 12

7:20 AM, Day 2

Rocker rose, scratched, made an impolite morning noise and got up to go to the bathroom. He kicked the chair in which Pinto was sleeping. "Move; I gotta go piss."

"Good morning to you, too, Rocker."

"Don't be a smartass; just move."

Pinto obliged, but getting up was easier than straightening up. He must have slept in one position; his neck was stiff and his right hand still asleep, prickly tingling making his wrist numb. He walked over to turn the radio on, trying to see if there was any news about the girl. He fiddled with the dial, looking for the local station, when he heard the announcer saying:

". . . ice have confirmed that there is a three state manhunt on for a Gloucester girl who was reported missing by her mother when she didn't get off a bus bringing her home after school yesterday. Anyone knowing anything about the girl, Carrie MacKenzey, described as 6 years old, blond curly hair, wearing a pink raincoat, red and white striped shirt, red jeans and yellow boots with little ducks on the toes, should call Gloucester police hot line: 978-288-1212. A reward is being offered. Now, when we return from this commercial, we will be . . ."

Pinto clicked off the news.

Rocker was walking back into the office. Pinto repeated what he had heard. Both men looked at the girl, as if to verify by the clothes that she was the missing child. Carrie had been awakened by the radio and heard the description of her clothes before the man had turned off the news.

"I want my mommy! You told me I would see my mommy. She told the radio man what I had on so you better take me home."

"Did you hear, Rocker? They got cops in three states looking for her."

"I heard. They gonna have to look in 47 others, too! Let's get us something to eat; I'm starved."

"Help yourself to tea and peanut butter. Room service isn't open yet. You watch the girl; I'm going to the bathroom."

Rocker stuck his finger in the peanut butter jar and licked the goop off. His finger wasn't long enough to get any more, so he threw the nearly empty jar against the wall. The girl flinched as the jar bounced near her and pulled the coat over her head. "I want my mommy," she said through the fabric.

"*I want my mommy. I want my mommy*. Is that all you can say, kid? Shut up before you get on my nerves again."

As Pinto came back into the room, Rocker told him, "Look, here's the plan. We get out of here and get over to the cabin where we want to be anyway. Nothin' to eat here and besides, we gotta mail the note to asshole MacKenzey. Give him the good news about gettin' the girl back. You ready?"

"I don't want my daddy. I want my mommy," Carrie said with anger.

"Yeah, you might want your mommy but we want your daddy's money, so Daddy it is."

"He never gives me any money. Why should he give you some when he doesn't even know you?"

Pinto suddenly remembered his own drunken father staggering into his bedroom to steal change from his only son. He couldn't remember the last time his father had given him anything except a slap across the mouth. The memory chewed at the pit of his stomach.

"Don't go worrin' about that, kid. He'll cough it up all right. Lots of it, if he wants to see you again."

"He doesn't want to see me now. He left me and mommy."

Pinto was grabbed again, remembering his own rejection, and let out his breath in a low whistle. Rocker slapped him on his upper arm: "What's up with you. Pinto? Losin' it?"

"Nah, jus thinking."

"That's dangerous for you; let's get outta here. You leave the thinkin' to me. Come on, kid; get movin'!"

"I'm not going anywhere until I go to the bathroom. You went; now it's my turn." As if she were in charge, Carried squared her shoulders and marched out of the room, as only a six year old could do.

"Got a mind of her own, that kid," Pinto observed.

"Let her go. Save us from having to stop anywhere. Listen: when we get to the car, you drive. I'm gonna get in the back with the kid so she doesn't pull any more shit like she did yesterday."

They waited outside the bathroom door for the girl to emerge, then all three walked out to the car. "You're getting in the back with me, kid, so hop in."

Carrie was clearly feeling a little bolder since her bathroom pronouncement. "I don't want to get in the back with you. I'm sitting with Pinto!"

"I don't give a shit what you want, kid. Get in the back before I put you there myself." He pushed her halfway in before she scrambled on her own to get as far away from him as she could.

Pinto had just made the beginning of the pathway when he hit the brakes hard and yelled," Rocker! Two men!"

Rocker looked up from the girl to see two men walking towards them with fishing poles and tackle boxes. Halibut Point was well known by the locals as a good spot for stripers, and early morning was a perfect feeding time. Rocker pushed the girl roughly to the floor and swung his legs over on top of her. "Keep going. Don't stop for anything," he hissed through his teeth. "Don't wave; don't nothing. Just drive!"

Pinto hit the accelerator, forcing both men to jump to the side barely out of the way of the speeding vehicle. As it went by, the car caught the tip of the fishing rod one man had lifted to protect himself and bent it back.

"You crazy bastard!" the man yelled at the speeding car. He tried to throw his pole at the car but it caught a branch overhead and the tip broke off, falling into the brush. The car kept going around the bend and out of sight as the fisherman ran after it. He was too out of shape from too many beers and the car drove away, but not before he saw the license.

"JF3 LV1. JF3 LV1. JF3 LV1" he shouted. "Frankie: you got anything to write with? JF3 LV1" he kept repeating.

"OK: J F 3 L V 1. I got it. Did you see the car?"

"Old gray Plymouth junker. Mass license. I'm going back to the car to call the police. That was my brand new pole, the bastard! Paid 600 bucks for it!"

"That guy was spooked. Did you see the other one in the back seat? He was breathin' fire! Wonder what that was all about? More to the point: what the hell were they doing in here in the first place? Park's closed, ain't it?"

Chapter 13

7:30 AM, Day 2

"Cape Ann Whale Watch calling Blyman, over."

"Blyman. State your request. Over."

"We're loading now. Expect to drop lines in 15 minutes and be at the bridge 12 minutes later. Can you let us through? Over."

"Roger, Cape Ann. We'll be expecting you, Dave. Out"

The last passengers were coming up the gangway, mostly excited kids, boys with their hats turned sideways, others with their sunglasses perched on their ears but with the lenses towards the back of their heads. *Never understood how that was cool*, Dave mused. *I mean, what's the purpose?*

Marshall called into the loud speaker: "Gail, everyone on board?"

The tanned summer intern standing at the head of the gangway turned and gave the thumbs up signal to the skipper. "One count shy, Dave. A girl in Ellen's class didn't make it. Safe trip."

"Roger. We'll be heading towards Block 125 just west of Stellwagon. Give me a heads up if the front speeds up."

Marshall skillfully backed the 57-foot twin diesel cruiser out of the narrow slip into the cut out and nosed out into the channel. Winds were from the west at a pleasant three to four knots; the Annisquam River was calm on a rising tide. He grabbed the mike again, clicked over to the maritime channel seven and alerted the drawbridge operator to his expected arrival in twelve minutes.

7:34 AM, Day 2

Valchon, who was listening to the exchange between Marshall and the bridge, knew that the computer program that operated the drawbridge required a three-minute window after the bridge had been lowered before it could be raised again. Three minutes before the two-lane road that ran over the bridge could be closed. He grabbed for his cell phone to speed-dial Rocker.

"Yeah?"

"It's me. Blyman is going up in about 12 minutes. Just heard it on the scanner. Thought you might be interested."

"Very. Thanks." Rocker told Pinto, "Pull into the high school parking lot."

From there it was no more than 30 to40 seconds to the bridge and the safety of the mainland, plenty of time to get off Cape Ann before the bridge could be raised and block their escape.

"Okay, kid. No sass from you. When I tell you, you're gonna lie down under my legs on the floor and you're gonna keep your mouth shut. Understand?"

Carrie sat with her arms crossed, as far away from the man as she could get. She held her chin up and looked out of the corner of her eye at Rocker and challenged, "And what if I don't?"

"And what if you don't?" Rocker mimicked. "What if you don't? You're goin' to be one sorry little kid if I decide to throw you and your smart mouth into the canal."

She looked at Rocker, not responding. Pinto caught her eye in the mirror and gave a slight shake of his head. Not a good idea to challenge him on this. Rocker got a dark blue beach towel, smelly with stale beer, from under the seat and spread it over his knees.

"I'm not getting under any smelly old towel," she announced.

"Yeah? We'll see. Go now, Pinto. There's the siren; the bridge is about to go up. Get up to the corner and wait there."

Pinto pulled out onto Centennial Avenue and coasted slowly up to the corner by the pizza store, As he leaned forward into the windshield, he could see the bridge going up. He could also see two cops sitting in a patrol car.

"We got company up there, Rocker. Two cops parked just this side of the bridge. Think there is another car on the other side, but I can't be sure. Can't see through the bridge grillwork too good."

"Yeah, I expected them. Just be cool, man. Don't even look at them. Just keep goin' with the flow." He turned to Carrie. "Okay, kid; show time. Get down here like I told you."

Carrie made no effort to move. She sat with her teeth clenched and her arms tight across her chest. She looked right at Pinto in the mirror with what he judged to be stubborn eight-year-old defiance.

"Do what he tells you, Carrie," Pinto said.

"I'm not getting near that smelly towel," she announced once more. Pinto put the car in gear, saw that the traffic had started to move and honked impatiently at the car in front of him. Rocker grabbed the girl's arm and shoved her to the floor. He put the towel over her and pinned her down with his knees.

"Turn the radio up, Pinto! Don't want nobody to hear anything this kid might yell. You keep your trap shut, you hear, girl?"

Pinto hit the horn again and pulled out around the car that wasn't moving. He got even with the rear fender when a pickup swerved right in front of him. Pinto swung the Plymouth back into line, hit his horn and flipped off the pickup before pulling out into the intersection.

"Stay cool, man," cautioned Rocker who, Pinto could see in the rearview mirror, had his arms casually across the top of the back seat, looking every bit the nonchalant tourist. Pinto could also see the cop and nearly panicked as he saw him open his door to get out. He started to say something to Rocker when the policeman pulled back in and reached for his radio. The traffic was moving, but too damn slowly. Pinto was sweating heavily and reached up to wipe his forehead with his sleeve and also to conceal his face from the cops. Moving forward bit by bit, he was now three car lengths in front of the policeman. Pinto glanced again in his rearview mirror. There was only one car between him and the cops when the siren went off.

Red warning lights began to blink and the bells were sounding. The gates started down. Pinto tensed, honked at the car in front, and looked back. Both cops were out of their car, staring intently at the cars making a last ditch effort to beat the bridge, now opening for *Whaler II.* The cops turned back to their coffee.

7:45 AM, Day 2

"Rockport Police Headquarters. May I help you?"

"Yes, this is Jim Cunningham. I'm at Halibut Point Park. Some crazy bastard came flying down the pathway and broke my new pole."

"Say again, Sir."

"My buddy and I were going fishing, and this car came out of nowhere and nearly hit me. His windshield snapped my pole. Brand new $600 Orvis fiberglass baby. Haven't even used it yet!"

"You say he was driving on the footpath?"

"Bet your life. Must have been doing 30."

"And when did this happen?"

"About 20, maybe 25 minutes ago. Would have called sooner but my cell was dead. Had to find Frank's."

"Did you get a plate number?"

"JF3 LV1.Did you get that? JF . . ."

"Got it fine. Did you say it was a Plymouth?"

"Dark gray one, pretty beat up."

The desk sergeant had typed the number into the computer connected to the state Bureau of Motor Vehicles. In seconds, the computer emitted a loud digitized voice: ALERT, ALERT.

"What's this?" Sergeant Powell yelled. "Gloucester's got an alert on this one! Mr. Cunningham: could it have been a 1996 Plymouth, 4 doors?"

"Could have been, but I don't know about the model year. Drive a Ford myself."

"But you're sure about the plate, are you?"

"Absolutely, JF3 LV1. We wrote it down."

"Listen, we have an alert for that car. You stay put. I'm sending a patrol car over to speak with you, Mr. Cunningham."

"No problem. I'm not going anywhere. Can't fish anyway."

Sergeant Powel put an all point out on the Plymouth and speed dialed the Gloucester Police.

"Gloucesterpolicestation,you'reonarecordedline."

"Jesus, Officer. How you expect anyone to understand you speaking that fast? Listen, this is Powell at the Rockport station. Just had a phone-in about the Plymouth you guys are looking for."

"Are you sure? Plate JF3 LV1?"

"That's what he said. Happened within the last 20 to 25 minutes. Two men in the car. I've got a car heading over there now. Will call you back when I get the details."

7:47 AM, Day 2

Sergeant Iacona bellowed over the open police net, "ALL CARS. Dark Grey Plymouth MA plates JF3 LV1 sighted 20-25 minutes ago leaving Halibut Point Park in Rockport under speed. Destination unknown. Two male occupants. Description coming. No word about any female passenger. Activate block on all off island roads. Click in your copy."

The two patrolmen stationed at Blyman's Bridge clicked the mike in acknowledgment and jumped out, hands near their service pistols. One walked along the growing line of cars waiting for the bridge to close and the gates to open, while the other ran to the bridge control and knocked on the window.

"Hey, Gino. Just had a call from the station. They want the bridge kept open. Better throw some Viagra in the gears; you might have to keep it up for a while! I'll let you know when."

Chapter 14

8:04 AM, Day 2

Once over the bridge, it was an easy drive past the Little League baseball field, through Stage Fort Park and out onto Route 127 towards West Gloucester. The road wound through a series of lazy curves as the tree cover thickened and the houses thinned out. Pinto turned off the main road onto a hard pack trail that snaked back into the woods. The road, long since abandoned, had at one point served as access for forest rangers to patrol the 400 acres of Ravenswood State Park.

The trail was hard going, at some points more assumed than actual. It twisted randomly around trees and huge boulders left in the debris of a moraine deposited eons ago by a long gone glacier. The wheels bounced violently over tree roots and fallen limbs. Branches scraped the sides of the car, whose undercarriage repeatedly thumped down on outcroppings high enough to catch the oil pan and cause a metallic noise like some sadistic sound system technician. Carrie held onto the door handle and pushed her boots against the front seat, but she was still thrown from side to side as the car wound deeper into the woods.

"I'm tired of this road," she announced. "It's making my bottom hurt."

"Mine, too," Pinto agreed, "but we're here."

He pulled into a small opening next to Valchon's pickup and killed the engine. To the side of the car was a cabin, built illegally on government property by deer hunters who had hauled in wood that was now weathered gray and streaked with water stains. The one small window was grimy and covered with spider webs.

As the three got out of the car, the door to the cabin creaked open and Valchon stepped out.

"Looks like you hit the drawbridge just in time. Cops have left it open so no one is getting through. You must have been one of the last ones over."

"Too freakin' close for my blood," Pinto shrugged. "We'd still be there if you hadn't called."

Rocker smiled thinly. "Why the hell do you think I gave Valchon the scanner in the first place?"

He pushed open the cabin door. He saw where Valchon had stacked the bales against the far wall, smiled broadly, and lifted the nearest bale onto the rickety plank of wood that served as a kitchen table. Flicking open his switchblade, he carefully cut off the rest of the cover. Released from the pressure, the contents spilled out onto the table and the floor. Rocker just stared, then ran his hands through the bags of OxyContin and the small bundles of heroin displayed in front of them. The blue OC's were pre-packed in bags of 20 or 80 tablets. Rocker picked one up, juggling it like a beanbag.

"That's a c-note right there. 100 bucks. Cost us 20. Not bad, eh? 5-600 bags of OC's in each bale. And the smack on top of that!" The three men stood nearly transfixed by what was in front of them. "Like having your own slot machine: put in 20, get out 100. Who the fuck needs Vegas? This is guaranteed payout!"

Having everything prepackaged made the distribution less risky, too. In and out. Nothing to touch, no residue on the hands. nothing to stick to the fingers then conveniently come off when the hand was casually put inside a pocket. It took the three men all day and well into the early darkness to inventory the load and break it down into delivery sizes. The sorting went smoothly, the men totally absorbed.

Not so absorbed, Carrie played make believe for just so long before she climbed down from the bunk and moved around the cabin. At first the men ignored her. She moved casually about the small space, stopping here to pick up the broken chair pieces, there to see what there was to eat, each time getting closer to the door. No movement very fast, sometimes circling back, sometimes just standing still, but each move brought her closer to the door.

Rocker became aware of her but pretended to be focused on the sorting. He watched the girl. Out of the corner of his eye he saw her purse her lips, sneak a glance at the three men, clasp her hands behind her back and ever so casually move closer to the door.

"One more step towards the door and I'll tie you down to the bunk" he said menacingly to Carrie.

She looked at him and cocked her head. "What door?" she said innocently, rocking on her heels, hands clasped behind her back.

"Look, kid. Don't sass me. I'm busy."

"I'm bored. I'm going for a walk."

"And the hell you ain't," Rocker threatened, placing his foot against the door. "Get back over there to the bunk and shut up."

"I don't want to sit on the stupid bunk. There is nothing to do there anyway."

Rocker unbuckled his belt, drew it out and wrapped the end around his fist, dangling the buckle end as he moved closer to Carrie. "What you want ain't no matter, girl. It's what I want. Get over there before I get more of a mind to see if this belt will convince you."

Carrie wrinkled her nose and tossed her head to the side. She looked around, rocked once or twice more then moved ever so slowly towards the bunk, stopping to run her hand along the wall, piling the broken chair pieces in the corner, straightening the blanket on the bunk, looking around at the ceiling and making no real effort to climb back on the bunk.

Rocker had no intention of being bested by a six-year old. He swung the belt several times in a circle just above the girl's head, each time bringing it closer to hitting her. In the very last arc before crashing into her face, he brought the belt down so hard on the mattress just inches from her hand that the dust flew. Carrie yelped, jumped back, eyes wide, mouth dropped open. He glowered at her and began swinging the belt again.

"Wanna see that again?" he asked, the belt inches above her head. She shook her head, ducked lower and scampered up on the bunk, shrinking into the back corner, hands covering her head.

"Smart decision, kid. You stay there till I say differently. Next time I won't miss." After one last glare at the girl, Rocker stared at the girl and put his belt back on. He had his hands full with sorting and didn't need the girl distracting him. First things first. Unlike most in the distribution chain, neither Rocker nor Valchon traded to support their own habit. They were clean. The only way to make it big was to stay clean. Give me money any day, he thought. Fuck the drugs. They're for losers he thought, not considering his own addiction to the money they brought. The scheme seemed so good. Snatch a kid of some rich bastard, ransom her for money, buy drugs, get more money. Nice part was the business was portable. Didn't stay put for too long and raise suspicion. Move to a place, scope it out, make your money, move out. This time was a little different: Revenge meant something more than move in, make your money, get even, then move out. Revenge meant MacKenzey was going to be missing something very precious to him.

8:50 AM, Day 2

Tony parked in front of the vanHawken place and he, Naomi and Lois got out. He looked back to the intersection. The CABA bus had been moved but he could picture clearly where it had been. He walked the street to the corner, a distance of no more than 50 feet, three or four car lengths at most. At the corner he turned and paced back towards where he'd started, counting his strides, calculating where a car might have parked while waiting for the bus. If his theory were correct, two men had to have been involved: one to drive and one to grab the girl. In order not to be exposed for too long, they would have parked near the intersection as close to the bus stop as possible, but on the "correct" side so as not to call attention. He slowed, examining the pavement for anything. Two bottle caps were in the gutter where a car could have parked, but they looked too old to have been from last evening. "Naomi: to be safe, you walk that side. See if you spot anything at all . . . anything that might have been discarded while someone waited."

After only a few steps, Naomi stooped over a small pool of bluish liquid. She put her finger in it and brought it to her nose.

"Anti-freeze," she said. "Could have come from a leaky radiator."

"Fresh enough. Can you sample it?" Tony asked.

Naomi nodded and scraped a quantity of the fluid into a vial. "May be useful if we ever find the get away vehicle." Just feet away were two rusty screws, which Tony pointed at with the tip of his shoe. As he started to say something, his cell phone beeped.

"Fiori here."

"Tony, we just got a make on the plates that Rockport called in. They're registered to a Sandra vanHawken, 6 Rocky Neck Boulevard."

"Say again?" He called quickly to Lois who was about to knock on the door. "Lois; wait one! Don't knock!" She heard the alarm in his voice and jogged back.

"S . . . something doesn't make sense, but this sure changes our entry plans." He paused, listening. "Yeah, I'll call you back when we're finished."

He hung up and explained quickly about the plate registration. Lois unclipped the flap to her holster then looked back at the house. Naomi saw a hand move as the curtain in the front window fell back in place.

"We're pretty exposed here, Tony. Let's get to the house or back to the car. I just saw the curtain move. If the girl is in there, then so is her kidnapper."

"Could be," Tony said. "Naomi, stay with the car and call for backup. Lois, you take the back, I'll take the front door. By the way, did George mention anything about Mrs. vanHawken having a son?"

"Don't remember. I'll ask when I call in." Naomi added sharply while pointing at his bandage, "I'd feel better if you waited for backup. You're in no shape for any rough duty."

Tony was torn; he wanted to move in fast, but Naomi was right. There were three of them against possibly two men inside who might be armed, odds not in their favor. He nodded to Naomi to call in for back up. Siren screaming, the patrol car arrived in less than three minutes. Amero and Santinello had their weapons drawn and down at their sides as they ran over.

"What have you got, Tony?" Amero asked without wasting any time.

"Truth is: I'm not sure," Tony said. "We were about to make a routine follow up to George's interview with Mrs. VanHawken last night. Just as we got here, the station called to report the plates on the car seen yesterday at the circle and again this morning in Rockport are registered to the woman who lives here. Naomi wanted backup in case the perps are in there, so we called."

"Glad you did. You're a detective not a one man SWAT team. How do you want to take this?" Amero asked.

"We've got an elderly woman and possibly the girl with one or two men inside. Worse case, they're armed and could use them against the girl, or us. More likely, but I can't be sure, is that the men hijacked vanHawken's plates for the gig and that there's no one inside except the old woman. In which case I look like a horse's ass for calling in the heavies when I go inside for tea and cookies."

Amero nodded. "So we play it safe, right?"

"Agreed. We don't over react, but we don't be careless either. Peter, you and Jimmy head around opposite sides of the house, check for back doors and block anyone attempting to leave. Naomi and I will take the front door. Lois, follow us but stand back till we see what we've got inside. Give me a fast read when the door opens. If vanHawken greets us and your quick reaction is things are cool, you tell me you'll go in with me. If your gut says otherwise, tell me you'll stay out here on the porch for whatever reason. Agree?"

"Agree. No heroics, though. I don't want to break in a new partner," Lois added.

"And I don't want to break in a new husband!" Naomi said with a tight smile.

Tony nodded, motioned to the two men to head off, and went up the walk. Lois followed a few paces back and to the side, where she had a clear view of the door and the window. Tony rang the bell, which they heard chime inside. The door opened and the smell over powered them. An elderly woman, early sixties, slightly stooped was blowing strands of white hair away from her glasses as she wiped her hands on her apron and asked, "Yes?"

Tony looked back sharply to Naomi and did a quick take on her reaction. Naomi was sliding her weapon back into her holster as she said, "Yes, Ma'am. I'm curious. Is it molasses or brown sugar you're using? They smell wonderful."

"Aren't you sweet to ask? Brown sugar, but I think you smell the caramel of the Skor Bar pieces I use. My niece loves these cookies and is coming over this afternoon. Now what do you people need?" she asked. "Do I have to contribute to a fund raiser?" she asked. Both women laughed. Tony remained alert, eyes rapidly scanning the inside of the woman's home "You are Mrs. VanHawken?" Tony asked holding out his police badge."

"Y-e-s." She drew out her answer as if still uncertain of what the police wanted.

"Are you alone, Ma'am?"

"Y-e-s, of course. But don't get any ideas, young man." Naomi saw a twinkle in the woman's eye, but Tony was looking over her shoulder and didn't notice.

"May we come in, please?"

It was more a statement than a question, as Tony was already moving forward. The woman hesitated, seemed confused about why the police wanted to come in her house, but moved aside as Tony stepped in front of her. After a brief inspection of the small home, Tony signaled to the two cops out back. "You can head back. All clear in here."

Naomi and Lois were already befriending the older woman, explaining why they had come in the first place. Tony rejoined them just as Mrs. vanHawken confirmed that, no, she had not used her car at all yesterday (didn't see well enough to drive when it was raining so hard, she had added), that, yes, it was still parked on the street in front of the house, and, no, she had not loaned it to anyone yesterday or today.

A thought struck Tony. He left and came back within a minute. Your license plate is missing, ma'am," he stated.

Naomi asked, "I don't suppose they switched the plates, did they? That could explain the two screws."

Tony agreed: "Just in case, I'm going back to get them. Meet me at the car." Naomi and Lois thanked the woman, apologized for the misunderstanding, and left.

Chapter 15

11:10 AM, Day 2

MacKenzey Enterprises sat in the back of Blackburn Industrial Park, just behind the Medical Center. Tony thought the building looked pretty plain, the factory portion a simple cinderblock rectangle, windowless and unadorned, while the floor-to-ceiling glass in the reception and office area was a subtle reminder of who had the privilege. The worker bees were crammed into a windowless box, while the boss could see daylight.

When Tony and Naomi introduced themselves and stated the purpose of their visit, the receptionist was polite but unhelpful. "I doubt that Mr. MacKenzey can be interrupted; he is, after all, a very busy man with a very busy schedule."

Tony showed his badge and returned, "We have a very busy schedule, too, but we've managed to make time for Mr. MacKenzey."

Within enough minutes to tell the unannounced callers they were interrupting something momentous to the future of American industry, a trim man in his early 40's came briskly around the corner. He was jacketless but handsomely tailored in dark suit trousers, white French cuff shirt and silk tie. His step was athletic; his 6 foot plus a bit frame carried no extra weight; and his face, though tan, was hard. There were no laughter lines around his eyes. There was no doubt this was the man in charge.

There was also no doubt that MacKenzey was a quick judge of character. While he approached, he scanned the man and woman waiting for him, guessed their business without needing to be told, and wasted no time in introduction or formalities. He stuck out his hand and crisply stated, "I'm David MacKenzey. May I assume you have news about my daughter?"

"Actually, no you may not, Mr. MacKenzey," Tony said. "We're here to get information, not give it."

"What more can I tell you than what I told the Chief last night?" His tone gave the clear message that he dealt on the Chief level and not on the detective level.

Unimpressed, Tony told him, "I'm interested in another aspect of the search for your daughter than what the Chief discussed with you last night. May we speak where it is less crowded, Mr. MacKenzey?" MacKenzey glanced at his watch with visible exasperation, then turned sharply away, saying, "Come with me," to the space in front of him as he walked back around the corner. Tony and Naomi exchanged glances and followed behind.

Naomi whispered under her breath: "He must think he is doing *us* a favor by letting us look for his daughter!"

MacKenzey's office had a magnificent view back into the woods, but was otherwise quite Spartan. There was a small conference table and chairs in the corner, but other than two wooden armchairs in front of the man's desk, the only other thing of any note in the entire room was a map of the world with multi-colored push-pins stuck into countries on every continent—oh, except for the desk. Must be the size of a U-Haul flatbed, Tony guessed, made from a curved piece of curly maple with the most magnificent graining he had ever seen. He could guess how Naomi must be reacting, he thought, livid that an original stand specimen tree had been sacrificed for one man's desk. Her clucking confirmed his guess.

MacKenzey motioned to Tony and Naomi to sit. His desk had been set on a small platform, subtly raised two or three inches above the level of the two chairs. It was sadly obvious that the purpose of the platform was to put MacKenzey on a slightly higher level than those seated before him. Tony remained standing as MacKenzey sat looking at his wristwatch, another reminder that time was passing.

Tony began, "Detective Fiori and I are looking at a different motive for the kidnapping of your daughter. The two of us are looking for the connection between you and the kidnapping."

MacKenzey's countenance darkened. Hands curled into fists, he said with barely controlled anger, "Did you come into my office to accuse me of kidnapping my own daughter, detective? If that's why you're interrupting me, then get the hell out."

Tony never flinched. "Actually, that's not my purpose for being here. But it did cross my mind. I mean, it would be a lot cheaper than paying the $600 an hour price tag of the legal suit you hired out of Boston. And it would be a nice diversion. After all, who would suspect you if you were suing your ex for custody at the same time?"

Something almost unreadable passed quickly behind the man's eyes. Tony caught it and wondered if he were getting through at all.

"Does your chief know you are taking this ridiculous tack?" MacKenzey demanded.

"I won't speak for the chief; he may have a totally different opinion. But I don't think you kidnapped her. You are capable of it, but it would require more finesse than I think you've got."

"I certainly appreciate your vote of confidence, detective. Made my day. Now how about telling me why you're really here. I have a few other things needing my attention."

"I'm sure there are more important things than finding your daughter, Mr. MacKenzey," Naomi said quietly. "But right now, nothing is more important than that to us."

Tony continued, "So if you could put aside your 'more important matters' for a moment and try being helpful, maybe we all could move along."

MacKenzey stared at him, jaw muscles working. "Go on."

Was there actually a hint of concern in the man's voice?

"I repeat, I think this kidnapping is more about you than any other possibility. Let's assume we have a kidnapping with a purpose." *And not some whacko who's got sick sex on his mind*, he added silently. "Then what's the purpose? To extort CABA? Not when it's public knowledge the place is mortgaged to the hilt.

"Your ex then? Is this about getting money from her? It's pretty widely known that you left her high and dry. I mean she has to work two jobs just to feed herself and the kid. She doesn't seem like the target to me."

"So you think someone is setting me up, detective? Because if you do, I am not giving the bastard a fucking dime!"

"Maybe not, but let's save the negotiations over money for later." "Right now I want to know who dislikes you, Mr. MacKenzey. No, that was too broad. Tell me who dislikes you enough to kidnap your daughter?"

Unexpectedly, MacKenzey picked up the phone, pushed a button and said, "Hold all my calls." He turned back to Tony with a tight smile on his face.

"I like your style, Fiori. You and I don't need to fight each other. Let's put a list together."

At the end of twenty minutes, they had a partial list. MacKenzey agreed to go back over the company's personnel records to identify anyone who might be carrying enough of a grudge to consider kidnapping. Considering kidnapping and carrying out kidnapping, Tony knew, were two different things, but this would at least give them a starting point.

They agreed to get back together at three that afternoon. With a hand on the doorknob, Tony hesitated and turned. "Ah, Mr. MacKenzey, now that we're cooperating, how 'bout we sit at the conference table this afternoon? The platform thing gives me a crick in my neck, you know what I mean?"

12:13 PM, Day 2

Rocker came back from the car with a beat-up portable typewriter with a ribbon so old it was nearly worn through. He punched out a brief letter, reread it, looked at the girl, reread it again and was satisfied. Short and sweet. Money for the girl and everyone could go about their business again. He thought about having the girl sign it so they'd know it was for real, but decided not to. The reference to the lunch box was sufficient. He folded it and stuck it in an envelope.

"Here," he said to Valchon ""Put this in the mail on your way. When you comin' back?"

"I guess between 8 and 8:30 tonight. No later than nine. I have traps to set before the tide runs and our first two transfers to turn some of this shit into money."

"Right." Rocker handed him the envelope. "Get some beer on the way back. This Diet Pepsi shit doesn't cut it."

Chapter 16

12:14 AM, Day 2

"What was the Jeckel and Hyde routine all about?" Naomi asked when they were back in the car. "Was I dreaming?"

"Seems like the man has a human side after all."

"Really, but why the change?"

Tony had thought about that question on the way out of the office. "I'm no shrink, but I think the approach you and I discussed beforehand paid off. He isn't used to not being in control. Take control away and the bluster doesn't work. I was worried, though, that being too tough right from the get go would get us thrown out. Let's see what he has for us at 3 o'clock. I think there's a 50-50 chance he'll blow us off. You know, personnel records are confidential, blah, blah, blah."

"For what it's worth, I thought it was brilliant standing up to speak with him," Naomi said. "That platform business is chicken shit."

"Want to bet where we meet this afternoon?"

"You mean at the conference table or the inquisition seat?"

"Exactly."

They drove in silence out to the circle. Tony looked at his watch and made a snap decision. "You hungry? Or can you wait a bit?"

"I'm Okay. What are you thinking? Valchon?"

"You double as a mind reader, Little Bird? I'm wondering if it really was a coincidence he drove by the bus just after the kidnapping."

"Are you thinking the girl was in the truck?" she asked.

"I don't know what I'm thinking yet. I just don't like coincidences."

"If you're bothered, Tony, there must be a reason."

She called into the station to get Valchon's address. They drove the rest of the way in silence.

12:16 PM, Day 2

Tony pulled into the yellow striped No Parking zone in front of The Stadium restaurant. Before getting out, he checked in with Chief Marren, found out there was no new information about the Plymouth, reported where he and Naomi were, and rang off.

Number 14B was on a wharf upstairs over an artist's studio that was part of the oldest art colony in the country. Rent was low, maintenance conspicuously absent. When artists starve, so do their living quarters, which makes them affordable for fishermen whose budget isn't much different.

Such was the case with 14B. Naomi started up the rickety wooden stairs, through which she could see the water below, and wondered how soon she would be swimming. The railing was splintered, held together by yellow trap line and what looked to be an old pair of suspenders. The door to the apartment had a handle, but where the lock should have been was a hole through which she could see inside and where glass should have been was an old phone directory, held in place by duct tape. Someone might have called it a statement of modern art; Naomi called it slummy.

She knocked, and the door pushed open. An old matchbook fell by her feet and on down through a crack in the landing into the water. The security system?

"Hello? Mr. Valchon?"

There was no answer. Naomi took a step inside. There were no windows. The only light was from the door she was standing in. The smell of mildew and wet clothing was overpowering. A sheet-less mattress was on the floor, so covered with discarded shirts and dirty jeans that she thought it served more as a bureau than a bed, or a clothes line during the day and a blanket at night.

The only furniture was a wooden chair whose seat was a piece of mesh that had been cut from an old lobster trap, a plastic tub turned upside down that served as a table, a Coleman cooler (no doubt the refrigerator, she thought), and a 12" TV with aluminum foil strung between the rabbit ear antennas. The unmistakable smell of raw sewage came from behind the door that she hoped lead to a bathroom.

Coils of ropes, bait buckets, rusty strainers, an air horn canister, a scaling knife and several colorful buoys completed the interior design. It was more of a statement of the well being of the Gloucester fishing fleet than any article she had read. She knew all about the onerous restrictions placed upon the New England fishermen. You couldn't live in this fishing port and not be aware of the effort the government was making to restore the fish. But seeing the condition of this apartment made Naomi realize the government might be saving the fish, but it was killing the fishermen.

Back out on the landing, Naomi took deep swallows of fresh air to clear the stench of sewage from her nostrils. She found Tony on the public wharf where a local gill net boat had been hauled. He was shaking hands with a man Naomi didn't recognize. Tony waved to the man and walked towards her.

"What did you find?" he asked.

"Next month's cover shot for *House Beautiful*," she said, "unless *Modern Baths and Kitchens* gets there first!"

"That bad, huh? That's Valchon's boat I was on. He hasn't been there today, but the man whose boat is tied up alongside thought he would be here within the hour. The tide is running."

"You want to wait?" she asked looking at her watch, "or catch a bite to eat?"

"The second one. Let's walk up to Sailor Stan's and grab a seat on the porch. Valchon will have to drive by Stan's so there's no way we'll miss him."

They found an empty table on the narrow porch in front of the restaurant. Tony closed his eyes, leaned back over his chair. Naomi turned her face to the sun. The warmth felt good. The storm had passed out to sea in the middle of the night, bringing in the crisp air of the high-pressure system that had blown in from Canada. A light breeze caused the water surface in Smith's Cove to dance. They could see a couple out in their sea kayak paddling the edge of the cove, drifting between the moored sailboats, not 200 yards from where the kidnapping had taken place.

"Funny how peaceful ignorance can be."

Naomi guessed where that remark came from and nodded. The waitress came over, jotted down the sandwich order and went back inside. She watched the girl walk away and wondered if her shorts were made of Lycra or just painted on her hips. If the latter, it was a damn small can of paint, Naomi thought.

They ate in silence, enjoying the chance to get off their feet and put the case aside for the moment. The coleslaw was spectacular. She put another forkful in her mouth and let it sit on her tongue. Must have made it with mayonnaise, she guessed, savoring another bite in the same manner. Mayonnaise and what, though?

"They make it with mayonnaise and sour cream." Tony said out of the blue. He took a bite of his turkey sandwich and gestured towards the dish of coleslaw. "Best on the island. Stan guards the recipe like the queen's jewels."

My husband reads minds, she thought.

"Only thing they are missing is a loaf of French fried onion rings. Ever had one?"

"A loaf of onion rings? What are you talking about?"

"Had them once down in Florida, just before you and I met. The place had coleslaw like this and onion rings that were battered then fried inside a cage, about the size of a loaf of bread. You would pick the rings off the loaf as you ate them. Mmmmm. Tried to get Stan to make the onion rings, but he said he wouldn't copy anyone. Never understood that logic. I mean he offers burgers and French fries. If you ever let me eat something like that now, I'd open my own damn place and serve them. Told Stan that, too! Told him I'd put him out of business but he could save himself the embarrassment of bankruptcy by just putting them on the menu."

"Bet he was really nervous, my Warrior."

"Hell no. He laughed at me. Told me the day you allowed fried anything in my mouth was the day he'd turn Indian Chief and serve food in a loin cloth!"

"Look: there's Valchon's pickup," Naomi said, pointing down the street with her fork.

"Let's move," Tony managed through the last bite of his sandwich.

He threw a twenty-dollar bill on the table and ran down the steps, Naomi right behind.

By the time they reached the wharf, Valchon was loading the traps onto his boat. They could see the man with whom Tony had spoken earlier talking to Valchon. He caught sight of Tony walking down the wharf, slapped Valchon on the arm and gestured towards the detective.

Valchon wore a dirty khaki shirt under the yellow, chest-high rubber overalls lobstermen favored. His cap had white salt lines from dried sweat and seawater. Valchon was chewing on a piece of rawhide, the same shade as the lariat around his neck from which the key to the engine hung.

Valchon was big, as tall as Tony but heavier in the chest. His neck was thick and creased where his muscles bunched. Lobster traps weighed 55 pounds each and Valchon was lifting two on board at the same time. His hands were huge, knuckles big from manual labor or fights. Naomi couldn't tell which, but knew she didn't want to get in the way of them in either case.

Valchon turned away from Tony, deliberately ignoring the detective. Tony stopped several feet short of the boat, put his hands on his hips and waited. The challenge was returned, a matter of who would give first. Valchon did, but as he turned, the lobsterman's face had such cold, hard anger written on it that Naomi stepped back. His right hand was wrapped around the handle of the scaling knife she had seen up in the apartment earlier.

"You the bastard snoopin' in my apartment?" Valchon asked. He spit on the deck in front of him. Tony ignored the question and continued to stare the man down. A minute or so passed as the standoff continued. Tony didn't move.

"Nah, I'm not that stupid. Have to get a rabies shot if I went in that shit hole. I knocked on your door, but your fancy lock didn't hold. That's why it was open."

Valchon grunted; at least the cop hadn't denied he was up there. "So why you botherin' me, then?"

Tony didn't answer right away. The lobsterman waited too. He tossed the knife in the air and caught it. Tossed it again and caught it. His eyes never left Tony's and his hand never missed the handle of the knife. Valchon flipped the knife one more time, caught the blade and with a lightning fast flick of his wrist, buried the knife in the deck of the boat. Naomi thought Valchon was readying to hurl the knife at Tony and dropped to her knee pulling her weapon out. The knife was quivering in the deck before she could get the barrel of her pistol pointed at his chest.

Valchon gave a derisive grunt and spit on the deck again.

"Shit, little lady. Had I wanted to use that knife differently, you'd a been too late."

Like a shot, Tony leapt over the gunwale and with full force drove his shoulder into Valchon's stomach. The speed of the attack caught Valchon totally off guard. He fell back, his head crashing against the wooden trap pulley, collapsing to the deck as he gasped for air. Tony stooped to free the scaling knife from the floor and stood over Valchon, tossing and catching the knife as casually as Valchon had done just seconds before.

"It's Detective Fiori to you, Valchon. Not 'little lady'. The name fits both of us, by the way. Got it?"

Valchon grunted, which was as close to a yes as could be expected; he was still getting his breath back.

"Now that we're properly introduced, I'm going to answer your question. I'm here to find out what you were doing last night. So fill me in."

"Didn't do nothin'."

"Tell me where you were driving last night."

"Went out. Why you asking me?" Valchon challenged.

"I want to know, that's why. Where did you go?"

"Went to a friend's. No one you'd know."

"Try me."

"Can't remember. It was a long time ago." Valchon said with a shrug.

"How come you were taking your traps to a friend's house?"

"Who sez I was?"

"I do. You were seen. Why did you take the traps when your boat was here?"

Tony saw the man's eyes look up. He hesitated before answering.

"I wasn't taking them anywhere. They were just on the truck."

"You always drive without tying them down? Looked like you were in a pretty big hurry. What was the rush?"

"Wasn't in no rush. I was just goin' drinking. So what's the big crime?" Valchon seemed to be recovering his stride.

"You hear anything about a kidnapping, by any chance?" Tony asked.

Valchon hadn't expected the question. He swallowed again, flicked his head to the side and said, "Maybe."

"Where'd you hear it?"

"I don't know, around"

"You got a radio in your truck?"

Another unexpected question. Valchon shook his head no, but Tony caught the hesitation.

"Then tell me. How'd you hear about it?" Tony asked, still pushing.

"I told you already. It was around town."

Tony stood there in silence, still tossing the knife, and nodded. He held the man's eyes for another minute. Nodding again, Tony said: "I'll bet. See you around town, Valchon. You watch those traps next time. They might fall off and expose what's underneath them. Know what I mean?"

When Valchon didn't answer, Tony flipped the knife one more time and stepped over the gunwale back onto the wharf. He took another step, spun fluidly on the ball of his foot, raised his hand, and, with a motion like a slingshot, whipped his arm down and threw the knife right at Valchon. It landed with a hard *thwap*, the blade buried in the deck between his legs, inches from Valchon's groin. Valchon looked down at the blade, the color drained from his face. His mouth dropped open. He just stared at the knife, still vibrating in the wood. He swallowed. Couldn't take his eyes off the knife. Swallowed again, his hand now covering his fly, checking to verify he hadn't lost anything important.

"Next time, don't lie to me, Valchon, or my aim won't be as far off."

Tony and Naomi headed off to get the car.

Behind them, Valchon still hadn't moved.

Chapter 17

3:00 PM, Day 2

As Tony and Naomi were escorted into David MacKenzey's office, they took one look around and smiled. Cooperation was the plan. On the conference table were various stacks of manila folders, some with Day-glo pink stick'em notes on the covers. MacKenzey was just closing one of the thicker folders as he rose to greet the detectives.

True to style, MacKenzey started right in without wasting time with a greeting. "Here's what we've done. My HR person and I have gone over every record of all the people who have worked here the past five years." He gestured towards the piles. "We've broken them down, male on this side, female over here. This may be a bias, but we pretty much ignored the female pile.

"Then we flagged the ones who were fired. I figured they might be even more likely to carry a grudge."

MacKenzey paused and looked to Tony for instructions. The man's demeanor and obvious effort destroyed any misgiving that Tony had about what cooperation he might expect from the executive.

"Frankly, Mr. MacKenzey, I'm impressed. You've saved us a lot of time. How many male records do you have?"

"167, of which 118 are current employees. About 50 left for various reasons," MacKenzey said.

"Do you record physical data on your employees? You know: height, weight, that sort of information?"

"Yes, on the hourly people, but not on supervisors or office people," MacKenzey replied.

"All right, then," Tony said. "Here's what we need next. Eliminate anyone under 5 feet 10and everyone whom you are certain left on a positive note. By the way, is your HR person here?"

"Carol Adams? Sure, I asked her to stay until you were finished. She's been with me since we started, probably knows everyone as well as I do."

"Then please ask her to join us."

After MacKenzey made a quick phone call, a stylishly dressed woman in her late 50's knocked and came in. Her glasses were held by a chain around her neck; her hair was gray, her expression alert and inquisitive. Tony sensed competence.

"Thanks for your willingness to help, Ms Adams. I guess you know Detective Fiori and I are here investigating the kidnapping of Mr. MacKenzey's daughter."

Tears came to the woman's eyes. "We all do. She is such a sweet little child. Whatever you need me to do, just ask."

"Thank you. Here's what I need for you both to do. We have about 30 folders here." Tony handed a piece of paper to both of them. "Put three columns on this paper. The column on the left is 'Positive', the middle is 'Neutral', and the one on the right is 'Negative'. Without making any comment to one another, I want you to read each folder, get a good recollection of the person, then write the person's last name in one of the three columns. Those you think might have had a reason to take Carrie go in the left hand column, those who didn't go in the right hand column and those you're not sure about put in the middle. If you have any doubt and can't decide, put them in the middle. Sound clear?" Adams and MacKenzey nodded and started in.

At the end, MacKenzey had two people in the middle. Carol Adams had only one. None of the three names was the same. However, MacKenzey was the more suspicious one; he had eight names in the positive column, Adams only four, but those four were on both lists.

"OK, tell me why these four."

"Hank Gentile was fired just before Christmas last year for stealing. He'd leave the production line in the middle of a run, claiming he had to go to the bathroom. The men have their own lockers where they keep their street clothes and personal stuff. Instead of going to the bathroom, Gentile was rifling the lockers, taking money, Lottery tickets and other personal stuff.

"The stealing went on for almost three months. We suspected Gentile but could never prove anything. Finally, we planted a gold plated penknife in the jacket pocket of Gentile's supervisor and had the man ride Gentile pretty hard. Long story short, we had an unannounced inspection at the end of the shift. Made everyone empty their pockets, open their lunch pails and take off their shoes. Gentile had the knife hidden inside his sock.

"Gentile claimed he was framed, he had never seen the knife before, and so forth. Swore he would get even with the supervisor," MacKenzey finished with an angry set to his jaw.

"Anything happen later?" Tony asked.

"No, lots of threats on the way out the door, some pretty ugly remarks actually, but, as far as I know, he never made good on the threats."

"Does Gentile live in the area?"

"He used to live with his younger brother on Portugee Hill but I think he moved out. Be easy enough to check. His brother Tommy still works here."

"I see you put Tommy on your suspect list too, Mr. MacKenzey. You think they could be in this together?"

"Tommy worshipped his older brother. Mimicked everything he did: wore the same clothes, drove the same type car, swaggered the same way. If Hank said sneeze, Tommy would grab a Kleenex. If Hank is involved, I'll bet money Tommy is too."

"You agree, Ms Adams?" Tony asked, bringing the woman into the conversation.

"Well, yes, of course, as far as Hank is concerned. He was the first to come to my mind actually. But as far as Tommy is concerned, call it a mother's instinct, but I think Tommy is all hat and no cowboy, if you know what I mean."

Tony picked up the second folder. "What about Anthony Pisano?"

Ms. Adams responded first. "That's easy. He was passed over twice for promotion to Line Supervisor. He thought he deserved it both times. Sued us for discrimination, claiming we were biased against people with Italian blood. At the hearing, all we did was show the Magistrate our personnel roster and the case was thrown out. You should know yourself, Detective; Gloucester has more Italians than the Vatican."

MacKenzey added: "After the court decision, Pisano hung around the parking lot and twice challenged the man who got the supervisor's position to a fight. Said he could prove he was the better man. We had to call the police to run him off both times."

"Your file says he was fired five weeks ago. So when did the cops run him off last?" Tony inquired.

"The second and last time was two weeks ago Friday. It was pay day and Pisano challenged to fight Mark for the paycheck he felt was rightfully his."

They discussed the third man, Ted Sullica; Tony was flipping through the man's file as MacKenzey was explaining why he listed Sullica. There was frequent mention of unexplained absence "for medical reasons". Mrs. Adams answered that they had fired the man because he was falsifying medical claims.

Setting Sullica's file aside, Tony asked: "How about this last person, Paul Connor? What did he do?"

"I'll answer that myself," MacKenzey said with obvious anger in his voice. "I hired Connor on a hunch. The guy was working at the Jiffy Lube in Salem. He found a leak in my engine and instead of ignoring it, reported it to me. I was impressed. Can't explain it any better than a gut reaction. I liked him. He had initiative. Offered him a job. Turned out the guy could fix anything.

"He had an edge to him which I was willing to overlook because he did his job. People actually asked to have Connor work on their machines, Then trouble started. Little stuff that got worse. I spoke with Connor several times, told him he needed to get his shit together. The last time was over an equipment breakdown that threatened our contract with our largest customer. I got hot, Connor got hotter and we got into a scuffle in my office. The security guard had to cuff him; then the police carted him off. I still remember him screaming 'you haven't heard the last of me" as the police took him out of here."

"That was what, three years ago? Any contact with Connor since then?"

"None at all. We got a threat in the mail a month or so after he was fired, but we couldn't say for sure it came from him."

"Do you still have the letter?" Tony asked quickly.

"We don't, but your office might. We gave it to them at the time but never heard anything back. I haven't seen nor heard from Connor since that night."

"So you don't know if he is still around then, do you?"

MacKenzey shook his head. “You can check to see if your office knows. I seem to remember that after we sent the letter to the police station, someone went to the address we had on file for him but he had moved out by then. Don’t think he left any forwarding address, but I don’t know for certain.”

The four of them went over the remaining files that were in the other two columns but nothing seemed to jump out at any of them to suggest a motive for kidnapping. The conversation had run its course. Tony received permission to take the four folders at which point he and Naomi left to go back to the station.

On the drive in, Naomi said: “That was a productive meeting. A whole lot smoother than I expected.”

“MacKenzey was almost likable, wasn’t he?. We’ll have to see if any of these four suspects run up the pole, but I think we can eliminate that Sullica fellow. Insurance scamming is pretty passive by comparison to kidnapping. Doesn’t fit the profile. I’ll check him out but I’m not putting money on his finishing first in this race.”

“What about any of the other three?” she asked.

“Gentile is listed at 5’ 10” on his application. If we can verify that, unless he wore elevator heels, he wouldn’t be tall enough to hit his head on the mirror. Besides, his hair color is listed as red and that’s not what we found. So that leaves me with Pisano and Connor. I have a hunch, but the circumstances seem to rule against it.”

“What hunch and what circumstances?”

“Both guys seem violent enough to have the temper for it. Pisano is in the area; at least he was two weeks ago, while Connor seems to have split. So for no other reason than opportunity, Pisano deserves a good look, but he wanted to fight Mark, the guy who got the job. That said to me that Pisano’s beef was with this Mark guy and not with MacKenzey. He waited in the parking lot for Mark, not for MacKenzey.

“By contrast, Connor’s relationship with MacKenzey seemed personal. MacKenzey discovered Connor, brought him along, gave him opportunity, promoted him. Seemed to me Connor had his ticket punched. Then wham, he’s in a fight with the boss and he’s on the street: like they were engaged and Connor got knocked out at the altar.

"I need to get the details of what the things were that MacKenzey said were going wrong that led to Connor's being canned. Maybe Connor didn't think he was getting a fair deal. Add in the fight with the boss and you've got a guy with an anger hemorrhoid so big that pooping only on one person isn't going to relieve it."

"Possible, but we don't have any proof Connor is any where near here," Naomi said. "I don't know. Pisano seems more likely."

"For that matter, if you want to play devil's advocate, we're basing this whole conversation on the assumption the perp was or is one pissed off employee,' Tony added, tapping the steering wheel. "What's to say MacKenzey overlooked a competitor he just beat out. He's not the most likeable guy to begin with."

Naomi was looking out the side window when she responded. "I don't see an established business responding that way."

"Just being the devil's advocate," Tony responded. "Leads and assumptions too early in an investigation can be like Jell-O. Push too early, they squish away. So we need to keep open about this. By the way, different subject: we should put a tail on Valchon. For a tough guy like him to be nervous of Jimmy, he had to have had one powerful reason."

"I meant to thank you for taking the rap on the apartment back there. Valchon scared me. But how did you know about the door?"

Tony smiled. "Old James Bond trick. He would put a hair across the door went he went out. If the hair were missing when he got back, he'd know he had visitors while he was gone. I saw the matchbook hit the water. You don't smoke, so I figured Bond was in town or we had a copycat. Either way, I wanted him focused on me and not taking it out on you."

"I thought he had you with the knife."

"Nah, part of the tough guy bluff. If he were for real, no way he would have let go of the knife. Rule one on the street: keep your weapons."

"What about you? You basically gave him his knife back."

Tony laughed. "Well I figured he'd have his hands full enough cleaning out his drawers to reach for the knife."

Chapter 18

5:05 PM, Day 2

Jimmy Santinello was pulling out of the lot as the Fioris drove in. Tony waved him down. "Where you headed?" Tony called over.

"Volunteered to tail Valchon; chief said you wanted to cover him."

"Thought you didn't like playing spy, Jimmy?"

Jimmy looked away before answering. "Don't, really. Just thought it would be useful for me to be the one."

"Well, watch yourself with Valchon. Just had a run-in with him on his boat. I may have given him a self-image problem. He may need to get even."

"What happened," Jimmy asked.

"I told him we knew he was up to something last night. He let it slip that he knew about the kidnapping. So how did he find out about that? And why was he leaving the Neck just after the kidnapping?" Tony paused. "You didn't see the girl, right?"

"No, no sight of her. I don't think there was a body under the traps . . . alive or dead."

"I'm wondering why was he in such a hurry."

"Maybe he was meeting up with the guy who did take her," Jimmy offered.

"Maybe, but the getaway car was long gone by the time you saw him, so what was his rush? I'm thinking it may be connected to why I was out on stakeout in the first place."

"You think Valchon was on the receiving end of the delivery?"

"I don't know, but according to you, he had a bee up his ass for some reason. That's why I wanted a tail on him. He may lead us to an answer." Tony slapped the car door twice and Jimmy drove off. Watching Jimmy leave the lot, Naomi said: "that was a little strange."

"What?" Tony said.

"Jimmy. He never volunteers to tail anyone. Why now?"

5:14 PM, Day 2

"Tell me what you've got, Tony," Marren asked as Tony walked into the chief's office.

Tony gave the chief an abbreviated version of the highlights: the initial meeting with Mrs. VanHawken, the two with MacKenzey and the last with Valchon. Tony failed to mention the knife, but told the chief why he wanted a tail on the lobsterman. He summarized in detail, however, the exercise he had put MacKenzey and his HR person through and the four leads they had come up with.

"I just asked Naomi to run the four men through the FBI's National Data Bank and the State net."

"Well here's what we know from this end," Marren started. "We've interviewed the old man who thinks he saw the girl at Grant Circle. Apparently the old man can circle the subject like the Indians circled Custer, so in the end, he didn't give us much more than a girl in a pink raincoat trying to get out of a gray car.

"The two fishermen in Rockport confirmed two white men in the gray Plymouth that nearly ran them down. You already know the license plate number was a goose egg."

"Too well. Felt like a jackass barging in on the VanHawken woman like that." Tony interjected. "Any description of the two inside the car?"

"Unfortunately, no. The fishermen were too startled, and the car went by too quickly. They did say that one guy was in the back seat and that he seemed taller than the driver. All in all, Chief Schilling said they were about as helpful as mud."

"That's funny," said Tony.

"What?"

"The guy in back. Did Schilling guess why one was in the back?" Tony asked.

"Didn't make sense to him either. No sign of the girl, though, unless she was in the trunk."

"Or unless the guy in the back was holding her down somehow. If it were the same two guys who took the girl, they never would have left her behind, at least not if she were still alive. Maybe Naomi and I should check out the Museum." Tony rubbed his forehead absentmindedly. This part of an investigation sucked, he thought. The things to investigate multiplied and the results couldn't get in the toilet fast enough.

Marren cut into his thoughts. "We got a list of dark gray Plymouths from DMV . . . all 2,460 of them! And that's just from Massachusetts."

"That sure narrows things down," Tony said sarcastically. "What about Walt? Did he finish the autopsy?"

"Yes. You can read it when we finish, but Martin died of a heart attack, not from a beating. Walt confirmed a different blood type off the mirror and is running a match through NDB as we speak. No prints were found on the door, but he got two good partials off the lunch box handle."

"Did the Rockport cops come up with anything at the museum?"

"Not that they told me."

Tony frowned. "I need to get over there. Do me a favor, Chief, and call your counterpart in Rockport and get the OK for Naomi and me to go over. Be nice if someone could meet us."

"You want to do this tomorrow?"

"No, right now before it gets any darker." Tony pushed himself out of the chair.

"Chief, one other thing. Do you remember a threat letter that was sent to MacKenzey Enterprises three, four years ago? MacKenzey said someone from here looked into it."

"Vaguely." Marren ran his hand through his hair several times before looking back to Tony. "I'm pretty sure Amero handled that. Ask him yourself. I'll call Rockport now and catch you on the radio."

"Chief? Did anyone else volunteer to tail Valchon?"

"Didn't get that far. I asked Jimmy to post the detail and he immediately said he would do it. Why do you ask?"

"No reason. In the past Jimmy always had an instant case of dysentery or some other excuse to get out of a detail like this. That's all.

Chief Marren gave a dismissing wave of his hand. "Get going to Rockport before it's too dark to see anything."

5:47 PM, Day 2

"How does your head feel, my Warrior?" Naomi asked, touching his bandage. Concerned about Tony's wound, she had filled a thermos with a mix her mother had given her of hyssop, lavender and juniper lime that she had boiled down in lemon water. According to lore, the combination increased concentration, slowed fatigue and helped prevent headaches.

"Other than feeling I should have a feather stuck in my headband, I feel fine. Some itching, but no pain."

They reached the parking lot at Halibut Point just as Tony finished the warm drink. A tall man, obviously angry about something, was pounding the hood of the patrol car and speaking heatedly into the radio. He had weathered features, a blossoming paunch and a light spray of spittle seemed to punctuate each word as he yelled at some poor soul at the other end of the call. He hung up and threw the mike down on the front seat and turned to great the Fioris.

"Sorry about that. Sometimes I think I'm a baby sitter and not a police chief! I'm Chief Schilling," the man said warmly.

"Good evening Chief Schilling," Tony said offering his hand. "I didn't expect to find you here. Have you met my wife Naomi?"

"No, I haven't, but the lady is why I'm here," he said and smiled at the confused look on Naomi's face. "Chief Marren said you would be bringing your wife so I figured it was about time I learned a thing or two from the expert I've heard so much about. I'm glad to meet you finally,"

Blushing, Naomi acknowledged the compliment. "You're very kind, Chief Schilling, but any talent I have came from my ancestors who are the ones deserving your compliment."

Schilling gave a short laugh. "Marren said you were modest." Changing the subject, he gestured towards the path and said: "Time is wasting. The museum is this way."

Tony got two flashlights and a digital camera from the trunk. At the head of the path, Naomi paused, raised her hands to the Great Spirit in the sky asking for His guidance. Tony was familiar with his wife's rituals but he could see that Schilling was taken aback.

As was their custom, Tony and Naomi flanked each other, walking several feet apart so as to cover the entire path. Neither spoke, but they pointed signs out to each other as they came upon them.

There were signs of bruising and scuffmarks in the vegetation. At one point, Naomi bent to study the mulch. She looked up at the tree limb above her, then turned, took two long strides, and pushed the undergrowth aside. Her hand came back with a broken piece of fiberglass with a stainless steel bale on the end.

"Here's the broken fishing pole. See the gray paint on the bale?"

Schilling saw the paint and shook his head. "Tell me how in the world you knew the pole was broken at that spot."

Naomi answered, "Wasn't very difficult, actually. You can see clearly here where the man jumped back away from the car, here where he lost his balance, right over here where he twisted on the ball of his foot, and up here where his pole caught on the tree branch."

"Looks only like a pile of mulch that was kicked around to me," the chief admitted, a bit chagrinned. "So how did you know where to look for the tip of the pole?"

"I measured the length of the pole by the distance from me to the branch up there. I already knew the height of the fisherman by his footprints in the mulch. Once I had the height, I paced off the same distance, allowed extra for the tip to have been thrown and, as you saw, there it was."

The chief clucked his tongue and followed along behind, still shaking his head. *Seen that reaction before, Tony grinned to himself.*

Where the path ended and the clearing began, Tony and Naomi knelt to examine the reflection of the light off the bent grass before continuing up the incline. Naomi pointed out to Schilling where a man had gotten out of the car, where the car had turned around and backed down the slope to the garage. Naomi examined the ground disturbances around the garage and came back shaking her head.

"It's quite clear that there now are three trails of footprints leading back up to the building. See the child's prints here in the middle?" she asked the Chief. Naomi stopped abruptly and knelt down to examine the dirt by the bulkhead door. "Tony, look!" she said in sudden excitement. "Here is the same footprint I saw outside the bus. See the cut in the ball of the shoe right here? Where's your camera?" Taking it from him, she snapped several pictures from different angles, checking on the digital screen to make certain the slice showed clearly. "This is the same person that was at the bus. We can assume the child's prints are Carrie's, but I wish I knew her print to be certain."

Tony agreed. "Too much of a coincidence not to be, Little Bird, but the good news is the confirmation she was alive and walking on her own. Let's see what else we can find," he added as he opened the bulkhead and stepped down into the basement.

Nothing down there of any significance. They proceeded upstairs, where Tony and Naomi split up, circling away from each other as they covered the first floor room-by-room, winding up in the office, which they examined with the same diligence as the Coroner used at the bus. Finished, Tony summarized to Chief Schilling what they'd found.

"This is the room where they stayed the night, the taller man on the couch, the little girl over there in the corner, and the shorter man here on a chair leaning up against the door. That much seems clear, Chief."

"Maybe to you, but tell me how you know."

"The distance between the oily residue on the arm of the couch and the dried dirt deposit on the other arm is about six feet. Compare that to these marks over here," Tony said, stepping over to the door and closing it. "See the sheen on the back of the door panel here? And the dried water mark here? If you lean that wooden chair against the back of the door like this, you can tell where the shorter man tilted his chair back and rested his head against the door. See the distance here?"

"Yes. Go on."

Tony borrowed his wife's cutting stick to measure the distance from the sheen to the floor. "The back of the seat is eighteen inches off the floor, but tilted back against the door like this, it's only sixteen inches. So if I tilt the chair and measure from the seat to the sheen, the man's upper torso is about 33 inches from butt to back of head and, adding the thickness of the seat and the distance to the floor where the heel marks are, we have 67, almost 68 inches. Allow another 2 inches from the top of the sheen to the actual top of the man's head; I guess he's right at 5'10".

"And the girl?"

"There's no lock on this door, so I imagine he slept there to keep the girl from getting out. She slept on the coat over there. There's no blood on the coat or anywhere in the room, so I think it safe to conclude that they didn't harm her. In fact, judging by the imprint on the coat, she didn't even thrash around."

"She could have been too scared to move, couldn't she?" Schilling asked.

"Yes, but if she were, she either would have slept upright or at least lain in a fetal position. See this indentation? And this one?" Tony added, pointing the shapes out. "That's from her head and this from her bum. And this dirt here on the coat is from her heels, so she spent most of the night in one position flat on her back. Pretty vulnerable position. You agree, Little Bird?"

"Tony is correct. I sense no fear in this position. She was trusting. I am happy to see the coat. It looks like it was put down to give her something comfortable to sleep on. That gives me hope."

"Chief, we're finished here, but I know you will want to dust the room for prints. You will need to print the people who work here to know which ones to eliminate. Ask your team to test the oil on the couch and the sheen on the back of the door. We may get a DNA sample to match."

Tony and Naomi headed back to their car. "Maybe we are looking for a local," he said "Someone who knew about the museum."

Naomi shook her head. "I am not sure of that. We both saw the footprints around the building and how they stopped at the windows. The men were looking for a way in before they opened the bulkhead."

"Maybe they were checking to see if anyone was there?"

"Maybe."

They got in the car and turned out to the main road.

Tony asked, "Still, how did they know to come here in the first place?"

Naomi looked back at the guard shack then pointed her flashlight out the window.

"There's how, my warrior." Illuminated by the flashlight was a sign: 'Museum Closed for the Season. Will reopen in May.'

Chapter 19

5:35 PM, Day 2

Four beers and a change of clothes had marginally calmed Valchon's anger. Taking a swig of his fifth beer, he climbed into his truck and put the half-empty bottle between his legs before starting the engine. He was startled by the figure that appeared at the passenger window. "What the f . . . . Oh, it's you, Jimmy. What's up?" he asked, moving his arm to cover the beer in his lap.

"Too late, Mike. I saw the beer, but you got much bigger problems than DUI."

"What DUI? I'm just sitting here."

"Yeah, and I don't hear the engine running either."

"So why you bustin' my balls, Jimmy? Marren got a quote to fill?"

"You remember last night when you were in such a hurry?" Jimmy asked, leaning into the open window.

"Nah, not really. Time's money, you know. I'm always in a hurry."

"Well, my memory's better than yours, I guess. So I hear a rumor about some shit being delivered to town yesterday via local lobstermen. Then I see you in a big hurry which, of course, you can't remember. Then there's a rumor that the deal went down just about when I saw you in such a hurry, which you can't remember . . . See where I'm going with this? See why I say you got much bigger problems than DUI?"

"What? What? So you hear a rumor. So what's that got to do with me?" Valchon feigned a hurt look.

"I'm guessing everything, but, then again, maybe nothing, Mike. Maybe what I saw, I didn't see. Maybe my memory can be altered, Mike." Jimmy paused. "Know what I mean? Think about it, Mike." Jimmy stepped back from the truck as Valchon pulled away.

Valchon polished off the rest of the beer and threw the bottle behind the seat. At a distance, Jimmy followed Valchon down East Main, through the S-turns and out to the stop sign, which Valchon ignored as he rocketed through the intersection. By the time Santinello caught up at the stoplight, three more cars were between him and the truck, giving him a bit more cover. Valchon drove past Rose's Wharf before skidding to a stop by the line of people waiting to get into the food kitchen for a free evening meal. Santinello pulled over to watch. Valchon honked. Even his horn sounded mean. A thin man with a cigarette drooping from the corner of his mouth and a glance that darted everywhere moved out of line. With a practiced hip-hop strut and his chin tucked into his collar, the Latino sauntered to the truck. His homeboy pants hung low on his butt, the sleeves of his T-shirt rolled up, his baseball cap on backwards.

As the man reached the truck, Valchon leaned over and rolled the window down. Santinello couldn't hear either voice but could see the Latino's glance darting up and down the street and almost missed seeing the glassine bundle expertly palmed in the man's hand. The Black Devil had just changed hands. Keeping his hand below the dash board, Santinello reached for his cell phone to call Tony, thought again, and put the phone down. *Let's see where this goes, he tho*ught. "Tony! Jimmy. I'm in front of the soup kitchen. Valchon just passed a BD bundle to some guy who is still hanging on the side of Valchon's truck, jawin' over something I can't hear. Want me to bust 'em?"

"No, no. What's the guy look like?" Tony asked.

"Like some white homeboy dude who's wore out the mirror practicing his strut. Black cap on backwards, rolled up sleeves on his T. Tattoo on his left wrist. 5' 8" to 5' 9", black hair and eyes set on high speed dart. Real thin,druggy-like."

"All right. You stay with Valchon. Don't lose him under any circumstance.I want to know where he's going. Maybe to the mother stash, for all I know."

"Roger. Gotta go. Valchon is leaving."

Valchon pulled away. Santinello let two more cars pass before pulling out behind him. The truck was heading west on Rogers past Chop Chop, the Chinese take out place. Valchon turned right up the hill on Washington Street and left onto the Boulevard, clearly heading towards the drawbridge and West Gloucester. Santinello tried to close up. Without warning, a pickup truck pulled out of the parking lot by Scoop's Ice Cream, cut in front of the police car, then skidded to a stop, blocking Santinello's view of Valchon. Santinello honked. The truck didn't move. Santinello honked again before the truck driver gave him a two-hand salute of the middle fingers, smiled and cut off another car as he headed back to town. Santinello, now three blocks behind Valchon, heard the drawbridge bells and saw the blinking red lights signaling the bridge opening. Santinello pounded the dashboard in frustration. Valchon had cleared the other side as the safety gates came down.

5:56 PM, Day 2

Tony leapt out of the patrol car before Amero had even come to a stop. He left the door open and jumped the two steps of the sidewalk in front of Lazarus House. Cigarette smoke hung like a shroud as Tony pushed through the door.

Inside was poorly lit. The smoke made it even harder to see. Tony could make out two long wooden tables around which thirty people were eating. The smell of sweat, street dirt, body odor and years of unfiltered cigarette smoke plugged Tony's throat. *How the hell can you eat and smoke at the same damn time? Tony wondered.*

The clinking of utensils stopped as if someone had hit a switch; silence was immediate. Thirty pair of sunken, furtive eyes stared at the detective. Thirty forks froze halfway between the plates and thirty open mouths. No one moved as Tony stared around the room searching for the white homeboy Jimmy had described. Amero rushed in seconds behind Tony and took a position against the wall to the left of Tony. Tony looked back at his partner, tossed his head to the left in a signal, and walked down the right side of the table behind the guests' chairs. Amero went down the left side, stopping at the end between the two rows of tables.

As Tony reached the end of the table Father Tom came around the corner, stopped short, then broke into an ear-to-ear grin and gave Tony a bear hug. "My, my," he said.

"Are we playing cops and robbers in my soup kitchen, Detective Tony? You know we only have the good Lord's children in here."

"Hey, Father Tom," Tony said, hugging the priest and slapping his back as men do when embarrassed by another's embrace. "Got a full house, I see."

Now that the two cops had been so warmly received by their host, the heavy tension drained out of the room and the "guests" resumed eating. The Lord blesses me with a full house twice a day, Tony. Here, have some manna from heaven. Made it myself." Father Tom thrust a piece of cake into Tony's hand. "Here's another for your friend. Now tell me what brings you to Lazarus House."

"I'm afraid one of your children has wandered off the straight and narrow, Father Tom. The white powder he was seen with wasn't exactly flour for your cake."

"We don't allow drugs in Lazarus House, Tony. Anyone caught with drugs is asked to leave and find another kitchen to frequent. Isn't that true everyone?" the priest asked to the room at large. Heads nodded all around the room amid a chorus of, "Oh, yes." "Absolutely true, Father." "Everyone knows the rules, Father Tom." "You know we would never do anything like that in here, Father."

But two people were noticeably silent, their heads down, slouched over their plates. Tony and Amero noticed, looked at one another, and each walked behind one of the two guests and stood, waiting. The silence dragged. The two guests pretended to ignore the cops, pushing potatoes back and forth through trails of brown gravy. The homeless street radar senses danger faster then the best Doppler senses a tornado. Chairs scraped back on the worn linoleum as guests, one by one, went for the door. No one spoke. Heads were down, eyes on the floor. No one wanted to catch the eye of either of the cops or the two remaining diners. Street code: avoid danger, stay alive. They shuffled out.

The two guests still hadn't looked up, but the food soccer had stopped. Both were waiting. Amero kicked the chair leg of the man in front of him and said: "So what's with you, huh?" He leaned over the man, crowding him.

"Just eatin' my food, man." "With a little extra sugar for the coffee in your pocket?"

"Don't know what you're getting at, man. Jus' eaten' my food."

"Let's see your pockets, Mister. Empty them on the table."

"Ah, man. What's your problem? I ain't done nothin'."

"Yeah, I know: jus' eaten your food, right" Amero put his hand on the man's shoulder and squeezed on the pressure point that made the man's fingers go numb. "Get up, now.'

With Amero still squeezing his shoulder, the man pushed back quickly, slamming his chair into Amero's thigh as he whirled to throw a punch at the cop's midsection. Amero grabbed the man's wrist, stepped aside and guided the fist right into the wall, pulled the man off balance, then pinned his arm painfully high against his shoulder blade. "Got any other moves you want to show me?"

"You're breakin' my arm, man."

"And you're breaking my heart. Try it again and I'll put your arm in your freakin' ear, elbow first. Now do as I asked and empty your pockets."

The second man, the one in front of Tony, watched the brief struggle and emptied his pockets without a word. The detectives frisked both men. Tony rolled the man's sock down and pulled out a table knife. He threw it on the table.

"Stealing from the hand that feeds you, eh?" But there were no glassine bundles, and no homeboy pants either. Tony knew the count. Wrong guys. To the man Amero had caught, Tony said, "Next time, do as you're asked. Now, get out of our sight."

The man stuffed his belongings back in his pockets and left. Tony stepped in front of the second man, preventing him from leaving. "So you're the smart one. Tell me your name."

"Greg."

"You got another name, Greg?" Tony asked.

"Just Greg."

"Right, Just Greg. Tell us where he is."

"Tell you where who is?

"The one you two were protecting with your tough guy act."

"Wasn't protecting no one. Look, Bobbie gave you the trouble. Why don't you ask him?"

I'll tell you why, Just Greg. You were smart enough not to fight with a cop so I figure you're smart enough to know who I mean."

"I'm telling you, I got no clue who you're talkin' about."

"Let's try another question, Just Greg. Where did you get the tattoo?"

Greg looked at his wrist, rubbed his hand over the coiled snake. "Initiation," he said

Tony nodded. "That's what I figured. That's a Lynn gang, right? The Vipers, right? What're you doing out in Gloucester? Recruiting?"

"Ain't doin' no recruiting. Jus' came here for dinner."

"All right, Just Greg. Listen up. Father Tom runs a nice soup kitchen here, but it's just for locals. You with me? You Viper bangers aren't welcome. Next time I hear you're back, you'll wish you had paid attention. Still with me?"

Just Greg shrugged a shoulder and left.

"I'm sorry we broke up your dinner party, Father Tom," Tony said. "We had a cop watch a drug exchange in the line waiting to get in here. We thought he might still be here eating, but he must have left right after the score. Did you notice anyone in the line out front who didn't come in to eat?"

"Usually I go out and greet my guests, but tonight I was short-handed and had to do the cooking myself. I never got outside, I'm afraid."

"The man we saw was skinny, 5'9" or so, tattoo on his left wrist, struts his stuff like a Hip Hopper. Baggy jeans below his knees. Ring a bell?"

"You put me in a hard place, Tony. No it doesn't ring a bell, but what folks do on the outside isn't my focus. Inside, here, is different. We get a lot of attitude, but drugs and fighting are not allowed. Everyone knows that. If I saw drugs in here, I would call you. If I saw them outside, I don't know. But as far as tonight is concerned, I can say to you I didn't see any."

"Okay, Father Tom. Look, I'm sorry again about interrupting before. We're dealing with a kidnapping of six-year old that may relate to a drug deal that went down last night, so we're watching the street pretty closely. There's a little girl out there that we want to find, and we could use your help. I respect your rules here, but I bet the Good Lord wouldn't mind either if I got an anonymous call with any information you might hear."

"You have a way of keeping my priorities straight, Tony. I'll let you know."

7:11 PM, Day 2

On the way back to the station, the two men reviewed the main leads they had and divvied up responsibility. Tony would question Anthony Pisano while Amero directed the hunt for Paul Connor. They agreed to meet back at the station by 8:30. Tony got his own car, called Naomi to tell her not to hold dinner and drove over to Tenney Court where Anthony Pisano lived.

Tenney Court was a block-long dead end street with dead-end houses and dead-end dreams. The buildings had once been single-family homes but were now rearranged into four, sometimes five individual apartments. Walk-up stairs were dark and littered with old trash and broken toys. Noise and food smells knew no walls, and privacy existed only if a neighbor had passed out.

Pisano's apartment was at the end of an alley on the second floor, accessible by outside stairs. Tony walked around trashcans overflowing with detritus that only the poor can generate and stepped over a urine-stained mattress. A collection of hubcaps leaned against one wall and a Harley Roadster against another, looking as out of place as directions to K-Mart at a Beacon Hill mansion.

As Tony knocked on the apartment door, he could hear kids fighting. A television blared in Italian. The door opened, and the unmistakable aroma of garlic reminded Tony of how hungry he was. The older woman who answered the door was a five-foot fireplug and just about as round. Her heavy breasts were covered by an apron stained with Marinara sauce. Her hands looked red and raw, still wet from doing the dishes; her look was dry and cold.

She said "Si?"

"Anthony Pisano home?" Tony asked, flashing his detective's badge.

The woman's expression darkened, but Tony couldn't tell if it was fear or out of 'what-the-hell-has-my-no-good-husband-done-now. She made no move to invite Tony in, nor did she close the door on him. She called something in Italian that sounded like Polizia. "Uno momento," she said, motioning for him to wait. She was a woman of more hand gestures than words, Tony thought. Anthony Pisano came from somewhere behind the door, pulling it further open to get by his wife. He said simply "What can I do for you?"

Tony showed him his badge, which Pisano dismissed with a wave. "I know you from town."

"You're Anthony Pisano, right?"

"So?" "You use to work at MacKenzey Enterprises?"

"So?"

"So, I want to ask you some questions. You want to talk here or are you going to let me in?"

"We can talk right here."

"Suit yourself. Tell me why you left MacKenzey."

"You came to my house to ask me that?"

"Among other things, yes."

Pisano shrugged and put his hands in his back pockets. Tony saw the man's posture relax.

"I got passed over for a promotion, one that should have gone to me. I got mad that someone less experienced got it and quit. It was a mistake. I need the money. We have a new baby." Pisano cast his head in the direction of his wife. "They tell you I wanted to fight the guy?"

Tony nodded,waiting for the rest of the story.

The man was looking down at the floor shuffling his toe over some imaginary object.

"Yeah, wasn't my proudest moment. Should have kept my fat mouth shut. Probably would have had the next supervisor's job in another month anyway. As it was, I lost our health insurance just when the wife needed it." Pisano stopped, shook his head. "So now we got this." Pisano cast his hand around, caught Tony's eye and resumed pushing the memory around with his toe.

"So what are you doing now?"

"Part-time maintenance over at the hospital. Work second shift waiting for something else to open up."

"You worked yesterday?" Tony asked.

"And the day before and the one before that. Just wish I could get back to MacKenzey. We're not making ends meet."

"Will I be able to verify you were on last night?"

"Just call the Commander. She'll tell you. Worked the ER, cleaned up after you left actually."

"Then you know what else I need to ask you, don't you?"

Pisano smiled. "Yeah, and no I didn't. I figured when you asked me about MacKenzey you were thinking I heisted the girl to get even. No, wasn't me, Detective. I made a mistake once over there, not twice."

"Any ideas who might have taken the girl?"

"Not really. I've been gone for a couple of weeks now. You certain it was someone from the company?"

"We're chasing different leads. You were a possibility."

"Were?" Pisano asked, eyebrows raised.

"Call it a gut feeling," Tony answered. "Look, I'm sorry to have bothered you. I'll be going." The men shook hands. Tony started down the stairs. Turning back to Pisano, he said, "I'll tell MacKenzey you'd like to come back."

"You would do that?" The hope in the man's voice sprung all the way from his shoes. Tony nodded and continued down the stairs. *Not very often you hear a man admit he'd screwed up, Tony thought.*

6:11 PM, Day 2

Carrie stood on the chair watching the truck drive up. "Here comes that other bad man," she said. Pinto looked up. "He's scarier than your friend," she added. "I don't like him." "We need him to get rid of this stuff." Pinto looked down at the girl. "But, He scares me, too."

"What's going to happen to me when you finish? Can I go home then?"

"I hope so," Pinto said, staring off into the distance of his mind.

Carrie looked at him. "Will you help me get home, Mr. Pinto?"

"I hope so, kid. I hope so." But Pinto knew down deep it would take more hope than he had to keep that promise.

Chapter 20

6:12 PM, Day 2

Valchon bounced over the rocks and pulled to a stop in front of the cabin. Rocker was leaning up against the porch post waiting for him. He spit out a twig he was chewing on.

"Where the hell you been? You're late."

Still fuming over the exchange with the detective, Valchon exploded out of the truck and stopped inches away from Rocker.

"Listen, asshole. I'm late 'cuz I'm late. Get off my back."

Rocker put his hands up. "Whoa, whoa. Easy, man. Chill. Somethin' go wrong?"

"Yeah, something went wrong. Something went wrong all right. That fuckin' cop got on my ass about what I was doing last night. I caught him nosin' around my place. Started askin' me a bunch of questions."

"Like what?" Rocker asked, concern in his voice.

"Something clicked through the anger . . . No way I'm telling him about the conversation with Santinello, Valchon realized.

"Nothing. Shit about where I was last night, what I was doing. Don't worry."

"Don't worry? You got a cop asking you what you were doing last night and you tell me not to worry?"

"Yeah, I'm telling you not to worry," Valchon said, averting his eyes from Rocker. "He left. Now do you want to know about the money, or are you goin' to bust my balls all night?"

Rocker backed off. He needed Valchon for another couple of days, until the rest of the drugs were delivered. An idea of how to handle Valchon was taking root in his mind. Now was not the time to piss the man off.

"Tell me," Rocker said.

Valchon took out a wad of bills. He held it in his fist and waved it at Rocker. "$41,000, Rocker. Two deliveries as planned, plus I got a little one on the way over. Caught Martinez at the soup kitchen on Rogers and scored a quick thou. Could have sold more, but that was the last bag. Told him I'd catch him later tonight behind Turner's."

Rocker counted the hundred dollar bills, handed ten of them to Valchon, and put a rubber band around the rest. "That's a bonus," Rocker said. "We'll divide the rest later." He palmed them into his pocket as the two strode inside the cabin.

7:28 PM, Day 2

The men ignored Carrie sitting on the bunk watching them work at the table. After they finished repackaging the rest of the drugs, the men made several trips to the truck, carrying an assortment of what appeared to be normal bags of groceries. The real contents were hidden under packages of pampers and Kotex, Rocker's idea of an innocent-looking way to camouflage the contraband—innocent, if Valchon had a harem of menstruating women.

They put the nets over the paper bags and Valchon took off with his load of sanitary napkins.

7:43 PM, Day 2

Tony threw his coat on the chair. The smell of the cheese steak and onion sub oozed through the plastic-coated paper as he opened it and took a bite. The juice drooled down his chin as the catsup smeared his upper lip. *Damn glad Naomi isn't here*, he thought, taking another bit of the greasy mass.

"Glad Naomi isn't here," Amero said. He carried a stack of computer print outs which he threw on the desk near Tony's dinner. "She'd be reaming you a new one. That isn't exactly health food."

"Whadda ya got?" Tony asked as more grease dripped on the paper.

"I can tell you anything you want to know about Paul Connor: his grade school, the name of his high school math teacher, the date of his promotion to

Private First Class in the army, his out-processing medical, anything you want to know about his hemorrhoids, his work record at MacKenzey Enterprises. Ask me anything you want to know, except where the hell he is. About that, I've got no damn idea." Peter slumped down on his chair, letting out a long sigh. "I've spent the last two hours looking for anything, *anything* that would tell me where the bastard is."

"What's the last we know about him?"

"When he walked out of this very police station three years and 34 days ago."

"What's your gut tell you?" Tony asked.

"My gut tells me that sub isn't good for you. Let me finish it for you. I'm starved."

"I mean about Connors."

"I know what you mean. Just a bite?"

Tony pushed the rest of the sub over, wiping his fingers on his socks. "Let me see what you've got."

He read through the printouts. The only detail that caught his eye was an article in the *Army Times* dated June 12, 1998, describing the awarding of an Army Commendation Medal to PFC Paul Connor for rescuing two men in his platoon, including one Private Rick Pinto of Somerville, Massachusetts.

"You keep in touch with anyone you were in the service with, Peter?"

"Not really. That was a while ago. Ran into one guy at an IPA convention in Vegas a year or so after. We had a couple of beers together, promised to stay in touch, you know: buddies to the end of the world stuff. I guess when we sobered up the next day, we each realized what an asshole the other one was and that was that."

Tony knew the International Patrolmen's Association was made up of a lot of ex-military police. "Were you in live combat with anyone?"

"I had to break up some pretty good fights in the NCO club, but if you mean with the bad guys shooting at me: no. I've had chairs and beer bottles coming at me, but no live rounds. You keep in touch with anyone?"

"No. I guess it's a guy thing. But let's say you saved some guy's life, you think you would stay in touch?"

"What are you driving at?" Amero asked, sitting up.

"Maybe just a long shot. I read the AT article about the medal Connor got for saving some guy's ass from Somerville."

"I saw that; close to home."

Tony circled 'Private Rick Pinto of Somerville, Massachusetts' and shoved the article across the desk to Amero.

"If you would. I'm going to call it a day. I hate to give up, but the throbbing behind my eye is telling me to quit. Call me if anything turns up, otherwise, let's regroup at 7:30 tomorrow and see where we are. I'll tell the night shift to keep an eye out for Valchon's truck. You get yourself some sleep, too."

"G'night. Hey, Tony! Don't forget the mouthwash. Naomi smells that cheese steak on your breath, it's not just the one eye that will be throbbing."

Chapter 21

10:36 PM, Day 2

Valchon pulled into the parking lot next to Fulton's delivery bays, backed into the row by the wire fence, and switched off the engine. He cracked his knuckles and looked around. From where he was parked, just beyond the play of the overhead lamps, he could see the entrance to the parking lot where workers from the night shift were outside on break, smoking.

This was his final and biggest delivery. He checked his watch: fifteen minutes early. Valchon grabbed handfuls of $100 dollar bills, which he sealed in individual Zip-lock bags, before stuffing some behind the truck seats and others in bait pails. He poured live bait into each bucket, completely covering the contents. Repeating the process until all the money was covered, he climbed back into the truck to wait.

A set of headlights played over the front of his truck as a car pulled into the lot, cruising slowly around behind the building. Two men got out and walked down each side of the parked row of cars, pointing their guns in each window as they walked towards Valchon. One of the two flashed his light directly into Valchon's eyes as the other man went silently around to the passenger side. The leader made a circular motion with his hand for Valchon to wind down the window.

"You got our delivery?"

"You got my money?" Valchon responded.

The other man nodded but didn't move. He had hard eyes, a scar on his cheek that looked like an exclamation point. Valchon felt his stomach tighten; in spite of the temperature, a line of sweat formed over his eyebrows.

"Show me," the first man said, his voice deep with a mix of command and impatience.

The second man tried to open the passenger door, which Valchon had locked before they arrived. The man rattled the handle. When Valchon didn't respond, he took the butt of his pistol, broke the glass and pointed the barrel at Valchon. The bead of sweat became a trickle.

"Let's do this together," the leader said. "Show me the goods; I'll show you the money."

Valchon held up his hands, motioned to the floor, then reached down to pick up the three remaining grocery bags. His movements were slow and deliberate. He didn't want the men to get itchy. He set the bags between his legs, out of reach of the man outside the passenger window, opened the door, and got out of the cab.

Nodding back to the floor, Valchon said, "You can see mine. Where's the cash?"

"Back in the car."

"Tell your sidekick to go get it and put it on the pavement between us." Valchon flicked his wrist and his knife slid down his sleeve into his palm. Not much against two pistols, Valchon knew, but if it got ugly, he might be able to damage at least one of the men. The leader flicked his head to the other man who ran back to the car and brought a black gym bag, which he set on the ground. Both men had their pistols still trained on Valchon's feet.

Valchon put the three paper bags with the three Kotex packages on the ground between them. The leader looked at the bags, looked up at Valchon and raised his pistol. If his eyes were bullets, Valchon would have been on life support.

"This some joke? You think I'm some pussy?"

"Relax, man. What's underneath is better than pussy. Now kick over the gym bag."

Valchon slide the first paper bag forward with his foot, causing the package of Kotex to fall out, exposing the contents beneath. The man nodded, now understanding. The packages and the money changed hands. Each man checked his contents quickly but carefully, and then the two men tucked their weapons inside their waistbands and disappeared into the dark.

Valchon wiped his sleeve across his forehead. It came back soaked. He waited until he was sure that the men had left, then drove out onto Rogers Street in the opposite direction. Close to three million dollars was enough to plaster an ear-to-ear grin across his face. Take me home, country road. Take me home, where I belong . . . Valchon whistled as he headed towards the bridge. He was too absorbed with the money to see the unmarked car pull out of the lot by Walgreen's.

10:46 PM, Day 2

Santinello switched on the flashing lights on the roof rack, flipped the siren toggle quickly and spoke into the loudspeaker mike: "Pull over to the curb: Now," he instructed.

Santinello got out of the cruiser and walked quickly to the side of the truck behind the driver's door. After looking through the rear window and seeing no weapon on the seat and both of Valchon's hands on the wheel, Santinello stepped up to the window.

""Twice in one day, Mike. How come I think I just saw something I shouldn't have?"

"I got no idea what you think you saw, Jimmy. All I know is I'm driving down the street mindin' my own and you flip on the lights."

"Right, Mike. Mind telling me what you were doing in Fulton's then?"

"What? I have to tell you every time I pull over to the side of the road, Jimmy? I gotta be on your phone to get permission to park?"

"You didn't answer my question." Santinello pointed to the black bag on the seat. "That new bag doesn't have anything to do with the visit to Fulton's parking lot, now does it?"

Valchon was silent, chewing on the inside of his cheek as he stalled for time. "Listen, Jimmy. I've been thinking about the memory thing you mentioned earlier . . . ."

"I'm listening."

Valchon made a decision and moved to climb down from the cab of the truck. Santinello stepped back as Valchon opened the door. Walking back to the rear, Valchon unhooked the tailate and hoisted himself up into the bed of the pickup. He reached into a bait pail and pulled out one of the smaller plastic bags he had hidden under the bait back at Fulton's. Wiping the goo off with a dirty rag, Valchon handed the bag to Santinello.

"About the memory thing, Jimmy. If my memory is still good, your little girl is still in the hospital, right?" Valchon didn't wait for an answer. "Maybe this could help with the medical bills."

Glancing quickly down each side of the street, Santinello accepted the bag. His head nodding, Santinello casually saluted Valchon and remarked: "Could help with my memory, too, Mike. See you around." Santinello got back in the cruiser, threw the bag under the seat, and waited, thinking, as Valchon drove off. Santinello pulled out and followed.

"Station. This is Santinello; come in.".

"Whadda ya need, Jimmy?"

"Patch me through to Tony, quick."

"Hold on."

Santinello kept well back from Valchon's truck as he followed him down Rogers Street past the Chamber of Commerce information booth. Without warning, the truck pulled over to the curb. Valchon hopped out and went inside Lumper's bar. Santinello pulled over a block back, just as the squad car radio squawked.

"You there, Jimmy?"

"Yeah, Tony. Listen. I was coming out of Walgreen's when I saw Valchon's truck pull out of Fulton's. He had this SEG on his face wide enough to stuff a Frisbee in."

"Where are you now?"

"Down the street from Lumper's. Valchon just went in there kickin' his heels like he was doing some Irish jig. Mighty happy about something. Thought you would want to know."

"Good call, Jimmy. Stay put. I'm coming over. If he leaves before I get there, follow him. Give me 15 minutes."

"Will do. Out."

Santinello put the mike on the seat and rolled the window down to try to get the fish smell out of the car. He was pleased with his sudden good fortune and a little surprised how easy it had been. He stretched his legs and settled back into the seat. *I'm going to have to be very careful with Fiori. Very careful. Could be another long one*, he thought, if *Valchon stays in the bar all night. Won't hurt to close my eyes for a second . . .*

10:50 PM, Day 2

Valchon was standing in front of the urinal when he overheard the exchange between Santinello and Fiori on the scanner in his pocket. He zipped up, pushed open the door to the hall and went out the back to the alley behind Lumper's, staying in the shadow as he circled around the dumpster. He could see Santinello parked in front of the bank.

The street was empty as Valchon crept up behind the police car, moving quietly as he neared the window. Santinello was snoring, his head tilted over his right shoulder. Valchon slammed his fist hard into the cop's jaw and left him unconscious. *Sorry 'bout that, Jimmy, Valchon thought. But then maybe you will thank me.*

11:08 PM, Day 2

Tony pulled in behind Jimmy's car and walked up to the passenger side and got in.

"So, what have we got?" he asked, closing the door and looking up ahead at the entrance to Lumper's. When Santinello didn't answer, Tony looked over at him. Sound asleep, he thought, and punched the man on the shoulder.

"Jesus, Jimmy, wake up."

When Jimmy didn't respond, Tony shook him harder. No reaction. Something was seriously wrong. Tony quickly felt for a pulse. He found a goose egg on Jimmy's jaw and knew immediately what had happened. Tony grabbed the first aid kit out of the glove compartment and broke open the smelling salts under Jimmy's nose. The strong ammonia smell revived Jimmy who groaned. He reached for his jaw.

"Ahhhhh, shit. Something moved my head off my neck! Ugggh."

"You Okay?" Tony asked, pushing the ammonia stick back under Jimmy's nose.

"Okay enough to know I didn't die but wish I had."

"You got chopped, Jimmy. Valchon if I make my guess."

"How the hell?"

"Must have seen you somehow."

"No way, Tony. He went into Lumper's like a laser. He never even looked my way."

"Okay, big game hunter, then how did he get the drop on you?"

"Last thing I remember was stretching out to wait for you. Must have fallen asleep, I fucked up, Tony."

"You sure did. Sit tight; I'm going inside Lumper's. Call the station. I want someone to check you out. Don't be a hero and follow me inside, understand?" Tony swung himself out of the car and leaned back in: "What's that fishy smell?" Jimmy kept rubbing his neck and feigned not having heard the comment, hoping like hell Fiori hadn't seen his jaw drop open.

The crowd inside Lumper's cheered as the cue ball ricocheted off two bumpers, spun into the eight ball and sent it home in the far corner pocket. Beer bottles chinked as people exchanged high-fives as if they had done something important. Smoke hung like a drab drapery as Tony made his way over to the bartender.

"Hey, Stan."

"I must be dreaming." Stan looked at his watch and pinched his wrist. "Can't be the real Tony Fiori. It's after nine-thirty. Naomi finally wise up and kick your ass out?"

"And I love you, too, Stan."

"Okay, I give; what's up? Must be something important. You don't even have your jammies on."

"Seen Mike Valchon in here tonight?"

"Sure. That's his beer right there. He went to the men's room a few minutes ago. Come to think of it, haven't seen him come out."

Tony left the bar and made his way through the crowd watching the pool game. Valchon was not in the bathroom, not that Tony had really expected to find him there. He stepped back into the hall and noticed the back door was unlocked and ajar. The alley was empty, but Tony knelt down, took out his flashlight and saw boot prints in the mud. Straightening, he went back inside.

"Stan, you keep your back door locked?"

"Have to. Liquor Commission laws," the bartender answered as he wiped a glass dry.

"When's the last time you were out back?"

"Probably after I opened up. Why?"

"Hope Valchon paid you for the beer, 'cuz he's skipped. Back door was open. No sign of him in the bathroom. Look, do me a favor? Call me if he comes back in, will you? I don't expect him to, but if he does, holler." Fiori slid his card with the phone number over the counter.

"Of course. Valchon was on some high; I'll say that. Is that why you're looking for him? Celebrating something he shouldn't be?"

"Could be." He stopped, turned back, a thought occurring to him. "Stan, you got a police scanner in here?"

The bartender shook his head.

By the time Tony got back to the squad car, the medic was finishing examining Santinello who was leaning against the car door, buttoning the collar of his uniform. The medic stripped off his latex gloves, made a note on his clipboard and reminded Jimmy to keep the ice pack on his jaw.

"Gonna live, Jimmy?" Tony asked.

"What did you find out about Valchon?"

"Like you said, he was in a celebrating mood, ordered a beer, went to take a leak then ran out the back door. His beer was still on the counter. Something spooked him."

"He get in a fight?"

Tony shook his head. "No. Went to the toilet then just split. I could see boot prints in the alley. No doubt they were his, but we've lost him for now."

"What the hell got to him, Tony?"

"Your scanner is portable, isn't it?"

"Sure. Why?"

"Give it to me. Give me five minutes then call into the station. I've got an idea what got to Valchon. Did you have a fish sandwich or something?" Smell's awful."

Santinello moaned and held his head. Tony gave him a look, took the scanner and walked back inside Lumper's to the men's room. As soon as he heard Santinello radioing into the station, Tony had his suspicion confirmed. Valchon must have a scanner and must have heard Santinello's call to Tony. That was the only possibility that made sense: Santinello had said where he was and Tony had said how long it would take him to get there. Valchon would have known exactly how much time he had to do what he had to do.

Now here's a thought. If Valchon has a scanner, and if Valchon and the kidnapper are working together, maybe I can use the scanner to my advantage.

Chapter 22

11:27 PM, Day 2

Rocker could see the headlights making their way up the path towards the cabin. When the lights dipped out of sight into the ravine, he grabbed the rifle and slipped out into the dark and made his way to the other side of the clearing. He knew it was Valchon's truck; the sound was unmistakable, but he didn't know who else Valchon might have with him. He flipped off the safety and held his aim at the passenger door as the truck skidded into a stop. Rocker lowered his weapon when he saw Valchon was alone.

He stepped into the clearing behind Valchon and asked: "How did it go?"

Valchon jumped. "Shit, Rocker; you scared me. Don't you ever knock?"

"Yeah, what is that goddamn stench?"

"That, my friend, is the smell of money. Lots of money!"

Rocker shined his flashlight into the bed of the truck. "All I see is your stinkin' bait. Where's my money?"

"*Our* money," Valchon corrected, "and let me show you."

Valchon pulled the gym bag off the front seat, handed it to Rocker, then hoisted himself up into the bed of the truck, grabbed two bait pails and slid them on to the gate. With a flourish he hoisted one pail and dumped the contents, splattering dead bait fish and smelly water on the ground and some on Rocker's shoes. "Dinner is served, sir."

Rocker jumped back, ready to curse, but when he saw the stacks of green bills inside the Zip-lock bags, he scooped two of them up and began juggling them, laughing with the realization of what they had pulled off. Valchon slid the other buckets over and dumped them, also. Drunk with money, the two men embraced, slapped each other on the back and called out to Pinto to join in the celebration.

11:30 PM, Day 2

Carrie watched from inside the cabin door. She had been awakened by the hollering outside and had climbed down from the bunk to see what was happening. Yawning, she wiped the sleep from her eyes, saw that it was only the men happy with their money, and turned to go back to bed. She stopped short. Sneaking back to the door, Carrie peered between the door and the jam. The men were totally distracted. Could she make it? The dark seemed so scary. All the monsters lived in the woods. Would they get her?

Carrie's thoughts skipped from being terrified to being tempted. Could she do it? Was she brave enough? What about the monsters? She wavered, then decided; the monsters couldn't be as bad as mean old Rocker. Moving quickly, she pulled on her boots, grabbed her raincoat, crept back to the door, looked out and saw Rocker walking right towards her. Carrie jumped back behind the door, holding her breath, trembling. She couldn't move; she knew she was going to be discovered. Her mouth went dry; she was certain Rocker could hear her heart beating. She flattened against the wall as Rocker stepped onto the deck.

Taking another step, Rocker stopped, reached down for the gym bag on the deck, then turned and walked back to the truck. Carrie puffed her cheeks and let out a long breath. She dared another peek, saw that the men had their backs towards her, stuffing dollar bills into the gym bag, screwed up her courage and snuck quietly out onto the porch, across the boards and around the corner of the cabin.

Pinto turned just as Carrie rounded the corner. He started to call out but stopped; maybe she was just going to the pottie. Neither Rocker nor Valchon noticed Carrie slip into the woods.

11:51 PM, Day 2

Naomi stirred and turned as Tony slipped into bed beside her. She kissed his neck, nibbling on his ear and draping her arm over his chest.

"You're late, my warrior. I tried but couldn't stay awake."

He slid his arm under her shoulders, feeling her warmth as he pulled her close under the covers. His hand stroked through her hair as he stared at the ceiling.

"You might be here in body, but your spirit is missing," she whispered. "Problems?"

"It's been a little more than 24 hours and I have nothing on the girl. No sign of her. One possible sighting of her in a car yesterday, but nothing since then. On top of that, I've got that Valchon guy twisted in a drug deal that I can't prove. I think he has a scanner. Jimmy called me from the street outside Lumper's and by the time I got there, Jimmy was out cold and Valchon was long gone. Only way he could have known we were on him was if he heard the conversation on a scanner."

He stroked her hair and ran his hand down over her shoulder. "Either that or we have a bad apple in the department feeding him news, but I don't even want to believe that," he said.

"I had a dream about Carrie just as you got into bed. All I remember was she was alone."

Tony knew Naomi's dreams could be uncannily similar to events neither of them could see, but which they subsequently found out actually happened. He held his breath, not wanting to interrupt her thoughts, not wanting to project his own onto hers. She was quiet. Tony knew she was deep inside, bringing up any subconscious detail of her dream that might help them find her. She shook her head.

"I can't see her. I can't bring up any details."

Tony remained still. Waiting. He sensed his wife coming back from within. He felt the difference in her presence by the sound of her breathing. She moved against him sliding her hand over his chest, down over his stomach and lower. She held him. "I can hear something moving in you, however, my warrior."

"Mmmm, you have ears in very strange places. Maybe I should see if my fingers can hear as well as yours," he whispered, as he moved his hand over her breast and his mouth onto hers, the frustration of the vague dream momentarily forgotten. *Funny, he thought of the smell in the cruiser.*

Chapter 23

1:14 AM, Day 3

Carrie got into the woods without thinking about where she was going or how she was going to get there. She had never been in these woods before, and while she was plucky, being in the woods in the dark was frightening. All she'd thought about was getting away from the cabin, rather than getting to get someplace safe.

Carrie just walked; stumbled would be more accurate. Because it was dark and she was deep in the woods, there was not much to see. She walked with her hands out in front of her, pushing aside branches and trying to save herself from bumping into things. That didn't work. Her hands were at one level, the branches at another. The raincoat protected much of her body but her face and legs got scratched frequently. She felt blood on her cheek but knew she couldn't stop to rest.

At last she reached a small clearing where she could see the moon and a few stars. Carrie found a boulder and sat on it to rest. Her mommy had told her about the Big Dipper but she couldn't see it through the trees and couldn't find the North Star. Carrie knew she couldn't stay in the clearing where she would be easy to see, so she stood up and kept going.

She had no idea what time it was, only that it was way past her bedtime, and she hoped her mommy wouldn't get mad at her for staying up so late. She was tired; her legs were getting heavy; her boots were making walking difficult. Carrie stumbled, caught herself, stood up, and smacked her head into a thick branch. It hurt; she sat down to rub her head. She started to cry. Carrie wanted to keep moving but she was so tired. Rest for just a minute, she told herself. Feeling around with her hands, she touched pine needles and pushed them into a little pillow, curled up with her hands under her head, and fell fast asleep.

5:19 AM, Day 3

Light snuck into the cabin through the dirty window and sat lightly on the sleeping men. Hours earlier, they had collapsed from a three million dollar celebration and had slept like the newly rich can, free of worry, laughing in the face of consequence. Their Zip-lock pillows held their dreams, smelly fish and all.

Valchon's arms were wrapped around bags filled with his freedom from fishing, a smile the only thing awake on his face. Pinto lay face down on a mattress of hundred dollar bills, one fluttering every time he exhaled. And Rocker, propped against the cabin door, sat on a cushion of Zip-locks filled with his future, as he slowly awakened from his past. He stretched, scratched, and opened his eyes.

He hadn't dreamt it! His eyes were open and the money was still there, all his. More than he ever thought he would see, let alone have. And he was just getting started. The girl asleep under the covers on the bunk was good for another million for sure. Maybe more, if he played his cards right. MacKenzey would cough up his arm for this girl.

He got up. The cabin door squeaked as he went out to relieve himself and the sound woke the other two. The three of them stood there in a line, three fountains of urine splashing onto the pine needles as the chipmunks ran for dry cover.

Still thinking of the money to come, Rocker went back inside to get food and noticed that the girl hadn't moved. "Hey, you! Girl!"

Nothing. Annoyed that she would ignore him, he went to the bunk and yanked the blanket down. "What the fuck?"

He was looking at an empty sleeping bag, bunched together in the shape of the child. Not believing what he was seeing, Rocker pulled the sleeping bag off, expecting to find the girl underneath, but she still wasn't there. He yelled to the other two, bent to look under the bunk, and then ran outside.

"Fuckin' girl is missing," he told them. They looked in the car, then the truck, then behind the cabin, finally realizing she was gone. Rocker turned on Pinto and balled his hands into fists.

"You let her go, didn't you?" he screamed. "You soft sonofabitch. You let her go!"

Caught by surprise, Pinto covered his head with his arms, drew himself up into a ball. Rocker wailed away, landing blow after blow until Valchon pulled him off. Valchon pinned Rocker's arms to his sides as he twisted to get free. He yelled at Pinto, "You sonofabitch. You sonofabitch."

Enraged, Pinto rammed his shoulder into the man's gut. Rocker and Valchon fell backwards, Rocker on top with Valchon's arms still around him. Pinto swung into Rocker's stomach, driving the wind out of him, punctuating each punch with "You asshole!"

Pinto stopped, stepped back, his chest heaving as he stood over Rocker who knelt on one knee, gasping air into his lungs and holding his stomach.

"Listen up, Rocker: you were asleep against the door. How the hell did I get her out? Walk over you? Huh! Walk right over you and pushed her out the keyhole? Huh! You stupid bastard. She must have gotten out when we were dancing around the clearing. The door was wide open and you know it. Now get off my case." Pinto stooped to pick up his hat, slapped it against his pants and jammed it on his head.

Rocker had regained his breath but he was still stunned at what Pinto had done. *Where the hell had that soft pussy gotten the balls to ram him in the stomach?, Maybe he was right.*

"Maybe you're right, Pinto."

"No maybe the fuck about it!"

"Right, right. Take it easy," Rocker wheezed, still regaining his breath. "We gotta split up and find out where she got to."

The men headed into the woods, agreeing to meet back at camp in two hours' time.

5:47 AM, Day 3

Naomi woke with a start. She had just dreamt she was asleep with the little girl, Carrie curled against her, both of them snuggled against a tree. She found herself curled like a comma against Tony and wondered if she had misjudged her dream for her own bed. Troubled by what the dream could have meant, Naomi slid out of Tony's embrace without waking him, and crept down to her garden for her morning mediation.

The sun had just begun to warm the boulder as she sat cross-legged on top of it. The birch trees were still, leaves at rest before the breeze could give them their daily workout. Naomi could see the early morning risers hunting for breakfast. Robins were pulling worms in the grass; a male cardinal bobbed and weaved in his undulating flight to the nearest birch where the low rays of the sun backlit him with a brilliant red glow. King of the birch, she thought! Two sparrows were bathing in the birdbath and a mockingbird was performing like a chamber ensemble.

Naomi Little Bird raised her face to her Father Spirit above and cast her hands down to the Mother Spirit below her, completing a communication channel that was as old as her people. The spirit of creation and nourishment joined within her to center her spirit, making her one with the natural world around her, filling her with reverence for the life surrounding her. Quieted, she drew within, losing herself, losing her boundaries, becoming her very thought as it flowed where the Spirit led her. She imagined herself the wind, swirling in curls, rising in thermals as she crested over the trees, brushing through the waving wands of the sea grasses, floating with the dandelion seeds as they tripped over the fields. She floated, absorbing the Life Spirit around her, rejuvenating, renewing, refilling.

She rested, her breathing slowed and shallow; her heartbeat quieted. She pictured herself above what she needed to see, looking down on what she needed to find, searching for what she needed to hold. She was hunting like the falcon, not to feed, but to see. *Show me, Great Spirit. Show me what you wish for me to see. Show me.* Naomi Little Bird hovered and waited, suspended.

Tony, awakened and dressed, had come down stairs and was watching from the kitchen, leaning against the screen door sipping coffee. Waiting. Naomi didn't like being interrupted. Tony glanced at his watch, scribbled a note on the message tile and left for the station. He had papers to shuffle before he could come back to get Naomi to drive to Somerville to find one Rick Pinto who might, he hoped, lead them to one Paul Connor.

Chapter 24

7:30 AM, Day 3

"Morning, Chief. Got a minute?"

"Sure, Tony. Sit down. Rotten break on Valchon last night."

"That's actually what I want to talk with you about. It was no rotten break. Valchon is onto us. I'm pretty sure he has a scanner. Santinello had him cornered last night, put in a call to me, and Valchon is history. Out the door. He had to have heard our conversation."

"Pretty much what I thought, too."

"That means we need to switch to cell phones, Chief. That will be awkward, but we don't have a choice. We can't keep broadcasting what we are doing to Valchon."

Tony stood up. "I've got to get going. I'll leave my cell number with Iaconna on the desk so you can reach Naomi and me, but while we're gone, see if you can get cells for all the guys and see if we can network somehow. If we get this guy cornered, we've got to be able to talk to one another without going through the switchboard."

"I'll work on that. Call me if you get anywhere with this Pinto character."

7:33 AM, Day 3

Rocker was tired and pissed. He'd been traipsing through the woods, pushing branches out of his face, tripping on tree roots, and yelling for the girl. He'd threatened her. He'd promised her cookies, ice cream, and a hot dog. He'd said he would harm her mother if she didn't come out of hiding. Now he was back to threatening. No response.

Stinkin' kid. Got a thousand more important things to do than stomp through the woods looking for the little brat.

He kicked a fallen limb. It bounced off a tree, came back and hit him in the chins. He cursed and threw the limb against a boulder and watched the wood shatter and the bark splinter off in strips.

I'll do that to her head if I ever catch the little bitch, he thought, as he broke back into the clearing at the cabin.

Pinto was already back and Valchon soon followed. Neither of them had spotted anything. The girl was still missing. Rocker swore again; Pinto looked worried. Valchon blew off Pinto's concern and bit into an apple.

"The girl will get hungry and show up. Don't get worked up over it." He wiped the juice of his apple off his chin with his sleeve. "You got the letter ready, Rocker? I gotta get goin'."

Rocker came out of the cabin licking the envelope closed and handed it to Valchon, who inadvertently got apple slurp on it while putting it in his pocket. He started the truck and was backing to turn when Pinto called out:

"Wait; I'm coming with you."

"What the hell for?" Rocker demanded.

"We're low on supplies. If we're going to be here another couple of days, we need food and toilet paper. I'm tired of using leaves," Pinto added.

"The hell you say. Valchon can get whatever we need. You stay here with me and look for the girl. She's more important than pampering your butt."

"And what happens if Valchon gets caught like he almost did last night? Then what?"

Rocker saw his point, but didn't want to search the woods on his own. "Then tell Valchon to leave the scanner. We will hear if he gets nailed. You need to be here."

Valchon handed Pinto the scanner, then drove off down the path.

7:38 AM, Day 3

"Tony, I got a patch through for you from David MacKenzey," Iaconna announced from the other end of the line. Tony, having swung home to get Naomi, kept driving with the phone cradled to his ear waiting for the connection. He heard the double beep.

"Fiori here."

"Tony, Dave MacKenzey."

"Yeah. What's up, Mr. MacKenzey?"

"It's Dave, not Mister. We got a letter about Carrie in the mail this morning. You want me to read it?"

Tony could hear the anxiety in the man's voice. The 'always in control, beat you at any cost' tone was noticeably missing. "First, tell me how did it arrive?"

"Regular mail. Our usual carrier brought it."

"Postmarked?"

"Gloucester. Stamped yesterday."

"That's some good news. Could mean she's still local. What's it say?"

"It reads: 'we have the girl, the one with the Scooby lunch pail.

To get her back in one piece will cost two million. Cash. Confirm your agreement by 12 noon today. No answer, no girl. Your choice.'

"And it's signed 'an old friend.'".

Tony put his hand over the mouthpiece and whispered to Naomi that MacKenzey had received a ransom note. He got a thumb up signal in return and checked his watch. "Put the letter down and don't touch it any more. Detective Fiori and I will be there within fifteen minutes."

He rang off and repeated verbatim what the note said.

Naomi nodded. "Confirms much of what you thought."

"I know. How do you read it?"

"Well, it confirms Carrie is the girl. It confirms they are local. It pretty much confirms they know MacKenzey can come up with two mil. And they want to move things along."

"What about the 'old friend' line?"

"I don't know how to take that. 'Old' implies a standing relationship, but 'friend' could go either way. Means what it says or, more likely, it's tongue in cheek."

"I think we can agree on tongue in cheek. It certainly keeps Connor on the possibility list, but it assumes he's local, which we can't verify. Here, call the Chief; see if he knows about the letter. Tell him we will be bringing it to the station within the half hour. Ask him to have forensics available to check for prints. Also, ask him to call the Post Master and see if he could meet us at the station in thirty minutes. I want to know if he can tell where the letter was dropped if he sees the cancellation mark. Also, get Laurie MacKenzey and have her join us at the station." Tony handed Naomi the phone and turned towards the industrial park.

7:51 AM, Day 3

MacKenzey was pacing at the front desk when Tony and Naomi arrived. The strain of the last two days showed on his face. His eyes were dull, dark circles around both. His skin seemed paler to Tony, like the man had lost some fight.

Guess I would have, too, Tony thought.

His straightforward manner was still in high gear, however. "Here's the letter and the envelope as you asked. I have put it in a clear folder so we didn't have to handle it."

Tony took the letter and read it with Naomi reading over his shoulder. It was typed, double spaced, on what looked to be common typing paper, available in so many places that trying to locate the source would just waste time. He examined the postmark closely and handed the letter to Naomi.

"Try and think clearly. Who has handled this since it has been here?" Tony asked.

"Just the receptionist and me," MacKenzey answered promptly, inclined his head to the woman behind the desk. "I had left instructions that if we received anything remotely out of the ordinary, no one was to handle it except me. What do you make of it?"

Tony inclined his head in the same manner as MacKenzey had. "Think we can discuss this in your office?"

As soon as MacKenzey had closed the door, Tony answered the earlier question.

"I think it is good and bad news. The good part is that your daughter is both local and alive. The bad part is obvious. Can you come up with that kind of cash in the next twenty-four hours? Because if not, then the news gets worse. We have to assume he's dead serious. Please excuse the expression."

"Why do you say twenty four hours?"

"Just a guess. He wants your answer in less than four hours, so he's moving things right along. If he communicates instructions for the money via mail, you can expect them no earlier than tomorrow, unless he sends them express mail, but that means someone will have to fill out the form at the post office window and my bet is that he won't take that risk . . . . So answer my question."

"It can be done. There will be one helluva tax implication but it could be done."

"There's one helluva life implication if it isn't."

"I didn't mean to sound like the tax was more important. Of course her life is worth every cent I have!"

"Mr. Mac, ah, David: I need you to come with us to the station. The Chief is expecting us to discuss how we will respond to this letter. There are a lot of decisions to make, some very difficult ones. You want to ride with us?"

"No, I'd better have my own car. Let me call the bank and my broker first, then I will come right over."

"Fine, but time is short. I suggest you tell both the banker and the broker that we can expect to receive a demand that the bills be non-sequential and fairly small denomination, say fifties and hundreds. I know most banks don't have that many large bills so it could take some time. To be safe, instruct them to bring the money to your bank here in town no later than noon tomorrow. Okay?"

"I'll tell them and be right over. You going to call Carrie's mother?"

"Already did."

8:02AM, Day 3

The postal clerk jumped down off the platform with the plastic bins and went out front to collect the mail from the drop-boxes on the sidewalk. He was two minutes late according to the schedule printed on the boxes, but the pickup truck wasn't due for another forty-five minutes. He was locking the last box when a truck pulled in behind him and a man got out with an envelope.

"I'll take that for you. Is it local?"

"Yup."

The beat-up truck drove off as the clerk lugged the boxes back inside to the sorting table.

Chapter 25

8:14 AM, Day 3

Pinto stuffed a couple of apples and a bag of crackers into his pockets, picked up a bottle of water, and joined Rocker in the clearing. The tension between them since the fight earlier had lessened, but Pinto could tell Rocker was still stewing. Was Rocker worried about the girl or about the money he might lose if they didn't find her?

The two checked their watches, agreeing to meet back at ten. Pinto headed out behind the cabin. It was not an easy climb. Pinto found himself ducking under branches, stepping over rocks and twisting around brambles as he moved into the woods. He tried to put himself in the mind of a six year old wondering how she would move in the dark. Little kid had some nerve, he realized, pushing aside a wild rose that grabbed his shirt.

His progress was slow thanks to the dense undercover, and the brambles were painful. No matter how he turned, thorns caught his clothing. Two steps backwards, one to the side for every three steps forward. Time dragged, progress measured in yards.

At last, after about an hour, the terrain opened. As he walked, the trees changed to more evergreens, taller pines in the upper canopy, shorter arborvitae, juniper, umbrella pines and cedar closer to the ground. The smell changed, too: like Christmas. More pleasant here and more protected, more hospitable. Pinto tripped, falling hard to his knees into the low hanging boughs of a hemlock . . . inches from a pair of very wide eyes. Carrie put up her hands to ward off a blow that never came.

Pinto put his finger to his mouth signaling Carrie to stay quiet as he strained to hear any sign of Rocker. Not hearing anything, he crawled under the boughs to examine the girl. She had a few minor scratches on her arms and her left cheek, a more major one on her calf. The blood had dried but had left a nasty trail of redness that he hoped didn't mean infection. Otherwise, he was surprised how well she had made it through the night and how clever she had been in finding the hiding spot. Had he not tripped, he never would have seen her.

"We have to be quiet so Rocker doesn't hear us," Pinto whispered. "If he finds you, I don't want to think what could happen! He's very angry that you ran off."

"I know; this morning I heard him yell he would hurt my mommy if I didn't come to him. I am scared of him."

Pinto had a real problem. He couldn't leave the girl where she was, but if he took her back, he knew Rocker would most likely harm her and he didn't want that. He looked around her little den and reluctantly realized she could stay here safely enough until he figured out what to do with her.

"I can't take you back right now," Pinto explained. "You would be in too much trouble. I want you to stay here while I figure this out."

Tears ran down her cheeks. Pinto patted her arm to reassure her, then took out his handkerchief and poured some water on it to wipe away the dried blood on Carrie's leg.

"If it starts to bleed again, press this handkerchief real hard on it until it stops. Okay? I don't have any Band-aids so this will have to do. I brought you some food. I don't know when I can safely come back so don't eat this all at once. Save it as long as you can so it will last. Do you understand me?"

Carrie nodded again. "When will you come back for me?"

Pinto shrugged. "I don't know. As soon as I can but if Rocker knows I know where you are, then both of us are in deep sh . . . . ah, trouble, so I'll have to be very careful. I want you to be real brave, Okay?"

She nodded. Pinto took out his penknife and cut some of the lower interior boughs both to give Carrie more room but also to give her something to cover herself with.

"You put these over you if you hear someone coming. Then they won't see your pink coat. If you get cold, you can use these as a blanket to keep warmer." He thought for a minute. "Have you ever used a penknife before?"

"My mommy and I used a kitchen knife to carve a pumpkin."

"Okay, I'm going to leave this with you just in case you have to cut more branches. But you be careful, you hear! I don't want any cut fingers when I come back here. I don't have any thread to sew them back on," he added with a laugh, hoping to make her more at ease. "I have to go now. You be brave."

"You promise you'll come back for me?" Carrie whispered.

"I promise." As he left the tree, he could hear her say 'you promised' in a loud whisper. Pinto looked around, marking her spot in his mind. Every so many yards as he walked back to the cabin, he snapped a small branch, leaving it attached as a trail mark to follow when he went back for her.

8:30 AM, Day 3

The conference room was full. Both MacKenzeys were there, chatting civilly, Tony noticed. They were about to get started when there was a knock on the door and Iaconna stuck his head in.

"Phone call for the Postmaster," he said nodding to the side table. "You can take it over there, line two."

The Postmaster listened to the call, explaining what he had learned as he walked back to his seat at the conference table. A clerk had been out front of the post office emptying the drop-off boxes when a man in a truck handed a letter to him. Somehow in dumping the bin on the sorting table, the clerk had read the address and immediately called his boss.

Minutes later, an out of breath postal clerk burst through the door and handed the postmaster a business size envelope. Tony recognized the type as the same used in the first ransom note to David MacKenzey, and reached for the envelope, picking it up by the edge to keep his own prints to a small area. "Chief, I'll make a photocopy of this and then let Gary dust the original for prints."

Minutes later he came back with the copy and read it out loud:

"We'll be listening on the scanner at noon. Since we expect your confirmation, here's how you will deliver the two million. all 50's and 100's, nothing consecutive, all used. Wrapped in four watertight bags strapped to four hard foam buoys tied together at 20' intervals on plastic floating line. Dropped overboard 1,000 yards on a SSW course from the green groaner buoy no later than 2300 hrs. Tomorrow night. Girl will be returned once amount is verified."

Silence filled the room as the instructions hit home. Laurie reached over and held her ex-husband's hand.

"Right," Tony said. "Let's review what we know and don't know before we discuss how to deal with this. We know or can reasonably assume that Carrie was kidnapped from the CABA bus, so someone knew she would be on it. We also know that they picked Carrie deliberately to get money from you, David, so they both know you and know you have that kind of money. We know that she is being held in the area, and since they expect an answer from us in another three hours, we know that they will still be within scanner range at noon. We're expected to comply with the instructions tomorrow night, at which point the money will be picked up by boat.

"What else did I miss? Chief, Naomi, anything?"

"We know Mrs. VanHawken's plates were stolen, probably by the kidnappers, and we know they stayed the first night at Halibut Point," Marren added.

"What we don't know," Tony continued, "is specifically where Carrie is being held, or by whom, or when or where she will be released. I hate to say this, but we don't know if she is still alive."

There was more silence as people realized the enormity of the unknowns.

"So, what do we want to do about this?" Tony asked, more to himself than the group.

"What the hell do you mean?" MacKenzey shouted. "You are going to get my daughter, that's what you're going to do about this!"

"Keep a lid on, Mr. MacKenzey. We all want to get your daughter. That's not in doubt. The issue is how. Right now we have instructions, deadlines, and no assurances. We also haven't established our position with the kidnappers. Let me ask you: are you willing to throw $2 million in the ocean without getting Carrie?"

"No, of course not."

"Hold on a minute," Chief Marren interrupted. "Does anyone think we should even pay the ransom? I mean, what assurance do we have they will give us Carrie back alive and not just run with the money?"

Laurie broke the silence: "But this is our daughter!" She cried.

"I know, Mrs. MacKenzey, but paying only encourages future extortion is the argument.

"It's not my money, but what do you say, David?" Laura asked turning to look at him.

"I think it is easier to be philosophical if you're the Prime Minister of Israel and you're talking about a couple of hostages that you don't even know. This is our daughter."

Tony, noticing that 'my' was now 'our' daughter, said: "It's more real when it's close to home, David, but the Chief is right in raising the question. Fact is: it's your call. We have no right to influence your decision but the answer greatly determines our response in the next few hours."

David looked at Laurie for a long minute, while each person wrestled with the decision. When he spoke, David MacKenzey spoke loud and clear:

"I'm paying the ransom. You make sure these bastards don't ask a second time."

Tony looked at Chief Marren who nodded back. "I don't know that we can guarantee that, Mr. MacKenzey. We're dealing with kidnappers, not Swiss bankers.

If you are making a decision based on their keeping their promise, I must advise you to forget the ransom."

"Chief's right, David. There is a more likely chance they will keep the money and Carrie. Maybe I should say they are more likely to keep the money than they are to return Carrie. Statistics aren't in our favor on this one," Tony added.

The group waited as MacKenzey wrestled with the implications. After a minute or so had passed, he said: "Listen, we know they are expecting us to reply by noon, but they have no idea that we know about the second note, because, technically, there hasn't been time for it to be delivered. We could make some demands of our own."

"Like what?" Laurie asked.

Tony answered first. "For starters, proof that Carrie is alive and safe. We could stall for time and claim $1 million was all we could get quickly. All we have to do to comply with the first note is to confirm we want to deal."

"You're right," MacKenzey replied. "Let's signal that we'll deal but doubt we can get more than one million together by the deadline. Suggest that we will try, but the banks aren't optimistic, etc. Sort of a cooperative good guy, bad guy response. I would be willing, but the banks are the obstacles. That way we could see how firm they are without our saying no to the two million."

"Good idea," said Tony. "If you are convinced you want to pay the ransom even after what we just said, then why don't you draft a response in your own words and plan to be here no later than 11:45 so we can go over the content, tone, etc."

The meeting broke up just as Santinello came in on the run, out of breath. "From what I can tell, it was Valchon who delivered the letter. The clerk got a glimpse of the truck and it fits Valchon's perfectly."

"Let's get him. I want a round the clock watch on Rocky Neck with every squad alert for his truck. See him, take him. Maybe he can tell us where the girl is. I want that bastard, fast." Santinello left to put things in motion.

"OK, so we have a full court press on finding Valchon. Naomi and I will head to Somerville and see what we can find out about Pinto. One other thought, Chief," Tony added. "Let's say MacKenzey wants to go through with the payout tomorrow. I suggest you call Commander Lewis in strictest of confidence, tell him of the delivery request, and have him come up with a game plan as to how we could pull that off. I have half a mind to put a bomb in the last buoy and time it to go off when it is hooked in!"

"I hear you, Tony, but we can't risk not getting the girl. I wonder how MacKenzey would feel watching $2 million dollars go up in fireworks!"

Chapter 26

8:36 AM, Day 3

Valchon drove out onto the wharf and parked. Before getting on his boat, he went up to the apartment. This would be the last time he would be there, if all went according to plan, so he wanted to take the few things of value that he had. Not that there was much. Mostly sentimental value, actually, but as he looked around, nothing seemed important enough any more. A couple of shirts, maybe, and the lamp his sister had given him.

He didn't bother with the security system, just turned and walked out. The matchbook was on the floor where it had fallen. This phase of his life was finished, *Maybe I'll head down to New Bedford and fish*, he thought. *Maybe just take a year off, charter a boat in the Keys, find me a woman . . . or two.*

Valchon headed out of Smith's Cove past Ten Pound Island and out to the breakwater. Valchon's boat made no special impression on anyone. He just slipped away. No ticker tape, no water gun salute from a local tug, no wave from friends on the wharf. Nobody would even know he was gone. With years of practice, Valchon stuffed the loneliness down deep, set the autopilot and opened a bottle of beer. Next stop: Beverly harbor where he was even more unknown and where he could wait out the next thirty-six hours until he became an even a richer loner. *Can I use Santinello to help pull this off*, he wondered.

9:02 AM, Day 3

Tony and Naomi drove down Route 128 towards Somerville, discussing what the chances were of finding the girl in the next 36 hours. They explored options for the money drop and even saluted the kidnapper's plan to have the money left at sea. They knew that in the cover of dark, it would be easy enough for the kidnappers to pick up the buoys and even easier to abort if they sensed other boats in the area. The drop area was far enough out of the harbor that no patrol boat could hide in a cove and surprise them when they retrieved the money, yet close enough in that the kidnappers could row out and pick it up. Either way, another boat would be easy to see on radar, but of course that worked both ways. Even the bad guys had radar.

They hadn't formulated a game plan by the time they drove into the area of Somerville where Pinto was last known to live. "Riverview Terrace" was a laugh, Tony thought, a developer's name to attract the easy-to-mislead crowd. There wasn't a river in sight. The only water in sight had been collected at a storm sewer so clogged with leaves and fast food wrappers that even the water turned its stomach at percolating though that mess.

Two-story row houses lined both sides of the street, most showing the neglect of absentee ownership, or tenants who barely made the rent. One or two tiny American flags were stuck in the occasional fence, but their colors had faded long ago; now a weathered cancer ate away at the cloth, leaving just stringy tatters on the once proud fabric. A child's pink pinwheel, missing one of its spokes, turned and stopped, turned again as the breeze worked up enough effort to make it spin. This was a neighborhood that took effort.

Tony and Naomi climbed the cement steps and rang the bell next to the paper that read 'P.i.n.t . . .' Tony wondered if the missing O was an omen. In a minute they heard someone shuffling towards the door and could see a shadow of a figure looking through the frosted glass. Two deadbolts clicked open and the door followed, before being stopped by a security chain.

The fingers that held the door were pudgy, the nails bitten to the quick. The woman's face that followed was pallid, heavily wrinkled, and sported a huge mole on the left cheek that was sprouting strands of curly black hair. Her eyes were dark and watery. Tony wondered if the woman actually saw him. She said nothing.

Tony flashed his badge and said: "I'm Detective Fiori and am looking for a Rick Pinto. Is he here?"

"Not at the moment," a quivery voice responded. "Rick isn't here much these days."

"Are you his mother?" Naomi asked.

"Yes, I am, young woman. Who are you?"

"I'm sorry, Mrs. Pinto; I'm Detective Fiori. We're both from the Gloucester Police."

"My, that's quite a ways. Why are you all the way down here?"

"We want to speak with Rick. Can you tell us where to find him?"

"He left a couple of days ago to meet an old Army buddy who had come to town."

"Do you know the friend's name, Mrs. Pinto?" Naomi asked.

"I don't know his real name," the woman said after a pause.

"Does that mean you know his fake name?" Naomi said, trying some humor.

What she said next made Tony's heart miss a beat.

"I don't know if it is fake or not, but Rick calls him Rocker, maybe because the man is off of it," she responded with a little chuckle of her own. Naomi laughed with her and exchanged a very pleased look with Tony.

"Can you tell us where we might find them, Mrs. Pinto?" Tony asked, taking back the lead.

"Didn't you say you were from Gloucester?"

"Yes, ma'am."

"Well, you could have saved yourself a trip. I think Rick mentioned something about heading to Gloucester. Said he would be gone a couple of days, I think. But you know how kids are these days."

"Mrs. Pinto, do you have a picture of your son that we could see?"

"Why, yes. Just a minute." Mrs. Pinto closed the door, latched both deadbolts and left.

"Can't be too safe in this neighborhood, I guess," Tony said.

"I don't blame her. You're pretty scary looking," Naomi offered. "Guess we're not going to be invited in."

"And your first clue was?" Tony asked as the two deadbolts were opened again.

Mrs. Pinto thrust a badly tarnished brass frame through the crack in the door. The picture showed two men in Army fatigues, their caps back at a jaunty angle, the taller man with his foot on the fender of an Army jeep and his arm around the other man's shoulder. Tony thought he might have won the lottery but asked just to be sure.

"Which is Rick, Mrs. Pinto?"

"That's my Rick on the left. The Rocker fellow is the one with his arm on Rick's shoulder. It was taken a couple of years ago just before they got out of the military. They've been friends ever since. I think that man Rocker saved my boy's life somehow."

Not just the lottery, Tony thought, *Mass Millions!* "Mrs. Pinto, do you know how Rick and his friend got to Gloucester? Did they drive?"

"I'm sure Rick did drive. He left here to go to the bus station to pick his friend up."

"What car does your son drive?" Naomi inquired.

"It's an old Plymouth. It was my husband Harold's car until he died five years ago. Rick has driven it ever since."

Not just Mass Millions: Tri-State Lotto as well!

"Mrs. Pinto, do you know if your son has a cell phone?"

"I know he has one of those portable ones."

"Yes, ma'am, they're the same thing. Did your son leave the number with you?"

"Yes, I'll get it for you." She closed the door and threw the deadbolts again.

"You old charmer!" said Naomi, punching Tony in the arm. "I'd keep the deadbolts on, too, if I saw you at my door."

The woman came back and re-opened the door, but still kept the security chain in place as she handed Tony a piece of paper.

"That's what he left me, but I don't think he'll like it if you call him. He told me to use it only in an emergency; I guess each call costs a lot of money."

"Thank you, Mrs. Pinto. We'll only use it if it's an emergency, don't you worry. We need to get back to Gloucester now. Let me give you my card. Will you call me if you hear from Rick?"

"All the way to Gloucester? That must be long distance."

"Just call me collect. Don't worry about the charge. Just tell the operator you want me, Detective Fiori. It's right there on the card."

Tony and Naomi turned to return to the car, holding the picture frame against his jacket, hoping Mrs. Pinto had forgotten about it. She hadn't.

"Say, Detective. I want my picture back, please."

Hoping she didn't mean right now, Tony answered. "I promise to return it, Mrs. Pinto. Just as soon as we see your son. Bye now!"

They nearly jogged to the car before the woman could demand it right then.

10:04 AM, Day 3

Naomi punched in the name of Harold Pinto into the computer connected to the Registry of Motor Vehicles to get the information about the Plymouth. Tony radioed back to the station and got Chief Marren.

"Chief, we got our first real break. According to his mother, Pinto left home a day or two ago in a beat-up Plymouth to pick up an old Army buddy at the bus stop before heading up to Gloucester. And guess who the buddy is? None other than our old friend: Paul 'Rocker' Connor."

"Jesus, Tony, great work! Where are you now?"

"On our way back with a present for you."

"What's that?" Marren asked.

"A photo of Pinto and Connor, yuckin' it up for the camera."

"Oh, man. Brass ring is right. I'll have the *Times* reporter here waiting for it. We should be able to get it in tonight's paper no problem."

Tony signed off, plugged the red blinker into the cigarette lighter, stuck it on the roof, and stuck the accelerator right to the floor. Amazing what a break could do for your morale.

Chapter 27

1:38 PM, Day 3

Commander Lewis stood up as Tony came into his office. "Well, detective, you look a lot better than the last time I saw you."

"Feel a lot better, too; I owe you and your men big time.

"That's our job. Glad we could help." He gestured for Tony to sit down, and sat himself.

"And now I'm afraid I'm here for more help," Tony said. "You know the girl that has been missing for two days?"

"The MacKenzey girl, right?" At Tony's nod, he continued, "I read about that. Damn shame. I also read between the lines that you cops think the kidnapping and the drug deal you and I were staked on are related. True?"

"A lot of things point in that direction, but we aren't positive. For the moment, we assume they are. We got a ransom demand from the kidnappers, which is why I'm here.

"Tell me what you need. If it's legal, I'll do what I can, you know that." "Thanks, Commander. Have you got a navigation chart of the area just outside the breakwater?"

Lewis stood up. "Got a blow-up right here on the chart table. Don't tell me they have the girl in the outer harbor?"

"Truth is, we don't know where they have her. My question has to do with where they are demanding we drop the ransom."

"They want to retrieve it by boat? Did they tell you where?" Lewis asked.

Tony read the instructions to Lewis, who pointed his finger at the buoy, set his straightedge heading SSW, then grabbed the calipers to mark the thousand-yard point.

"That would make it right about there," Lewis said. "That's in sixty fathoms of water. They could bring a sub in to make the pickup. On the other hand, it's close enough to shore they could use a rowboat. Jesus! Pretty clever. Do you know anything more?"

"Only that we have to lash four bags of bills to buoys tied at 20' intervals by 11 tomorrow night. No other instructions, so far anyway."

"So, we've got a nighttime pickup in deep water." Lewis examined the chart. "What are you looking for me to do?"

"Frankly, I don't know. A lot depends on if we find the girl beforehand, but that may be a long shot. All we know right now is that the kidnappers can monitor our radio transmissions, which we can work to our advantage, if we need to."

"All right, I get the picture. Either you have the girl by eleven tomorrow or we assume the girl is still at risk at the time of the drop and plan accordingly."

Tony nodded. "That's the way I see it. We have two opportunities to interact here: one on the water, and one when the boat that picks up the money gets to land. In either case, we could use your men."

"The water part is clear. But how the hell are you going to know where the boat will land? We'll run out of men before you run out of land where he could put ashore. Here, look at the chart."

Lewis took his straightedge, started at the edge of the outer harbor and pointed his way around Norman's Woe, Coolidge Point, down the coast of Magnolia, to Lobster Cove in Manchester, Manchester Harbor, and all the way to Beverly and beyond to Salem. "You could land a day boat in hundreds of places, a small outboard in thousands of places. Look here: the drop point is close enough for you to even swim out, if you wanted to be really quiet."

"Not good news" Tony agreed. "Too many possibilities. Could we improve the odds if we put a transmitter in one of the bags and just track him?"

"Sure, unless he finds it and tosses it overboard first. Then what are you going to track?"

Tony voiced the obvious answer: "My way to the unemployment line."

Lewis scratched his head. "Let me ask you this: are you giving me any limitations on what we can consider doing here? I mean, I've got lots of options to work with: underwater divers, the inflatable you were on the other night, helicopters. Hell, I could even throw the 52 footer out there. Its speed is classified but I can tell you that if you could do forty knots in a race with her, you'd lose your ass."

"Commander, this is your area. All I can say is, we're going to need to cover different scenarios and be silent no matter what. If they know we're there, they could radio back to shore and harm the girl."

"I have enough to go on for now, Tony. Let me get with my guys, come up with some options, and I'll call you later this afternoon."

"By four if you can."

1:41 PM, Day 3

Pinto was growing more and more frustrated by his own indecision of how to help Carrie. The longer he thought about it, the more certain he was that he must get her safely back to her mother. Screw Rocker. Screw Valchon, too! But how-in-hell-am-I-going-to-do-that kept rebounding in his head, like an echo in a vacant room. One option would mean using a phone, but his battery was dead. Getting to Rocker's would be tricky.

Rocker interrupted his thoughts by storming into the clearing, swearing and beating anything in his way with the stick he was carrying. He was alone, so Pinto knew Carrie was still safe.

"I hope you're satisfied I haven't hidden her," Pinto stated, brushing pine needles off his arms.

"Screw you, Pinto."

"Look, Rocker, I want to find her too, so how 'bout you and I work together instead of you thinking I'm working against you all the time, huh? I'm getting tired of you being on my back all the time."

Rocker ignored that. "I've got an idea how to flush her out." He paused. "Get me some matches. We're going to start a fire. Burn her out!"

"And bring every fireman within twenty miles right here? Great idea!"

"Well then you tell me, Mr. Know-it-all; what's your idea?"

"I don't have one any more than you do. We keep looking. But I'll tell you this: We need to stay here out of sight. We both know the cops want us in the worst way. Even if we do find the girl, where are we going to go till we hook up with Valchon? No, we're stayin' right here, if you ask me."

"Well, I ain't asking you. Besides, I've decided to stay here anyway. Freakin' girl." Rocker took a long swig of water.

"Rocker, have you thought about what you're going to tell the cops? Or are you just going to blow them off and not answer?"

"Haven't decided yet. If I don't tell them anything, they are going to have to go through with the drop. Otherwise they know we'll do something to the girl. Right now, I don't have to tell them shit, so I'm going to wait."

Rocker's phone rang and they both started. "Valchon," Rocker said shortly, and answered the cell. "Yeah, what's up?"

"You're a celebrity, man," Valchon said. "You and Pinto made the front page of tonight's paper. Now every dickhead on Cape Ann will be looking for you. If they find you, guess what? They come into 5 large!"

"$500,000?" Rocker asked. "They got my name?"

"And a pretty picture of you standing with your arm over Pinto's shoulder. Both of you in front of some Army jeep, looking' just like John Wayne himself!"

"A picture of me in the Army? How the hell? Wait a minute." Rocker took the phone from his ear and looked over at Pinto. "You know anything about a picture of the two of us in the Army?" he asked. "With my arm over your shoulder by some jeep?"

Pinto thought. "Sounds like the picture my mother has on her mantle, but how would they get it from her?"

"Valchon?" Rocker said back to the phone. "Pinto said it might have come from his mother."

"If you had kept your powder cool, I could have told you that myself. Says so in the article. Same hotshot detective that came bustin' my balls the other day somehow put you and Pinto together and went looking for him in Somerville. Found Rick's old lady straight off."

"Shit!"

"It gets worse. The article identifies Pinto's car and license plate, so you're goin' to have to stay put, unless you can get yourself another set of wheels."

"How the hell am I going to do that? No, you get them; can't use your truck anymore anyway, and then you have new wheels to pick us up tomorrow night."

"I'll work on it," Valchon mumbled.

"Just don't get anything hot." Rocker clicked off and started to smile.

"What's so funny?" Pinto asked.

"Just got me a new plan," Rocker said.

So did Valchon. He thought *if Rocker's wheels are hot, and an anonymous caller told Santinello where he might find the car, then the ransom money wouldn't have to be split with anyone but me!*

Chapter 28

4:14 PM, Day 3

"Fiori," Tony said answering his phone.

"Lewis here. Got a minute?"

"Sure." Tony looked at his watch. "You're a man of your word. Your call is right on time."

"Sure try, anyway. Listen, we've been shooting some options around over here. I think we have a game plan for you. You want to come over?"

"Give me 20 or so and I'll be there."

Tony finished briefing the night shift, making certain they had the picture of Connor and Pinto and of Pinto's car and Valchon's truck, none of which had been seen all day. "The easiest target is Valchon," he told them. "You see him, you nab him. I don't care if he's at Mass at Our Lady: nail him. If he's in the crapper at Lumper's, get him before he zips his pants. I want him badly. If we can find him, maybe we can find the other two. We find the other two, I think we find the girl. And she's the home run. You've got my cell. Call me anytime you see any of them. Doesn't matter what the clock says. Now go get 'em."

Tony folded up his notes and looked over at Peter Amero. Trying to sound upbeat was beginning to sound a little false.

"How you holdin' up, Tony?" Amero asked.

"Getting nervous, Pete. I thought we had a break getting the connection between Connor and Pinto. There's no doubt that it was Pinto's car that the old man saw at the circle and the guy at Halibut Point saw. My gut tells me Valchon is in this up to his ass with these guys, but where the hell are they? They have to be near by. Now Jimmy tells me Valchon's boat is gone and his apartment door was wide open. They've gone to ground."

Amero nodded. "Could use a break right about now."

"Talk to me," Tony said; "anything we're not doing?"

"I don't know. That's why you make the big bucks, Tony. I'm just the flunky."

"Yeah, right! I'm going over to the Coast Guard station. Ring me with anything, will ya?"

4:31 PM, Day 3

Valchon changed out of his fishing gear. He had tied off at the old construction site underneath the Beverly/Salem Bridge where there was little traffic, sort of a no-man's land that neither Beverly nor Salem cops patrolled, just the sort of place where a strange boat wouldn't be suspicious.

After climbing up the embankment to the road, he set out on foot towards downtown Salem on a road littered with tenement houses and marginal businesses, right where a character of his description would fit in. Valchon was on the make for a set of wheels.

He walked by the roast beef stand; the smells of barbeque sauce and fried onions were tempting. Wheels first, he told himself, then eat. Next on that side of the street was a dry cleaner with its van parked alongside the storefront. He decided against it. The signage on the side of the van was too visible if the stolen van was reported to the police.

The Harley store caught his eye. *Man, I could see me prancin' in all that chrome and the thundering tailpipes: shhheeeeeeit! Ridin' pretty!*

The thought of tooling down 128 with the wind in his face and the machine purrin' was quickly drowned out by another thought: some tattooed biker with a burr up his ass comin' after him for stealin' his bike. So he left the Harley where it was, but he did pat the seat on the way by.

The next lot was more promising. The sign on the door advertised money orders, bail bonds and rental cars, one way and round trip. At the end of the second row, there was an old Chevy, just dying to be taken for a spin. He jimmied the door and reached under the dashboard, pulling down a bunch of wires. He crossed the right ones and the car just seemed to say, "Take me. Take me." Valchon obliged, headed to the package store he had passed earlier, got a six pack of Bud, drove back down to the boat and settled in. Checking his cell phone, he noticed Santinello hadn't called back.

4:40 PM, Day 3

When Tony got to Commander Lewis's office, there were four other men there. He recognized Jones and was quickly introduced to the other three: the head of the dive team, a demolition expert and the other with pilot's wings on his lapel. The five of them huddled around the charts while each man presented the options his team could provide. Each scenario was thoroughly explored, refined, and tweaked again until the give and take had formulated a series of plans for personnel assignments, transmitter placements, back-up boats and so forth for the following night. Tony was impressed and told them so before the meeting broke up.

5:10 PM, Day 3

Rocker had been in the cabin behind the closed door for over an hour. When Pinto knocked, Rocker yelled through the closed door, "Go find the girl and quit bothering me."

Pinto realized he had an opportunity, ran to his car, grabbed a towel, an old sweater and a cap, and raced into the woods. The trail he had left was easy to follow and he came up on Carrie's hideout in less than twenty minutes. She looked happy to see him and ran out to give him a hug.

"Listen, Carrie, I only have a minute; I got away while Rocker was doing something in the cabin. I brought you some stuff from the car I thought you could use tonight, Okay?"

"You mean you didn't come to get me?" she said wrinkling up her brow and dropping her shoulders.

"No, sweetheart, not yet. Probably by tomorrow night, unless I can figure out something sooner. Will you be Okay till then?"

"I guess so, if the wolf doesn't come back."

"What wolf?" Pinto asked in alarm. "There are no wolves in this neck of the woods."

"It looked like a wolf, anyway, big and all gray, with real scary eyes. And it ate Mr. Chipmunk, right over there," Carrie answered, pointing to the clearing just feet away. "I could hear the wolf chewing Mr. Chipmunk; it was so awful. I want to go home, Rick. I miss my Mommy and I'm getting hungry."

Now Pinto had a problem. Which was worse, bringing Carrie back to face Rocker or leaving her here to face the wolf? A lose-lose decision, no matter what.

"If I bring you closer to the cabin, Rocker might see you," Pinto said, more to himself than to Carrie. "But if I leave you here . . . Damn, I don't know what to do!" Pinto saw the look in Carrie's eyes and knew he should stay to protect the girl. But if he stayed, and if Rocker found him, then he would be dead too. Shit!

"Do you have any of the food left?"

"Just some water and two more crackers. I tried to save them for supper."

"Good girl. Look, I've got to get back. Otherwise, Rocker will suspect something and if he finds us, he'll kill us both. I just know it! You keep the knife I gave you and if that old wolf comes back and bothers you, you use it. Okay?

"You mean stab the wolf with it?" Carrie asked, crossing her arms across her chest, her eyebrows rose. "How would I do that?"

Pinto was flustered with indecision. *No matter what I do*, he thought, letting the end of the sentence trail off into avoidance. "I'm pretty sure that if he didn't bother you before, he won't bother you again," he said at last, trying to convince himself more than the girl. "I'll do my best to bring you something to eat first thing in the morning. By then I should know more about what's going to happen. You'll be Okay. You stay put now, promise?"

"I promise. That man Rocker almost found me this afternoon. I was so scared. He was so close, he beat the branches over my head with a stick and all the dead pine needles came down in my face. I almost went pee-pee, I was so scared."

Pinto gave her a quick hug, made her promise one more time to stay put, then hustled back to the cabin where Rocker was waiting.

"And where exactly have you been?" Rocker looked at him closely. "Did you just see the girl?"

"I saw trees," was all Pinto answered.

5:35 PM, Day 3

Back at the station, Chief Marren was deep in thought, running his hands through his hair. Kicking the chair away from the desk, Tony sat and waited for the chief to arrive at his decision, or to have his hair fall out, whichever came first. At the rate he was going, Tony mused, he could need a toupee pretty soon.

Marren finally said, "Seems like we've hit a wall, Tony. I just spoke with MacKenzey and he hasn't heard anything from the kidnappers either. I'm worried we might have our hand forced without knowing if the girl is alive."

"We ran that risk with the script MacKenzey read, Chief. I still think it was the right decision. Otherwise, the kidnappers knew they had us; now they only think they do."

"Either way, we are going into this blind. I haven't dealt with this sort of thing before, but I don't like having no option except for shelling out a bucket of money."

"I don't like it either. Commander Lewis came up with a couple of options, including how we might track the boat once it has picked up the money."

"Thinking about bugging the bags?"

"Yes. Lewis agrees that anyone with a brain will check the bags for transmitters before leaving the pick up site, so Lewis's demolition guy suggested having a diver with air tanks waiting underneath the bags to clamp a fresh transmitter on the hull of the boat so we'd still be able to track him."

"Could also turn the guy into shark bait if he gets near the prop."

"I asked that, too. They have some fancy fiberglass pole that telescopes like an umbrella handle when you push on a button. Lets the diver remain eight feet below the hull and out of danger of running into the props."

"What holds the transmitter in place, a magnet?"

"They have some fast-drying putty-like adhesive they use because it can stick to any surface. A magnet wouldn't work on Valchon's boat; it's wooden planked. They seem very confident it will hold. I like the idea because the kidnappers could get a little careless if they think they are scot-free after tossing our dummy transmitter."

"I'd hate to be the diver, hanging out under water for some unknown length of time just to run out of air as the kidnappers show up. Sounds risky to me," the Chief said, "but if it works, it would give us time to have a vehicle stationed where they come ashore. I like that part." Marren paused: "Still, we won't know where the girl is. I can't imagine they will take her to the money pick up. We can't take them when they come ashore without knowing she is safe."

5:45 PM, Day 3

Valchon picked up his phone after checking caller ID. "So what would you do for me if I knew someone who might know where the girl is?" he asked.

"Probably could put in a good word for you to get some of the ransom money. You hear the word 'some'?," the cop called

"I'll check. Might know more tomorrow."

Santinello said "when?" to a dial tone. Valchon was gone. *What do I do with this information*, he wondered.

Chapter 29

6:37 PM, Day 3

"Anything yet?" Tony asked.

"Nothing that has come in," said Naomi. "They're sitting tight." She put down the cell phone. "They're waiting us out. You need to learn patience, my warrior."

"I need to learn finding kidnappers first. Feel like all I'm doing is stirring the pot when nothing is cooking."

"I'm going to the lady's room, then let's go home for dinner. Neither one of us has had a decent meal in three days and besides: I feel as if things have settled in for the night. My Spirit is quiet."

"Does that mean you are cooking?" he asked, hoping for time for a beer.

"Yes, but I need time in the garden first. Then I will cook." She left the room.

The day was ending, Tony thought. The chores were all but complete.

And Carrie was still missing. Tony made one last call to Santinello, telling him not to give up on his stakeout of Valchon's apartment for the night. Then Naomi was back from the rest room. He checked out with the watch officer then put his arm around his wife's shoulder as they walked out to their car. They had reached the point in the day where further effort was unproductive. There came a time when there was so much to do that the best thing to do was nothing. Even a soufflé needed time to rise to its performance.

7:04 PM, Day 3

Rocker could feel the quiet descend, and he knew the girl wasn't coming in. There was no movement in the forest. Either she had holed up or had gotten lost. He had a strange feeling that the girl was playing with him, that she was somehow beating him. He kept coming back to the belief that Pinto was involved, a thought that had consumed him all afternoon as he packaged the money and finalized his plans for the following day. Tomorrow he would know for certain where Pinto had hidden the girl. Tonight he would lay the trap.

7:18 PM, Day 3

After changing into more comfortable clothes, Tony grabbed a beer from the fridge and went out to the garden. Naomi was sitting cross-legged on the boulder, her arms lay palm up across her knees, head bowed, eyes closed. Tony sat on the ground in front of her, leaning against the same boulder and crossing his legs in a similar manner. Neither spoke, but Naomi placed her hands on Tony's head almost as if she were blessing him.

The setting sun behind them cast a deep red glow on the grove of paper birch before them, highlighting the scrolls of bark that had peeled back from their trunks. A very light breeze made them rustle, like the deep notes of a xylophone. At the edge of the grove, the purple tips of the switch grass caught the last rays of light as they danced in their own end-of-day ballet. Two robins were making a last minute rush to the worm convenience store to bring home nibbles for those back in the nest.

Tony could feel the warmth of the sun that had been stored in the boulder that day relax the muscles in his back. As much as he watched Naomi, and as often as he listened to her describe the sensations of her meditation, he never felt he ever reached her level of peacefulness. But then what did a seamstress mother and an Italian laborer father know about the natural world? How to make a world-class tomato sauce, yes. How to intertwine a violet etoile clematis with the light pink of a New Dawn climbing rose, yes. But Tony was pretty certain that the only spirits his father had communed with were at the far end of the bar at Lumper's.

His thoughts gradually slipped out of gear, tip toed around in neutral for a while, and then seemed to disappear altogether. Naomi's hands could do that, he realized. At some point Tony felt her hands move from his head and begin to massage his temples then his neck and shoulders. He tilted his head back into her lap, moaned with pleasure and said, "I see you got the right message from the Spirit of the great Masseuse in Heaven, saying 'take care of your husband, take care of your husband'!"

She tweaked his earlobe. "I must have been on another channel, my warrior. I seemed to have missed that connection." She noticed his beer. "Ahhh, I see. You're having your own communication with the Spirit of the Great Malt Hops."

"Well, a balanced intake, I've always said. Speaking of intake, did my growling stomach wake you out of your meditation?"

"I'm going. I'm going." Naomi blew him a kiss and went inside to start dinner.

4:37 AM, Day 4

Pinto lay awake, worrying about Carrie out in the woods for one more night. Pretending to sleep, he really had been waiting for Rocker to dose off. He knew he needed to get help for Carrie, which meant getting word to the police and that meant using Rocker's phone . . . without Rocker knowing. Small stipulation! The only chance he would have would be while Rocker slept.

Rocker's snoring had been pretty steady for quite a while. Pinto had been timing it against his own breathing to see if Rocker was faking, but after getting slightly out of breath, he was convinced Rocker was dead to the world.

Pinto slipped off the bunk. Finding Rocker's shirt on the table, he felt for the phone, found it in the pocket and slipped it into his hand. At the door, he stopped, listened to the snoring for a moment more before creeping outside. Walking quickly to the other side of the clearing behind the car, he punched in 911. He held his breath, hoping the chimes of the keypad didn't carry far, knowing he needed to get back inside before Rocker woke.

He heard a rustling in the woods behind him.

As Pinto spun around, the male voice said: "911 operator. State your emergency." Even though Pinto had rehearsed what he would say, the noise in the woods distracted him. Not connecting the voice to the noise, at first, he then realized it came from the phone. Still looking for the source of the rustling, Pinto said, "We have the MacKenzey girl. She's safe but I'm worried about what will happen to her after tomorrow. She's in the woods about 20 minutes from the cabin. I . . ." Pinto heard a "beep beep" and nearly dropped the phone. He froze with fear, expecting to see Rocker come around the car. He turned. Another "beep, beep." Pinto swallowed, looked back towards the cabin, then down at the screen on the phone and saw "low battery." Realizing where the beeping was coming from, he let out a soft sigh.

Then he heard the rustling again.

The low battery had disconnected the call. Pinto hit end and jammed the phone in his belt at the small of his back, petrified that he had been heard. As he crept back to the cabin, he looked again towards the noise. Still nothing. With one hand on the door jam, Pinto heard more snoring before he tiptoed to the table to replace the phone. He was sweating, his nerves firing like a car engine cooling after a long trip. Rocker rolled over, coughed and, after a minute, resumed snoring. The phone made another "beep-beep."

Pinto held his breath, terrified, sure that Rocker had heard it also. He didn't move. Waited. Certain the pounding of his heart would wake Rocker.

There was no more chirping. The snoring started up again. Pinto was safe. He was still angry that he hadn't said everything he planned to the 911 operator, but knew flat out he couldn't risk using the phone again. He had been lucky once, but twice would be pushing it.

But if it hadn't been Rocker he'd heard beyond the clearing, then who was it? Or what was it? The animal Carrie had seen?

4:45 AM, Day 4

Officer Jenkins swore, entered the caller ID in his log and redialed the number on the screen. The screen signaled trouble with the other phone. Jenkins swore again and hit replay on the answering machine. He listened to the full message and immediately reached for the cell phone.

"Come on, answer the friggin' thing." Jenkins was temped to redial when the phone was answered. Jenkins heard the phone hit the wooden floor, then "Oh, shit," then, "Fiori here."

"Tony, Jenkins. Pick up the phone."

"Hmmmm."

"You awake?"

"Hmm. I'm awake, unless this is a dream. How many fingers am I holding up?"

"That's my line, for chrissake. Are you listening? I just had a call from the kidnapper."

That had the effect of a cold bucket of water. Tony's voice was suddenly fully alert. "What did he say?"

"Hold on." Jenkins hit the Play button and held the phone to the speaker. He hit Pause and asked, "Did you hear that?"

"Loud and clear. When did it come in?"

"'Bout 60 seconds ago."

"Was that all of the message? It sounded cut off?"

"It was. I tried redial but couldn't get through. The line was dead."

"Keep trying. Get a hold of the Chief. Tell him Naomi and I are coming in; see if he can join us. Be there in twenty minutes at the most. Call me right away if the kidnapper calls back."

"Right. See you."

#

Tony put the phone down and turned back to look at Naomi. She was sitting up, rubbing her eyes and pushing the hair back from her face. "Could you hear any of that?" he asked.

"Your side. I gather we got a phone call."

"Not a phone call, the phone call. From the kidnapper. He said 'we have the MacKenzey girl. She's in the woods about twenty minutes from the cabin. I'm worried what will happen to her tomorrow,' and then he was cut off." Tony was pulling on his pants as Naomi was pulling off her T-shirt. Tony stopped, looked at her walking nude to the closet.

"Don't even think about it," she said, swishing her rear end from side to side.

"Whaaaat?" he asked as innocently as he could muster. But he could see her smiling in the mirror on the closet door. They both dressed on the fly and raced out the door to the car.

Chapter 30

5:23 AM, Day 4

Tony paced as Chief Marren, Naomi and Peter Amero huddled around the speaker. "Play it one more time, will you, Jenkins?"

Once again, they heard, "We have the MacKenzey girl. She's safe but I am worried about what will happen to her tomorrow. She's in the woods about twenty minutes from the cabin . . ."

The voice that spoke was hushed, just above a whisper, with a slight echo that suggested the man had his hand cupped around the speaker. The words were clear, thought out, spoken hurriedly, with a hint of a Massachusetts accent. There was no sound in the background.

Naomi spoke first. "I would bet that's Pinto. He's speaking so softly, he doesn't want to be overheard."

"Makes sense," Tony cut in. "Connor's the Alpha dog there. Maybe we have a guy on our side out there."

"And no damn way to reach him," Amero added. "If we use the scanner, Connor hears everything."

"True. But can we count on Pinto to help the girl?" Tony asked.

"I don't know," Naomi said thoughtfully. "All he said was 'I'm worried.' My read is that he feels powerless to affect what will happen 'tomorrow'. I don't feel we can count on him at all. His voice didn't send that sort of strength to me."

Chief Marren nodded. "I tend to agree. Look at the sequence of his words. Of course, we don't know what he would have said next, but my take is that if Pinto were going to help, he would have suggested what he was going to do instead of telling us where she was."

"And why was she twenty minutes from the cabin, anyway?" Amero asked. "Why not in the cabin?"

Marren suggested, "Maybe Connor put her away from where he and Pinto were because he was worried Pinto might help the girl."

"But Pinto seemed to know where she was," Tony replied. "If I were Connor and I was holding a kid for two million bucks, I'd want her under my thumb 24/7. No way I'd let her out of my sight."

"Remember my dream the other night, Tony? When I thought I sensed danger and safety?" Tony nodded and Naomi went on, "I wonder if Pinto hid her."

Amero asked: "Are you serious? The same guy hid her who a minute ago we thought didn't have the power to save her tomorrow?"

"Today, you mean."

"Tomorrow, today. Whatever."

"Or maybe she sneaked out and Pinto knows where she is" Tony said thoughtfully. "That makes more sense to me."

"It also could explain why we haven't heard from the kidnappers." Naomi. added, "MacKenzey demanded to know the name of her favorite animal, remember?

They haven't called with that."

"Good point," Tony said. "But let's play that out. The girl runs away somehow. Connor knows she's gone, thinks Pinto helped her or knows where she is. He has less than eighteen hours until the money drop, can't call us with information he can't give, and therefore doesn't know for sure we will go ahead with the drop. What would you do if you were Connor?" he asked rhetorically. "What would I do?"

"I'll tell you what I'd do," said Amero. "If I thought Pinto had hid her and was holding out on me, I'd sweat Pinto. And I'd sweat him hard and I bet Pinto knows that, too. Why else would he sneak off and call us?"

Tony nodded. "My thought, too."

"And what happens if he sweats him too hard and Pinto doesn't cough?" Amero wondered.

Naomi said what none of them wanted to hear. "Then we lose two people, Carrie and Pinto."

And they all were silent, not wanting to consider that reality, but knowing how close to likely it was. Still pacing, Tony finally stopped in front of a large-scale map of Cape Ann that was pinned to the conference room wall.

"Who's got a red marker?" he asked. Chief Marren handed Tony one from his desk drawer. "Okay, where are all the wooded areas on Cape Ann? We've got Dog Town here, Nugent Stretch here along the tracks, Ravenswood here in West Gloucester. Where else?"

"Up behind the self-storage facility on 133," Amero added. "The whole area on School Street in Manchester. You know, down from the tennis club."

Tony circled both areas. "Isn't School Street sort of swampy?"

Naomi answered. "Yes, too swampy, in my opinion. You and I tried to hike in there this spring, Tony, remember? We gave up in fifteen minutes."

"You did; I gave up in five! Think we can rule that area out. Anywhere else? Anyone?"

Chief Marren offered, "How 'bout the Audubon area out on the end of Eastern Point?"

Tony shook his head but circled it in red anyway. "If you walked twenty minutes from there, Chief, you'd be in someone's back yard or in the middle of the harbor. Think we can rule that out also."

No one could think of anywhere else so Tony capped the marker and sat down as they all stared at the circled areas.

"I like Ravenswood the best," Tony said breaking the silence. "Dog Town is surrounded by too many homes. I've hiked the trails behind the self-storage a lot and I don't remember a cabin. Do you, Naomi?" She shook her head. "Ravenswood is off Route 127, which can get pretty sleepy. I know the High School cross-country team practices in there on a maze of old hiking trails. You could get a car in there pretty easy without being seen, if you timed it right. And we're talking over 400 acres, aren't we?"

"420 some-odd, to be exact," the Chief answered.

Tony slapped his thigh, startling everyone. "Shit! Why didn't I think of this sooner? Peter, start calling the cell phone companies and see who's got Connor's contract. Maybe we can work backwards if they can pinpoint where the call came from."

"You got it." Amero left the room muttering, "No wonder he gets the big bucks!"

"All right, let's assume Ravenswood is it for the moment. We don't have time to search 400 acres. We've got to narrow that down."

"Town Building Inspector should have plans of the area, shouldn't he?" Marren asked.

"Probably, but what we really need are the USGS topo maps," Tony said. "Wonder who would have them in town."

"Would they be on the Internet?" Naomi asked.

"You could check. Why don't you call over to the fire station and see if they have a set. The Building Inspector won't be in for a couple of more hours, any way. Probably not till eight. Besides, this is a state park, so he may not have anything. Let's focus on getting the topos and go from there. It's light enough now; while you track them down, I'm going to take a quick run over to Nugent Stretch. If I'm not mistaken, there's only one way in there, which I can check in a heartbeat and be back here in less than thirty minutes. You should have a good idea about the topos by then."

6:06 AM, Day 4

Rocker woke in a foul mood. He had been sleeping on his side and his right hand was asleep, tingling with that numbing sensation that makes you wonder if the hand is still attached. He shook it, trying to get the circulation back, and stood up, hitting his head on the wooden rail of the upper bunk. Swearing, he headed for the door, grabbing his shirt on the way out. He heard a very faint beeping. It seemed to be close by, but he couldn't locate it. As he spun to look behind him, the beeping repeated and Rocker, still not completely awake, realized it was coming from the phone in his pocket. He pulled the phone out.

The screen read 'Low battery". What the hell? How could it say 'Low battery'? He had turned it off after speaking with Valchon. He was certain of that. He punched the redial key and 911 came up on the screen.

"Oh, shit!" he yelled. The realization of what that number meant blew the lid off his anger meter. "PINTO!" he yelled.

Rocker hit the off key and ran into the cabin, bashing the door against the wall as he strode to the bunk where Pinto had just sat up, awakened by the crash of the door. Rocker yelled, "You double crossing motherfucker!"

He grabbed Pinto by the shirt, ripping him off the upper bunk and throwing him to the wooden floor. Pinto landed hard on his chest, his right arm trapped underneath him as Rocker crushed his knees into Pinto's back, knocking the wind out of him.

Pinto fought for air. Nothing was coming. He wheezed, thrashed around with his left arm to push Rocker off as he tried to wrench air back into his lungs. It was useless. He gasped, trying to ward off the barrage of punches coming at him.

Rocker got up, kicked Pinto in the groin. Pinto rolled into a ball, air finally rejoining his lungs. Somehow he scooted under the table, then out the other side, putting the table between him and Rocker. The respite was brief. Rocker, out of control with rage, threw the table aside with such strength that it shattered against the bunk. Rocker grabbed one of the broken table legs, wrenched it free, then swung it with all his might against Pinto's knee.

Pinto screamed in pain and reached down to hold what was left of his kneecap, now totally splintered and bloody in his hand. Rocker swung again, this time crushing all the fingers of Pinto's right hand. Pinto, mercifully, passed out. The only sound was the heavy breathing coming from Rocker as he stood over the unconscious man on the floor, the table leg still raised over his head to strike again. He threw it against the wall and kicked Pinto in the groin one more time, the final punctuation of his last "motherfucker."

The cabin was deathly still. His chest heaving, his fists still clenched, his fury unsatisfied, Rocker looked down at Pinto. He ran out to the car where he grabbed the coil of rope. Dropping it on the front step, Rocker went inside, dragged the still unconscious man through the growing pool of blood and gore out to the porch, and threw him against the post. Pinto's head fell back against the wood, then dropped forward limp over his chest. Rocker uncoiled the rope and tied Pinto's hands behind his back and around the post. The flies were starting to buzz around the open wounds of the unconscious figure.

6:18 AM, Day 4

Nugent Stretch was a several mile long strip of no-man's land that stretched between Gloucester and Rockport, bordering the western side of the commuter rail tracks. The woods were not as dense as Ravenswood. Nugent Stretch was a much newer stand, one reason being that the teenagers who snuck in there to drink and make out managed to set the undergrowth on fire nearly every summer. The result was neither a lot of undergrowth nor a lot of places to hide.

Tony drove onto the coarse gravel turnoff, bounced over the tracks and came to a halt in front of the chain that the Rockport police kept across the dirt access road. He tried the padlock and found it holding fast. The chain was too high for a car to drive over, but with not enough play for a car to drive under. There were no tire tracks anywhere. Tony walked the brush on either side of the cement-filled columns, where he found no evidence of recent footprints or tire tracks either. There were partial boot prints, the stride regular enough that Tony knew the man had not been carrying weight on one side. No child's footprints were anywhere.

Back in his car, Tony turned towards Gloucester, went a half-mile, and pulled into the parking lot of the Babson Museum, a small, one-room seasonal museum that generally attracted little interest. There was a path around the back that extended for a ways into the southern end of Nugent Stretch, where the lawn maintenance company dumped grass clippings. Tony walked down the pathway, examining the tire marks as well as the piles of clippings that were strewn haphazardly along the trail. Nothing. No tracks wider than a wheelbarrow, certainly none as wide as a car tire. This was not where the kidnappers were hiding out.

On the way back to the station, Tony called in to Peter Amero, who had just hung up from speaking with the area supervisor for Verizon Wireless. She had confirmed the phone was Paul Connor's and that the 911 call had come from the 281 Gloucester exchange. Her engineers were attempting to pinpoint the location of the microchip inside his phone. She had seemed doubtful, but had promised to call back within thirty minutes with their results.

The net is closing in, Tony thought. *Now, if only we can close it before tonight. I'm damn good at proving where they aren't,* he realized. *Only five hours left to prove where they are.*

Chapter 31

6:41 AM, Day 4

Pinto stirred, opened his eyes, reached to feel the unbearable pain in his knee, spent several excruciating seconds trying to determine whether his hand or his knee or his balls hurt the most, decided it didn't matter and passed out again.

The longer Pinto was out, the angrier Rocker became. By the time Pinto moaned and raised his head, Rocker's fuse had all but ignited. He wondered if Pinto were faking in order to buy time, half expecting the police to jump out of the woods any second. The more rational half of him knew that if Pinto had told the cops where they were, they would have been here long ago. The fact that they weren't gave him hope that maybe the 911 call had not gone through in the first place.

But he couldn't take that chance; he had to revive Pinto enough to question him. Rocker went into the cabin, fetched the canteen, shook it to make certain there was still some water in it, came back outside and poured the contents on Pinto's face. Pinto blinked, then opened his eyes enough to see Rocker standing over him, glowering down, itching for an excuse to kick him in the balls again.

"The 911 call was real cute, you asshole," Rocker spat.

"Never . . . got . . . through" Pinto managed to get out.

"Yeah, my ass." Listen up, motherfucker. I've had enough of your shit. One last time: where's the girl?"

"Don't . . . know . . . need water . . ." D . . . o . . . n . . . 't k . . . n . . . o . . . w. Need w . . . a . . . t . . . e . . . r."

"Screw your water, Pinto. Where's the girl?" R ocker shouted, shaking Pinto by the shoulders, then and slamming his head repeatedly into the wooden post. Grabbing a handful of Pinto's hair, he slammed his head back one more time, still yelling,: "Where is she?"

This time there was a sickening noise as Pinto's head struck the post, with a hollow sound like a watermelon splitting open. His neck had snapped, his head flopped to the side like a rag doll, a very dead rag doll.

"Shit!" Rocker yelled, letting go of the handful of hair he still held. Now he had a real problem. He didn't know where the girl was, he had just killed the one person who might have known, and his phone was dead . . . and the cops could on their way. He paced the clearing as he tried to think what to do. Mid way around the clearing, Rocker stopped dead in his tracks, made a decision, and headed for the cabin. Maybe the problem was ancient history. Who needs the girl? Screw 'em: I got more money than I need right here. My share, Pinto's. and Valchon's, too. Shit, who needs Valchon?

6:52 AM, Day 4

Naomi had called an old hiking friend of hers, who worked for a surveyor out of Danvers, catching him just as he was on his way to a job in the western part of the state. He had agreed to drop them off the topo maps on his way out of town. She had been studying them for several minutes before Tony joined her.

"I caught Sam Stevens on the way out of town and he dropped these off a few minutes ago, According to Sam," she said over her shoulder, "these maps less than a year old, so they should show all the structures in the Park. Hopefully, any cabin also."

"Show me Route. 127," Tony asked.

Naomi pointed to the curving black line near the bottom of the page. "Here. This is the main entrance off 127 to Ravenswood and this is the beginning of the cross-country trail here, if I read the contour lines correctly,"

"That symbol there must be the maintenance shed," Tony suggested.

"I think so; it would be in the right location for it, but I couldn't find that symbol in the key directory. A building looks like this small box here. See it?"

"It's not a house, that's for sure. God, I didn't realize Ravenswood covered as much territory as this. We've got four maps to examine. You take those two; I'll do these. Just identify any structure, particularly any that has an obvious trail leading to it."

After a few minutes of silence, broken only by the scratching of the felt tip pens, Tony looked over at his wife and asked, "found anything?"

She shook her head no. "I thought I had, but the trail ended in a marshy area, so I crossed it off. There are too many possible sites for a cabin; if I circled each one, you wouldn't be able to see the topo. Here's the trail you and I hiked this spring. Remember? It took us all afternoon and look at what a small part of Ravenswood we covered! I figure it would take two days to cover my two maps, not counting yours." She raised her eyebrows and grimaced. Tony said, "I followed trails or contour lines that seemed passable for a car. Remember they don't have a Jeep, so with that fat old Plymouth, they're going to need some easy going. There are two that come off 127 and another off to the east, accessible from what could be a logging road. All of them wind back into the Park for some distance over a gentle enough incline that, from here anyway, the Plymouth could handle. Want to take a ride?"

"I'm on. We can tell better there than here." Tony rolled up the four maps.

"I'll tell the Chief where we're headed. You check with Amero and see if Verizon got back to him?" He checked his watch. "See you in the car in five."

7:11 AM, Day 4

The light woke Carrie. She sat up, pushing the boughs off her and stretching. Her Stomach growled. She searched her pockets for something to eat, found nothing, before realizing she had eaten her last bit of food last night. And then she got scared.

I hope Mr. Pinto will bring me something soon, she thought. She could tell by the light that she had slept a little later, which made her hopeful that she wouldn't have to wait too long for him. She peeked out through the branches of her hideout but saw no one. Carrie thought her hearing had gotten better since she had been hiding in the woods. She could tell when Mr. Pinto or that mean man Rocker was coming because they made a different noise than the small animals. She giggled. *Of course, silly: they're a hundred times bigger*, she told herself. Carrie piled the boughs on top of one another and neatened her hideout, just as she made her own bed in the morning at home. She wanted her Mommy to be proud of her. Tears came to her eyes and dripped down her cheeks. *I hope I see my Mommy again,* she thought, as she climbed through the branches to the clearing. She ran down a short path to a stand of wild berry bushes she had found by accident yesterday while looking for a place to potty.

7:19 AM, Day 4

Amero cradled the office phone and immediately picked up his cell phone. Tony answered on the second ring. "Tony, we got some good news!" "Verizon?" "Spot on. Their engineers were able to pin point the phone to West Gloucester."

"How close?" Tony demanded.

"Well, that's the problem. Pinto didn't stay on the call long enough to be more exact. Just somewhere in West Gloucester."

"So, Ravenswood is looking better all the time," Tony said, excitement in his voice.

"My thought, too," said Peter. "Oh, and the lab confirmed the DNA on the second envelope was Connor's. They got a match from lab work he had done in Vietnam."

"Good news. Naomi and I are on our way there now. Will let you know what we find," he paused to check his watch, "within the hour."

7:23 AM, Day 4

Rocker finished loading the bags of money into the trunk of Pinto's car, pawed through Pinto's pockets to find his wallet, took his license and the few dollar bills that were there and jumped in the car. He hadn't driven on the way in and had trouble in a few spots controlling the car as it side swiped a couple of saplings. He miss-judged one curve; wrenching the wheel wildly, he missed an elm tree, over-corrected and slid his rear fender into a boulder on the opposite side. But he kept going.

At one point he made a wrong turn, but, after a hundred yards or so, hit a dead end, forcing him to back the whole way to the trail. Turning the opposite direction, he sped down into a glen he recognized from the way in, climbed up the other side and finally reached the main road, where he turned right and headed west towards Manchester. He had to ditch the car, but where?

Chapter 32

7:41 AM, Day 4

Naomi was moving her finger along the map as Tony slowed. She looked up and said, "Should be around this bend."

Tony braked as came out of the curve, spotted the dirt trail and pulled off. The house on the right was a nondescript cape in bad need of paint. The clapboards looked as if they had leprosy. Overgrown bushes hid the front door. Rusted-out lawn mowers and metal chairs with no seats were strewn in piles in front of an enormous collection of hubcaps. The carcass of a Day-glo pink doll carriage was stuffed with a scarecrow clothed in an Army fatigue jacket and a faded NY Yankee baseball cap with its bill facing backwards. A piece of weathered driftwood with faded white letters that read 'my children's inheritance' was hanging unevenly from the jungle gym cross member.

"Didn't know we had a Museum of Modern Art here in town," Tony snorted.

"I was thinking it was quite a social statement of our times," Naomi responded.

"Lucky kids," Tony sarcastically observed.

They both got out of the car, proceeding on foot down the dirt trail. Without needing to exchange another word, they assumed positions on opposite sides of the path and walked slowly, eyes cast down to read the story the path would tell them. The map had indicated that this was an abandoned logging trail, which was why it was of interest to Tony. The footing was hard-packed, but was littered with branches and weeds. In less than twenty yards, the two stopped, convinced that no vehicle had driven on the path since the last rainstorm. There were no footprints, no branches broken by a heavy boot, no regular indentations in the soil, in short: no evidence of any human activity.

They returned to the car and drove another quarter mile to the second objective, another abandoned logging trail that immediately looked more promising. Naomi got out first and was kneeling on the trail when Tony walked up.

"This has had a lot of traffic, Tony. Look here," she said, indicating a clear set of recent tire marks. Tony knelt beside her, put his eye close to the ground and looked down the trail.

"This last set was left by someone on the way out," he said eventually.

"I am sure of it, too." Naomi answered. "This clump of grass has just begun to recover." She stomped heavily on the grass and knelt down quickly, watching the grass spring back, and counting. "I would say the car went through here very recently, probably within the last fifteen minutes."

"We may be too late." Tony continued to crawl down the trail. After covering fifteen to twenty feet, he stood up. "I count the same truck coming and going twice plus a car that left after it. What do you see?"

"I see that you had a good teacher, my warrior," she replied. "But what we don't know is who, if anyone, is still at the other end of these tracks."

"Or if they have a weapon trained on us," he added.

"Not here; there's not enough cover. Maybe further down beyond where I can see from here." Naomi paused. "This feels right to me. Want to go in?"

"I do, but if we're right about the car and the truck leaving, we could we be walking into nothing, or an ambush. I don't know which. The kidnappers might just have run out for a short errand and might be on the way back while we stand here."

"Go hide the car and hurry back," Naomi suggested.

Tony backed out, did a 180 and disappeared around the bend. After pulling off the road, he opened the trunk, took out the jack and propped it against the rear wheel. He put the spare on the ground next to the jack, making it look enough as if the tire were being changed. He took a long look at the topo, memorizing the details of the trail he thought they would have to follow.

Checking his watch, he called into the station to report where he and Naomi were and what they were intending to do. With a few quick instructions to Amero, Tony put his phone on vibrate, and walked back to the trail where he had left his wife. She wasn't there.

8:06 AM, Day 4

Valchon's mouth tasted like the bottom of a birdcage. For some reason he couldn't understand, he was lying on the deck with each foot inside a separate lobster trap and several coils of rope in a pile on his chest. A quick thought passed through his mind that someone had tried to bury him in his own traps. He tried to sit up, but the pain behind his eyes put him back on the deck. Too painful to lift. Better to try just turning, so he moved his head while remaining flat on his back. Better. At least the neck worked. Next he tried moving his hands; the left one came up with an empty bottle in it.

It took a second for the thought to go from his eye to his hand and back to his brain. Then he remembered. Last night he had run out of beer before he had run out of celebrating and had found the bottle of cheap vodka stashed in the opened case of motor oil . . . for emergencies, of course. Can't run a piece of machinery if it's not well oiled, he had reasoned. And after a six-pack and a bottle of vodka, he was as fine a human machine that had ever been invented. Need more oil was his first thought as he pushed himself, slowly, very slowly, off the deck. His second thought was throwing up, which he did, all over his shirt and the cell phone that he belatedly noticed in his lap.

He hit the redial button, but couldn't understand why the ringing didn't sound right. He found pieces of what vaguely looked like his dinner on the earpiece, wiped them off on his pants, and put the phone back to his ear. Much clearer, he thought. But all there was was ringing. *Where the hell was Rocker,* he wondered as he punched in a new number.

"Thought about my offer?" Valchon asked.

"Of course, but how are we going to work this out?"

"Well, I've been thinking that my safety is going to be a little risky after I collect the ransom, so I might be willing to share some of it with you for one small favor in return."

"And that is . . . ?"

"If I knew where the cops were positioned, it would make a big difference in your share."

"I can arrange that, but how will we meet up? I mean, I tell you where the cops are, and I get cut out of the deal, you win, I lose. So I'm going to need some sincerity money first."

Valchon thought for a moment: *where can I get to easily? . . . and safely?* "Do you know the Harley dealer on the left just over the Salem Bridge?"

"Yeah."

I've got quite a drive to get there, so give me an hour. I will leave a down-payment for you behind the seat of the Roadster to the left of the office trailer."

"You better make it a significant down payment, enough to make it worth my while to cooperate."

"Trust me. You won't be disappointed."

"So how will we meet up later? Afterwards?"

"I will let you know." And Valchon clicked off the call.

8:08 AM, Day 4

Tony made the whistling call of the red hawk. Waited. Made it again and immediately—to his relief—heard the responding call coming from the brush down the ravine on the left. Following the sound, Tony saw where her tracks had left the trail and found her behind the clump of Mountain Laurel. He repeated the arrangements he had made with Amero.

"All I want to accomplish right now is to follow the vehicle tracks and see where they lead. No contact until we have proper reinforcements."

Naomi nodded but asked, "What if the girl is in danger?"

"We'll play what we see, but I don't want you playing hero. First priority is your safety; we can't help her if we do something stupid."

Naomi nodded. "Same approach as usual?"

Tony knew she was asking for stalking instructions. "Usual" meant they would leapfrog each other on opposite sides of the trail, one person always out of sight, waiting for the whistle before going ahead. No whistle, no movement. Under this arrangement, with limited ability to communicate, the waiting could be nerve-racking. You never knew if your partner were waiting or had been compromised and couldn't whistle. In any case, only one person was at risk during any movement so, in theory anyway, the other person could retreat for help. In theory.

Tony pointed at himself, held up one finger and left. She didn't take his going first as a sexist thing. At first, years ago, she did, but when he explained he'd rather take the bullet than watch her get it, she understood, but she also remembered that at the time, he had no answer for why it would be acceptable for her to watch him get the bullet. Men, she thought, and waited for the whistle.

It came within a minute and she stepped out. The person in the lead wouldn't proceed without verification he was still on track. Nor would the lead go more than twenty-five yards, with or without verification. In most circumstances, that still allowed them the option of a visual signal if something came up and it kept them close enough together that they could still support one another.

Find cover, verify the trail, move forward, and don't be seen. Sounds simple in the classroom. In the field, nothing was simple. For the first several hundred yards, the tracking was easy. They made good time through the glen and up the other side of the hill. Naomi was in the lead when she encountered the first branch of the trail. There were tire tracks in both directions.

After giving the cackle of a quail (their signal for "I'm checking"), she knelt to the ground to examine the imprint. The ground was too hard for her to get a clear read, so she went forward on all fours until she found a softer section of soil. There were identical set of tire markings, one nearly on top of the other, but she couldn't verify the direction of the marking on top. She cackled again and scampered forward and found a spot where the tire spray clearly indicated the vehicle was going back to the main road.

She took another minute retracing her steps to where the trail had diverged and gave the red hawk whistle for Tony to leapfrog ahead on the main trail.

And so it went for the next half hour, except for the last few turns, they had stayed to the side of the trail moving quietly through the underbrush, daring to step out on the trail only to verify that they continued to follow the tire marks before returning to the protection of the brush. They were good at this. They moved without touching branches or stepping on twigs, the snapping of which would give their presence away. They knew how to step, first on the outside of the foot rolling into a firm placement on the ball of the foot. They knew how to blend in, move with the breeze, with the natural rustling of the leaves.

Tony was in the lead when he saw the light of a clearing ahead. He paused, quieted, listening for anything that didn't belong. He heard nothing human, but there was a buzzing. He waited, the buzzing continued. He gently parted the branches of the heavy cover enough to see through into the clearing. A strong smell of human urine verified that a human had been there recently.

He surveyed as much of the clearing as he could see without moving his head or parting more branches. No one was in sight. There still was no noise, but the buzzing troubled him. After guiding the branches back into their natural place, he turned silently to trace his steps back to Naomi.

He moved in with her, gave the universal circling sign for "we're here," put his finger to his lips, nodded back down the trail and set out in the lead, still leapfrogging as before but moving more quickly. They reached the glen before Tony spoke.

"I found the cabin. It was quiet enough to be empty but there was a quality to the silence that I didn't like. A buzzing, insect buzzing. Probably around a dead body. Men had definitely been there; the smell of their urine and feces was unmistakable, fresh. Couldn't see in front nor inside the cabin; didn't want to do more until we were better prepared."

"Buzzing isn't good news," Naomi whispered.

"I was afraid to think about whose body."

Tony could feel Naomi tense. "Then we need to get Amero and get back there immediately."

10:12 AM, Day 4

Staying in the brush to the side of the trail, Tony and Naomi traveled quickly out to the main road. Amero was waiting right where Tony had asked him to park.

"Call the other two cars in.," Tony instructed Amero. "I'm going to run back to the car and get the topo map. Be right back."

With the map spread out on the hood of the cruiser, Tony gathered everyone around. He described the trail in to the cabin and then the clearing in detail. They could see there was only one apparent way in that a vehicle could handle. That meant there was no back door escape other than the obvious one of plunging deeper into the woods. Tony gave out assignments.

"Naomi and I will go in just like before," Tony said to the group. To Naomi he said, "we reach the clearing, you skirt west around, I'll go east around and we'll meet up on the far side. Shoot for this outcrop here," he indicated a spot of the map, "but if we miss it for some reason, whistle and I'll come to you."

Naomi nodded her understanding.

"Peter, you and Jimmy come behind us. Stay to the trail but if you hear this whistle," and Tony imitated a red hawk, "get in the bushes out of sight until you hear it again. If you hear it twice in a row, real close together, come on the run, weapons live. It'll mean Naomi or I hit something we can't handle. Okay?"

Amero nodded, remembering the drill from previous experiences with the Fioris.

"Good. George, take Peter's wheels back towards town, pull in behind my car and hang there, engine running. You hear any kind of call for help, come fast, block the trail with your vehicle and assume the bad guys are coming at you. I want them live, if at all possible. Shoot to wound, particularly Pinto; he may be the only one who knows exactly where the girl is. Clear?"

"Like a bell, Tony."

"Unless we hit a snag, it's going to take Naomi and me about twenty minutes to get to the clearing and another ten to circle it and decide what to do. Peter, I want you and Jimmy to hold position at this point here—" Tony pointed to the rock outcrop clearly marked on the topo—"while we scout the clearing. Stay put at all costs until you hear the whistle.

"Now, that leaves you two." Tony said to the remaining two patrolmen. You guys are our eyes out here. Get back in your cars where they are hidden. If anyone at all heads onto that trail, you ring my number and keep ringing until it blisters your finger. I mean until they bleed. I want no Indians sneaking up my backside here."

"Gotcha," the patrolman said and both men left for their vehicles.

"Make damn sure you stay awake!" Tony yelled after them. Both waved and kept going.

Naomi spoke up. "Weapons, Tony?"

"Peter, what have you got in the squad car?"

"Usual shotgun and reserve sidearm, plus what I'm carrying, of course," he said motioning to his holster.

"What about the others?"

"Same," Amero confirmed.

"I need your shotgun. What's your preference, Little Bird?"

"If I'm going to be in the woods, the sidearm will do. Shotgun would just get in my way."

"Okay, then, get Peter's reserve, check for ammo and let's move out. Peter: you and Jimmy grab the other two shotguns before you follow on. You will be mostly on the trail and won't have to worry about them getting in your way. Any other questions?"

Peter and Jimmy looked at each other, shrugged and shook their heads. "Been through the drill, Tony. We'll be there. Just watch yourselves. It's too far for Jimmy to have to carry you out."

"Jimmy, eh? Pulling rank?" Tony asked with a smile.

Peter answered with a seriousness that Tony hadn't expected. "No, I figure if you're down, since I ain't leavin' your side, there's a good chance I might be down, too. Just givin' Jimmy chance to be forewarned, that's all."

Tony and Peter held each other's eyes for a long moment, knowing full well the implication of that remark.

"You're a good friend, Peter," Tony said. Seeing that Naomi had her weapon, he slapped Amero on the shoulder, gave Naomi the move out signal and they left as quietly as they had arrived.

Sensing an opportunity, Santinello said: "I need to get some more ammo from the cruiser. Be right back."

Amero nodded and resumed checking his weapon. Out of sight, Santinello dialed Valchon.

"Where are you?" he asked after Valchon picked up.

"Oh, sure! Why you calling?"

"Fiori is onto some trail in Ravenswood and he's moving in now. Thinks he's found something at a cabin he didn't want to approach without back up. You there?"

"Interesting. No, I'm not, but thanks."

Valchon dialed another number. No answer. Dialed again. Still nothing. *Well, it's your ass, Rocker, not mine.*

Chapter 33

10:31 AM, Day 4

Tony and Naomi moved quickly over the now familiar trail. They kept up the hurried pace until the last hundred yards before the clearing, when they stopped. Both checked the wind direction and took a quick drink from Tony's canteen, readying their weapons and flicking off the safety buttons. They embraced, touched foreheads together and separated. They exchanged no words; the look they gave each other said everything. Naomi pointed at herself, kissed her finger, put it to her husband's lips and left. Had Tony had his eyes closed, he would not have known she had gone.

Giving her the normal count, he headed out to begin the leapfrogging until they hit the clearing. They covered the remaining ground without incident, Naomi pulling in even with Tony on the other side of the trail. He gave her a thumbs-up before moving to the right.

Carrying the shotgun made the going difficult through the heavy brush. He had to watch where he pointed it at the same time taking care where he put his feet. Clumsiness would give him away. He ducked, twisted, bent around branches, and went through the movements that he had learned from his wife. Progress was slow, but he was able to keep moving without having to backtrack. When he came up on the other side of the cabin, where he could see through an opening in the branches, all that was visible was the weathered wood. Still no sound, except the insect buzzing.

It took another ten minutes for Tony to reach the outcrop where Naomi was waiting. He put his thumb and middle finger together asking if things were okay. She shook her head no. With rapid sign language, she told him one man was dead, the girl wasn't visible and no one else was there, she thought, shaking her hand side to side with their sign of uncertainty.

The smell of death reached Tony's nose; they were down wind of the cabin. They waited. Nothing moved. Tony took a small stone and, with careful aim, threw it into the open door of the cabin. They could hear it rolling. Nothing happened. Either the person inside was one cool dude or not there at all.

He signaled he was going in and handed the shotgun to his wife. As she trained it on the cabin door, Tony took out his revolver and crept across the clearing. He could hear the insects buzzing around the body, getting nourishment from what humans flushed down the toilet. He made no sound as he approached the cabin from the side, out of view of either the door or the window. Not wanting to risk a squeaky floorboard, Tony stayed on the dirt as he inched out across the clearing, now doing a soldier's crawl along the front edge of the narrow porch. Just outside the door and right alongside the body, Tony stopped completely and cocked his head to listen. His mouth was open, better to hear with. Nothing.

Still on his stomach, he inched up on to the boards, set his foot against the post, took a breath and propelled himself forward and through the door, pistol out in front sweeping the room side to side and back. He rolled on his side to examine both bunks. Nothing.

With a long exhale, he stood up went to the door and motioned Naomi in. She completed another sweep around the perimeter of the clearing, noticed no additional footprints and joined Tony, who was kneeling over the body.

"Pinto," he whispered. "See what you can find inside." Tony gave the birdcall, which brought Amero and Santinello on the run into the clearing, weapons out, pointed down.

After a quick scan of the clearing, Amero motioned Santinello to the boulder where the Fioris had been minutes before as he took up position by the cabin wall. Between the two of them, they could see the entire perimeter.

With one final, thorough sweep of the room, Naomi finished her examination of the cabin. "Looks like the fight ended right here," she said, standing alongside the body.

"Sure ended here," Tony agreed, "but there was no fight. Look at his hands. He was caught by surprise, I would say. No swelling on his knuckles, no skin under his fingernails. He was cold-cocked before he could put up a fight. Must have been alive when he was dragged out here, otherwise, why bother tying him up? Someone, no doubt Connor, snapped his neck when he slammed Pinto against the post."

Tony fished through the dead man's pockets and inside his socks, hoping to find something useful. He came up empty and stood up. "What did you find inside?" he asked.

"Other than signs of a good brawl, nothing helpful. Pinto was dragged out of the top bunk, but I don't know why. No sign of the girl, though,"

"That would have been too much to hope for. Okay, what now?"

"My take?" said Naomi. "Something got to Connor. Maybe somehow he found out about Pinto making the 911 call. He got pissed, jumped Pinto and beat him up with that broken table leg. But why drag him outside and tie him up?"

"I think to question him. Look at the dirt marks on Pinto's pants. Perfect shoe prints. I think he spread Pinto's legs to make him real vulnerable, then stood on his pants so he couldn't move. Probably trying to get Pinto to talk. Then he killed him."

"So the question is, what did he want to know? What Pinto told the police?"

"Or maybe where the girl was," suggested Amero . . .

"Sounds more likely to me," agreed Tony. "This man was tortured. When was the call to the station? 4-5 o'clock?"

"About 4:30," Amero confirmed.

"Well this body hasn't been here for any six hours, that's for sure. He hasn't been dead more than a few hours. 'Course we don't know when Connor found out about the call, so maybe I'm moving too quickly to believe the torture was over the girl's location and not over the call."

Naomi had walked over to the tire marks where she stooped to study the area around both marks. "There were a lot of trips made to the car before it left, but there is only one set of foot prints, an adult's."

"He could have carried her," suggested Santinello, secretly relieved that his future nest egg seemed still intact.

"Could have, but only two adults slept in the cabin last night, so if Carrie were in the woods at 4:30, and if this fight took place a couple of hours ago, then I bet she's still out there somewhere."

Tony nodded. They now had two deadlines: one for the money drop, and one to find Carrie. He checked his watch. Just after 12 noon. Eleven hours left for one; who knew how many left for Carrie. Her deadline was closer?

"Peter, give your men a call and have one bring in the topo I left in your car. Naomi and I will need that. Then you head back to the station. I need you to work out the details with Commander Lewis and his gang for the drop tonight. Until we find Carrie, one way or the other, we have to assume that the drop has to be live. Real money. You have to get MacKenzey to get his cash to the Coast Guard Station no later than four o'clock so they have time to pack it and set up the buoys. That could take a while.

"Unless you need Jimmy, I'd like him to stay here to give us some support," Tony added.

Realizing the opportunity, Santinello interrupted quickly: "I'll be happy to go back and coordinate with Lewis, so Amero can stay here and help you guys."

"Just Jimmy?" Peter asked, ignoring the offer. "Don't you need a crew to search the woods?"

"Unfortunately, Naomi and I are going to have to do this ourselves. No one else can track and we don't need a whole bunch of well-intentioned people messing up the signs. The biggest help to us would be for Jimmy to have water, food and a good phone.

"Oh, put out an ABP for the Plymouth. Connor's out floating in it somewhere. Better check with surrounding towns from here to Somerville for any cars that have been reported stolen. Connor may dump the Plymouth early, if he hasn't already.

"One last thing: remind Lewis to keep up the search for Valchon's boat. He said he would, but wouldn't hurt to make sure."

12:10 PM, Day 4

A patrolman arrived with the map and left immediately with Amero.

"Think we can take the 'twenty minutes' in Pinto's message literally?" Naomi asked. She and Tony were examining the map.

"Didn't look like a woodsman to me, but you know how easy it is to lose track of time in the woods. Let's err and say thirty minutes. That's a pretty big circle."

"Yes, but terrain will make a difference in how far they could have traveled in that time."

Tony knew she was right, particularly if his assessment of Pinto's ability in the woods was correct. "Here's what I suggest," he said. "Let's forget the main trail in. Too obvious, besides I saw no footprints on the way in here, either time. We examine twenty, maybe twenty-five feet outside the clearing and identify all the markings of people coming and going. That distance should eliminate the piss stops. We'll flag them, divvy them up and see where they lead."

"Works for me." She drew a line in the dirt on both sides of the clearing. "This side's mine. Give a whistle when you're finished flagging."

Fifteen minutes later, Tony whistled and they met back at the clearing. "How many did you flag?" he asked.

"Four. You?"

"Five. I was thinking, of my five, two were single trails. How 'bout you?"

"One. Why?"

"Let's assume Pinto knew where the girl was. That means at least two people walked there: the girl and Pinto. So unless those single trails converge further out, I say we forget the three singles and concentrate on the other six. It goes without saying that any with the child's prints would be top priority. Agree?"

"Right. And as a double check, you track my three and I'll take your three. If we run across any more, we can flag them as well."

"Good thinking. Track as far as you find duplicate prints, unless just the adult's continue on; then give up. Come back and go to another track. Make sense?"

"Agree again."

"How's your phone?"

"Still have five bars."

"Wish that's where I was; we might need a drink after this effort!"

"Funny. Call when you eliminate or when you hit the jackpot, okay?"

And they split up. Tony checked his watch and noticed it was 12:20. Time kept moving. *Why does it always move more quickly than my progress*? he wondered.

1:35 PM, Day 4

Tony had lost the trail twice. The outcrop made tracking impossible. The only way to recover the trail was to keep searching in increasingly larger circles until the tracks resumed. Twice he recovered the trail, only to find it meandered around until he lost it a third time. Another twenty-five minutes of frustrating circling were wasted before he found another print heading back towards camp. He checked the location of the sun and realized he had gone in a gigantic circle and was rapidly approaching the clearing. Being on your knees with your eyes to the ground and you could lose sense of direction in no time, he thought.

On the plus side, one trail was crossed off. He left a flag with a tare halfway through it, signaling dead end. He found Naomi's second flag and set out again. This trail looked promising. There were multiple sets of tracks, two different footprints, both going and coming. No child's prints, but maybe, he thought, the adult's had overridden them.

This trail was easier to follow; the ground was softer, the markings clearer and the trail wider. He had concluded that two men were walking side by side at some points, then in step at others. The two different footprints confused Tony. On one hand they were easy to follow, almost as if someone were going out of their way to make it obvious. On the other hand, when the prints diverged, there was no sign of a child's print, nor did the adult prints have a direction to them. They meandered. Tony thought it could only mean two men out walking. Maybe Connor forced Pinto to walk with him. Maybe not.

Then the tracks changed. Earlier, one footprint had been on top of the other; now it was the reverse. He could tell by the treads. The one with the distinctive slash mark that he had seen at Halibut Point was now on top. Before, it had been covered by another print. Two men walking the same trail at different times? What did that mean? One man in the lead at first, the other taking over later? Two men covering the same trail at totally different times? Well then, why one print on top for part of the time, the other for the rest?

And why no child's print? He had no choice but to continue to track. But then the signs disappeared altogether. No broken branch. No depression in the soil. No leaves over turned. No scattered detritus. No bent grass. Nothing. Cold. He circled, and circled again. It was only by luck that he picked up the trail when he was forced to climb over a fallen tree. Right on the other side, a beautiful heel imprint with the slash, just like earlier. He was back on track! Then without warning, a set of animal tracks appeared. He bent to look more closely at the paw print: definitely the three toe markings of a coyote.

He froze, one foot up, balancing on the other. He had heard something and didn't dare move. His heartbeat quickened. Keeping his body immobile, he turned his head to try and catch the sound again. Something had definitely moved. He twisted his head in another direction and opened his mouth to hear better; still nothing. Gradually he put his foot back on the ground and readied to rush the bush when he heard the red hawk whistle.

"Shit, Little Bird; you scared me."

"And you me. I was following this trail in reverse because it looked promising. I was tracking two men hoping it would prove to be them coming back from Carrie. Then you! Not that I'm sorry to see you, but you're not what I was looking for."

"Neither are these," Tony said pointing to the coyote prints.

"That explains this feeling I've had," Naomi answered, bending to confirm the identification of the paw print. "I've sensed the presence of something for the past ten minutes, like I was being stalked. If it is a coyote, we better find the girl before it does."

"Coyotes don't attack people."

"A child might be something else again. And if Carrie alarms it . . ." Tony looked at his watch and wiped his sleeve across his forehead. "We've been on this for almost two hours. Dead end. Shit! Now it's going on four and I still have one more to go. How 'bout you?"

"Two more. I could use some water before I drop."

"Me, too. Let's head back. I can call Amero and see how he and Lewis are doing."

They reached the clearing and sat down against Santinello's 's car, exhausted. Tracking was hard work by itself. Coupled with the pressing deadline of the money drop and the frustration of not finding Carrie, they were nearly spent. Tony laid spread eagle on the ground as Naomi drained a water bottle. She sat and loosened the laces on her boots, and took them off to massage her feet. Lying on her back, she put her feet up on the rear wheel of the vehicle to let the fluids drain from her legs.

Tony wanted to sleep. Instead, he dialed Amero, who asked how things were going.

"Shitty. After nearly four hours, we have eliminated only three trails. Worse, we're worried a coyote might get there first, so I'm calling in for some good news."

"Well, you may have the wrong number. No trace of Connor or the Plymouth, and the same for Valchon and his boat. The only good news, and that is a matter of opinion, is that MacKenzey is here at the Coast Guard Station with a Brinks truck backed into the loading dock."

"How's he doing?" Tony asked, working his shoulders in small circles to relieve the kinks.

"For a man about to part with 800 big ones, he's remarkably calm."

"Guess if you can come up with that much, you have more where it came from."

"I wouldn't know," admitted Amero.

"Me either. How 'bout Lewis and his crew?"

"Those guys are pros. Scary how cold they are: so matter of fact."

"Yeah, Wouldn't want them batting for the other team."

"Me neither. They've wrapped most of the money and there is a bogus transmitter in each of the bags so far and a real one on each flotation device. They figured Valchon or Connor or whoever would be more likely to search the bags than the buoys."

"I like it. And plan B?"

"Already done. Kinda risky, Tony. You sure you want to proceed with it?"

"At this point, yeah. The longer I crawl on my hands and knees in this forest, the more pissed I get. Just make sure MacKenzey has no clue."

"No problem. I worked it out with Lewis."

"Keep it that way. Put both plans into play and we can decide which one to activate right at the deadline. I'm going back out. Keep me up to speed if anything changes."

"You do the same. Out."

"Okay, Little Bird. Ready for more bushes? We're out of here, Jimmy."

"You'll find her, Tony", said Santinello. "No one tracks like you two." *God, I hope I'm wrong,* he thought.

Chapter 34

4:12 PM, Day 4

Rocker had been trolling the airport garage for nearly half an hour, looking for the right spot to drop the car. He had driven into the queue for Terminal B, saw the security men get out of the booth to inspect the trunk of the car two ahead of him, and promptly drove out the exit ramp. He circled over to the Central Garage where no one was inspecting trunks. *What assholes*, he thought! *Who gets paid to run this security system?*

Once in Central Parking, he cruised the different levels, spotted the dead ends, and checked for maintenance or security patrols. Seeing none, Rocker grabbed an orange cone and placed it at the entrance to a darkened aisle where he had removed the bulb from the light fixture earlier in his circling, and drove in to the end, next to a dark blue Honda. After jimmying open the door with a wire coat hanger, he transferred the bags. hotwired the Honda, and drove off in a vehicle not yet known to be missing.

4:27 PM, Day 4

Valchon had slept off as much of the hangover as he was going to lose until he started drinking again. He finally felt well enough to change the shirt that had grown stiff with the detritus he had recycled from last night's dinner and realized he was ravenously hungry. He wrapped twenty hundred-dollar bills inside an old cloth and stuffed them into a small plastic bag, which he slipped in his pocket as he climbed ashore. Leaving the bag on the bike as he had promised, he retraced his steps to the restaurant.

Dinner from the fast food restaurant at the end of the bridge consisted of extra large roast beef with mayo, onions and extra sauce that coincidentally looked strangely like the front of the shirt he had just discarded, so for variety he added an order of French fries, another of fried onion rings, and a large Pepsi and he was good to go.

5:45 PM, Day 4

Tony's frustration level was out of control. He could feel the clock ticking. The sand was running through the hourglass faster than he could push bushes aside. The dull, late afternoon light had begun to settle on the woods, making it difficult to see the reflection of the light off the weeds. He was beginning to track on intuition, which he knew was a fast road to failure. *Stay to what you see*, he kept telling himself.

He was working on talking himself out of giving up just as he lost the trail for the umpteenth time. Shit! He went into circling mode and found nothing. Widening the circles brought no results either. He drank the last of his water as he retraced his steps back towards the clearing, totally discouraged, drained, feeling like a failure and questioning whether it had been a dumb mistake to discard the single person tracks.

He pushed through a patch of wild rose bushes that he had passed earlier. A thorn caught him on the cheek as he backed out. A trickle of blood began running down his cheek, inside his collar. The blood running out reminded him that time had run out. The girl was not here after all. Suddenly Tony thought he heard a red hawk whistle. He stopped and heard it again. This time he answered with a whistle call of his own. It was answered. Forgetting any effort at silence, he plunged ahead towards the whistle.

What?" he asked Naomi, his throat dry.

"Look at these broken branches," she said, pointing out one then another branch further on. "Someone deliberately broke them. I've seen eight so far, and I think it marks a route."

"God, I hope so. We're going to have to give this up soon. My eyes will quit before the light gives out. My patience has already quit."

Naomi had moved ahead. *How does she have such energy*? Tony wondered. *I can hardly put one foot in front of the other and she is nearly at a run.* "Wait up!" he yelled.

"No time. This is our last trail."

He followed, keeping up with his wife, as the broken branches were easy to follow, although it was getting noticeably darker. Losing sight of the next broken branch, he whistled; Naomi answered from up ahead to the left. He looked at his watch; it was already ten after eight. They'd have to turn back. Neither one had a flashlight. He whistled again, nearly bumping into Naomi before he realized she was there.

"Damn; I didn't see you. It's too dark; we've got to turn back."

"Shhh," she said, putting her hand over his mouth. She waited, listening. "Carrie? Are you here, honey?"

There was silence. Naomi spoke again. "Carrie? I'm Detective Naomi Little Bird with the Gloucester Police. We want to take you to your Mommy. Are you here?"

A rustling in the evergreen off broke the silence to the left. Tony walked towards it. "You're safe, Carrie. You can come out," he said, suddenly excited, but realizing he was talking to a bunch of branches. Had he lost his mind? Then Naomi rushed past him and knelt to hold the little girl who had just pushed out of the branches. She squeezed Carrie, rocking back and forth, holding her tightly to her chest.

"You poor girl. You poor girl. You're safe now. You're all right, Carrie."

"I was scared no one was going to come for me. Mr. Pinto told me to wait for him. Where is he? He promised me?"

"Mr. Pinto kept his promise, honey; he led us to you instead. He was your friend, wasn't he?" Naomi asked still holding the girl, stroking her hair, mothering her.

"Oh, yes; he didn't tell that bad man where I was and he even brought me some crackers and stuff. But I'm real hungry now."

Naomi released Carrie, stood up and held her hand. "Well, then, let's go get you something to eat right now. Now that you mention it, I'm hungry too."

Tony had his phone to his ear waiting for Santinello to pick up. He didn't answer. Tony hit redial and saw 'low battery'. The phone had been on vibrate which overrode the low battery chirp.

"My damn phone just quit. You got any power left?"

With her free hand, she held the phone out to Tony. "Check for yourself," she said as she pushed on through the woods with Carrie in tow, the two of them chatting as old friends.

"Good, you do. Do you know Santinello's 's cell number?"

"Sorry, haven't a clue," Naomi called back over her shoulder.

"That's just great," he said. "I've got the number but no power; you have power and I don't know his number."

"Call the station then; have them call him."

Tony did just that. "Peter! Tony; we found her!"

Tony could hear Amero yell, "They found her" before he came back to Tony, "Fantastic news, Tony. Where did you find her?"

"Naomi found her huddled underneath a tree."

"Amazing! You went to the wire, didn't you? Is she okay?"

"Seems fine. Can't see my hand in front of my face, if you want to know. If it hadn't been for not wanting to admit defeat in front of Naomi, I'd have given up long ago. Listen, call her parents. No, first call Santinello and tell him to turn his car towards the trail, the second flag to the left of the cabin, and turn his headlights on. We've got to follow them in or we'll be spending the night here ourselves."

"Will do. Call me when you get to the car. We've got to finalize with Lewis in the next twenty minutes. Finding Carrie changes everything."

"There's the clearing, Carrie," Naomi said, trying to reassure the child. "As soon as we get there, you can call your Mommy."

"I can't wait," Carrie said, still animated and bursting with conversation. "Mommy is going to be proud of me for making my bed in the woods. I did it every day. Will I be able to thank Mr. Pinto??" she asked.

"Maybe later, sugar. I think maybe he has already gone. Tony, do you want to call and see if Pinto will be waiting for us?"

Tony got the message and was already dialing Santinello as they walked towards the headlights.

8:25 PM, Day 4

"If we are going to get everything in position, Sir, we need to leave now," Jones informed his commanding officer.

Lewis checked his watch for the tenth time in the last five minutes. He had been pacing, waiting for the call from Fiori with instructions on the final plan. His team was in the inflatable, ready to go, gear checked, outboards idling, missions clearly understood, nerves calm. He was the nervous one. What the hell was holding up Fiori? The briefing from Amero had been clear: Plan A was the operative one unless Fiori personally called for Plan B. He checked his watch.

"Okay, listen up. Fiori hasn't called, so our instructions are to put the buoys out as specified by the kidnappers. Everyone clear?" All three men grimaced, faces tight with disappointment, but they nodded affirmatively. Lewis paused, knew he was taking a career level risk, then added: "I did not order Plan B to be activated, but let's say there was a great deal of commotion as you shoved off, the outboards made hearing difficult, you were bent over getting gear ready and you definitely thought you heard me call for Plan B. I'm pretty certain under the stress and all of the circumstances that any Board convened for an Article Ten inquiry would be inclined to dismiss any charges."

All three men broke into immediate smiles, Jones executed a snappy salute and called out: "Sorry, Sir, I'm having trouble hearing you. Must be the engines!" He waved and threw the throttles into reverse.

Lewis returned the salute, gave a thumbs-up signal and headed up the incline to the office, sincerely doubting the Article Ten Board would give him the same benefit of the doubt.

8:26 PM, Day 4

She could no longer muster the courage to answer the phone. Laurie MacKenzey knew if she didn't answer the phone, then they couldn't tell her Carrie was dead. Simple as that. That was the only way she knew to keep her daughter alive. If they couldn't reach her, she couldn't get any bad news. She sat unmoving in the chair and listened to the ringing.

It stopped. Thank God for that, Laurie thought. No answer, no bad news. She closed her eyes. The ringing started again. Nooooo, I'm not answering. She started to cry and put her hands to her ears. The ringing continued. She wiped her tears, staring as if in a trance into the dark room. The ringing kept on, now bothering her with its persistence, forcing her to answer and get the bad news.

In an angry motion she jerked the phone off the receiver and shouted, "Just leave me alone, do you hear me?"

"Laurie, this is Peter Amero; they found Carrie! She's fine!"

The time for the news to get from her ear to her brain was an eternity. Denial. Not possible. This is a crank call. They found her? Alive? My Carrie?

"Who is this really?" she asked, not willing to believe it could be true.

""It's true, Laurie. The Fioris found her. Carrie's fine."

"She's alive?" Laurie yelled. "Really alive?" She exploded out of her chair. "You're sure?" She jumped, twirling in joy and pulled the phone line right out of the wall. She was dancing, oblivious to the dead phone. Alive! Then she heard ringing from the kitchen phone, and ran to get that one.

"Laurie, this is David. They found Carrie! In one piece! I'm coming to pick you up in five minutes. We're meeting her at the Police Station. Five minutes. Be ready!"

He hung up, not before Laurie thought she had heard him crying. David crying? Must be true! She blew through the front door still holding the two phones as she raced outside.

Chapter 35

2/3

8:47 PM, Day 4

"Mommy!" Carrie yelled, seeing her mother waiting in the parking lot as Santinello pulled in. She had been sitting quietly in the front seat for the fifteen-minute ride back from Ravenswood, but as soon as the cruiser stopped, Carrie jumped out and ran open-armed straight to Laurie. "Mommy!"

Carrie leapt into her mother's arms nearly knocking Laurie over. Laurie couldn't speak, but she didn't need to; hugging was what both of them needed and that's what they were doing. Hugging, swaying and crying.

"I missed you, Mommy. I was so scared."

"I know. I know. I missed you, too. Just hug me." And if it were possible, Carrie squeezed her mother harder. "You're here safe and sound."

"We missed you, too, sweetie," her father said joining them, putting one arm around Carrie, the other around Laurie. "We missed you a lot."

Laurie finally put Carrie down, grabbed a tissue to dry her eyes. Still holding Carrie's hand, Laurie went over to Naomi, hugged her and started crying all over again. "Thank you. Thank you!" she said between sobs.

"Oh, God; I'm a wreck!" Laurie finally said. "There isn't enough make-up in the world to cover these red eyes," she joked, reaching for another tissue. "Thank you both,"

Naomi squeezed Laurie's hand, and said: "We're just as happy as you are that Carrie is back safe and sound."

"I doubt it," Laurie laughed and picked Carrie up to hug her some more. Turning to her daughter, Laurie added: "Let's go get you something to eat. You must be starved!"

"Can we get a big Mac, Mommy? Please? Please? Just this once?"

"Of course, sweetheart."

"Maybe some French fries, too?" Carrie asked, sensing it was okay to press her luck. "Please?"

"Yes, some French fries, too! I may even have some," her mother added.

Now Carrie knew her Mother was really glad to see her. "Is Daddy coming, too?" Carrie whispered.

"Yes, he is."

"Oh," Carrie said, wondering if she could push for an ice cream cone.

"I don't mean to be a damper on your dinner plans," Tony interrupted, "but before you go anywhere, you better take Carrie to the hospital to have her properly evaluated."

Carrie looked at her mother, shaking her head. "I don't want to go to any hospital, Mommy. I'm fine. I'm just hungry."

Naomi had made her own examination of the child, noticing that her fingernails were not as pink and healthy looking as she would have liked. "I think Tony is right, Carrie. You haven't had much to drink for a couple of days now and I bet the doctor will want to take care of that."

"So will a super-Coke at MacDonald's," Carrie countered.

The adults laughed at the child's suggestion. Naomi tussled Carrie's hair and knelt to look into her eyes. "Don't you worry; maybe even the doctor will give you a soft drink as well. Then you'll get two!" As Naomi rose she turned to Laurie and said: "You will need to take Carrie to Beverly Hospital as Addison Gilbert closed its pediatric unit. Do you know how to get there?" "Unfortunately, yes," Laurie replied as she ushered her daughter to the car.

8:49 PM, Day 4

Santinello stayed behind in the cruiser as the others ran off. "Did you leave the deposit?" he asked into the phone.

"Of course. Didn't you find it?"

"No yet. Been tied up. You decided where we're going to meet?"

"You find out where the cops are going to be stationed?"

"Not yet. Just got back to the station. Should know within the hour. Don't know if I will be assigned a detail, but tell me where you want to meet and I will see if I can at least get nearby. I'm going to need to make the connection with you quick."

He's pushing, isn't he? Now why does he keep pressing? Wondered Valchon, warning bells going off in his head. *Setting up a trap*? "Haven't decided yet, but as soon as I do, I'll call. Don't worry. Gotta go."

8:51 PM, Day 4

Rocker drove north out of Logan Airport heading up Route 1 through Saugus where he found a no-tell motel that would accept cash payment without requiring a driver's license. The young clerk with multiple piercings in his ears, nose and lower lip asked Rocker, "You want the room for more than an hour?"

"I want it for the next twenty-four hours."

The clerk snorted: "Like I've worked here for almost five months and you're like the second person who's stayed like, you know, that long."

#

After showering, his first one in several days, Rocker dialed Valchon.

"Yeah?" was Valchon's response.

"It's me."

"Jeez, where the hell you been?"

"Phone died. Had to get new wheels, find a place to recharge the phone, and call."

"You find the girl?" Valchon asked.

"Not yet," Rocker answered, not wanting to give out any more details. "You set for tonight?"

"Yep. Figure I hang here for another couple of hours, start out after eleven, make the pickup, and be back after midnight. So where do you want to hook up? Back at the cabin?"

"No. Could be too risky by then." Rocker paused, making it sound as if he was deciding where to suggest. "I'll come to you. Since I've got safe wheels for the moment and you might not, I can pick you up when you land."

"That could work as long as you're here when I get back. I don't want to hang out with my thumb up my ass waiting. Might have people tailing me."

"I'll be there, don't worry. Give me directions. We need to get off the phone."

9:01 PM, Day 4

Master Chief Jones checked the GPS and pulled the throttles back into neutral. The motors idling, the inflatable rose and fell on the sea as the three men silently readied the gear. Two separate lines, each with four bags tied to individual buoys, were checked a final time. Jones pressed the switches to activate the transponders; after making certain he was getting a reading, he ordered the buoys to be dropped overboard as they drifted slightly downwind.

When the last buoy was away, Jones nudged the throttles into gear, motored ten yards closer in towards shore and ordered the second line of bags and buoys to be deployed. The demolitions expert, Seaman Andrews, already in his wet suit, rolled over backwards into the water. He entered without noise and Jones immediately handed him the telescoping pole.

Seaman McGrath, also wearing an all-black wet suit, put his air tanks, fins, flare gun and waterproof lantern into a rubber raft. He rowed silently away from the inflatable to a prearranged position a hundred yards to the northeast of the first line of buoys. He lay flat on the bottom of the raft in the dark of night so that he would be nearly invisible.

Jones radioed in and reported: "cargo away. Returning to base."

9:12 PM, Day 4

Valchon cast off and with the receding tide and paddled out into the channel, waiting until he was outside of the bridge before starting his engine. Noise carries well over water. Once clear of the shallow rocks at the mouth of the harbor, he fed the gas and felt the evening breeze in his face. He was motoring to the northeast, hugging the 4-fathom line on his sonar just off the craggy coastline.

His destination was Misery Island, an uninhabited granite outcrop with a small, sheltered cove on the inland side. The sea was calm, traffic non-existent and his night vision good enough to make out the outline of the island in the distance. After making the cove without incident, he turned bow into the wind and dropped anchor. Valchon spread out the rubber dingy, opened the aircock and began the monotonous job of filling the air chambers of the dingy. He had plenty of time.

9:21 PM, Day 4

The tension in the conference room could have been spread on a slab of bread. Chief Marren was wearing out his hair, running his hands through it. Amero paced. Tony tried to distract himself by doing the crossword puzzle in the *Boston Globe*, but the amount of erasure filings on the table belied his concentration.

He had filled 24 down six or seven times and erased it six or seven times. The newsprint was nearly worn through.

Even the room seemed to hold its breath when the phone rang. Tony hit the speaker button.

"You are on speaker," Tony said tersely.

"Lewis here. The crew is in place and the buoys are out. Nothing is moving yet."

"Are you getting readings on the transponders?" Tony asked.

"Loud and clear. Because of how close they are, it's tough to tell which we are hearing from but when they are moved, it will be obvious."

"When do you plan to move the chopper?"

"In about twenty minutes. The station on Eastern Point is expecting us before 21:45 hours. Any later than that and the engine noise could scare off the bad guys."

"I'll be right over then," said Tony, throwing his pencil down, still frustrated by 24 down. It was a short jog to the Coast Guard station and he was walking through their front door as the Jayhawk helicopter was warming up on the pad.

9:36 PM, Day 4

Rocker sealed the last of the extra large Zip-lock bags and stepped back, admiring his work. If he looked quickly, he couldn't tell that the center of the bag was stuffed with newspaper. All he could see were the ten dollar bills he had carefully positioned all around the paper which he had dampened to make it seem heavier. He was convinced that in the dark, Valchon would never know the difference.

If his calculations were correct, Valchon would wind up with less than $400.00 from the original take; Rocker would have the rest. Seemed like a fair division of the initial $3 million, he thought, humming a mindless tune as he made the final trip, closed the trunk and went back inside to wipe down anything he remembered touching. He used Windex, knowing that the alcohol would obliterate any prints. After that, he turned on the TV to the all news station, flipped the Do Not Disturb hanger on the outside doorknob, and drove off.

Chapter 36

9:39 PM, Day 4

The unmistakable *thwoping* of the Jayhawk's twin GE turbines was nearly deafening. Instinctively, Tony crouched lower as he sprinted for the side door to the helicopter. Even though Lewis had told him the blades, even at their lowest point, were still 12 feet off the ground, Tony was happy to give it a good margin of error. He was fond of his head.

The crew chief, wearing a bright orange life vest, reached out a hand to haul Tony up and inside. Over the noise, he pointed Tony to a seat, demoed the shoulder harness, then turned to the pilot and twirled his finger up. The pilot pushed the throttle forward and the 3,200 horses lifted the chopper a foot or so off the pavement, where it lurched, spun 90 degrees and climbed out over the wharf, heading southwest towards the lighthouse at the end of Eastern Point.

In less than a minute they approached the Coast Guard annex adjacent to the lighthouse. The chopper leveled off, hovered, then settled down in the middle of the large yellow X that had been painted on the grass. Undoing the harness, Tony crouched and hurried away from the chopper to the office. The whining of the engines slowed, then stopped. Though fifty yards from the now silent chopper, Tony was still bent over when he heard a corpsman inquire:

"First time on a chopper, detective?"

9:44 PM, Day 4

Valchon scurried up the deck along the side of the boat and tugged on the line; the anchor was holding fast. He checked for reference points on the island to make certain he wasn't drifting. Satisfied, Valchon lowered the rubber dinghy over the side and slid the oars into place before lashing them down. He put the two canvass bags on the floor of the dingy and pushed clear of the anchored boat.

As he rowed quietly around the small cove, Valchon looked for any other craft that might be moored or hauled up on the beach. He made way around to the northeast on the leeward side of the island, still out of the slight wind.

When clear of the rocks, he set his GPS to the proper heading to the drop point, about a quarter mile away. He would be rowing backwards so wouldn't easily be able to follow the line of sight towards the lighthouse. Placing the GPS on the floor between his legs, Valchon spit on his hands, rubbed them together and set out towards his retirement fund. The rubber oars made no noise at all.

9:51 PM, Day 4

The man was dressed in dark jeans and a maroon pullover. Maroon worked just as well as black and was easier to explain should a night watchman want to know why he was poking around in the dark at the Manchester Yacht Club. He stepped carefully over the coiled rope on the dock, moving quietly, looking down both sides at the yachts that were tied up for the night. The mooring lines stretched and creaked as the boats pulled against them in the gentle wind. Music from a dinner party at the mansion on the point drifted across the narrow harbor.

Near the end of the dock he found what he was looking for, took out his knife, cut the lines, and guided the rowboat around the last yacht before jumping in. Once clear of the dock, he hauled the oars and pulled on the rope to start the small two horsepower electric motor. Electric motors are quieter than gas powered ones and quiet was first on his menu.

He motored out, keeping the green channel markers on the starboard side, staying in deep water. He could see the outline of Misery Island and made straight for it, knowing he had about 45 minutes to get out, do his work, and get back. He rounded the island and came into the cove alongside the lobster boat. Quickly tying off, he jumped on board, unlatched and lifted the engine cover, felt around for the plastic fuel line, found it and cut a deep notch into the line. Then he severed the cooling line altogether, latched down the cover, and, dropping down into the stolen dinghy, returned to the harbor.

10:14 PM, Day 4

Tony keyed the mike twice. Petty Office McGrath keyed back and whispered: "still no sign."

Jones was on the same channel and responded, "Nothing here either, Tony. Nothing has left or entered the outer harbor. temp's dropping; and fog's rolling in pretty steadily now."

"How's visibility?"

"Fuzzy. Can no longer see town. What's the plan if the chopper is grounded?"

"Hang on." Tony held the mike to his chest and turned to Commander Lewis. "Jones is asking about the chopper."

"If it stays like this, we've got a go. Ceiling drops any further, could be iffy."

Tony spoke back into the mike: "We may have to abandon the chopper plan. Call you back at quarter to. We'll decide then."

"Roger that. We may have to think about yanking Andrews before the visibility shits the bed."

"Will get back to you on that."

Tony went back to the chart of the coastline between Gloucester and Salem. He traced his finger south along the shoreline, held it over Manchester harbor for a brief moment and shook his head.

"Isn't going to be Manchester. It'd be too obvious, Valchon's lobster boat, I mean. Would stand out too much with all those fancy yachts." He tapped the chart at Beverly. "Would take too long for him to haul down to Salem after the pick up; they need time to transfer the money and run for it. It's got to be Beverly, Commander; that's got to be where they will come ashore. Where does Salem have its boats positioned?"

Lewis joined Tony at the chart table and indicated two separate points in a line that extended in a slight curve from 100 yards off shore, across the northeastern channel into Salem, to a third point where the last boat would block a run around the island, in case the kidnappers decided to come in via the southern channel.

"I'd have them move north, closer in to Beverly. If this fog gets worse, whoever picks up the money will want to make land quickly. Could you get them to tighten in more on Beverly? Set up a block further north?"

Lewis reached for the phone as Tony turned to leave.

"I'm going to head down to Beverly harbor now before the fog gets any worse." He stopped at the door. "What about Jones? Will he be able to watch our harbor entrance by himself if this fog worsens?"

"No. I'll call in the bigger boat right now. We'll need its radar in this soup."

"Good. Get them in position as quickly as possible." Tony checked his watch. "We've got about half an hour before their deadline,"

"My boat will be at the groaner in less than ten minutes. No problem."

"Listen, here's my cell. Call me at once if your men have any contact at all. Oh, shit, I forgot. My car's at your station in town. Don't suppose you could fly me back, could you?"

Lewis stuck his head out the door. The lighthouse, only twenty yards away, was invisible, as was the helicopter, only slightly further away. He couldn't even see the sundial at the edge of the walk. It was as if a bag of gray cotton candy had been dumped in front of the door.

"The chopper isn't going anywhere, Tony. I can't even see it from here. Hold on: I'll drive you back myself. First, I'm signaling Jones to pick up Andrews. This fog is bad and getting worse by the minute."

"That will mean we won't have anyone at the drop site."

"Can't help it. I won't risk Andrews. You have no idea how disorienting the fog is. On top of that, the tide could take him out and it would be hell to find him. No way. He's coming in, now. Meet me at the car; it's the blue Ford by the door you came in."

10:17 PM, Day 4

The drive back from the lighthouse was painfully slow. Tony kept pushing his right foot harder on the floor, trying to make the car go faster, but since he was in the passenger seat, the only thing he was accomplishing was making him tenser. He could feel his shoulders tightening and tried rolling them to loosen his muscles. Flipping open his cell phone, he called in to the police station and found Amero there waiting.

"We got major problems. The fog has grounded the chopper and the Coast Guard is picking up the two men out by the drop site as we speak. That means we have no way to follow Valchon or Connor or whoever the hell it is once they make the pick up."

"That means we won't get a transmitter on their boat, so if they find the transmitters on the buoys, then we're really screwed."

"Exactly."

"Where are you now?" Amero asked.

"On my way to you. I'll be there in about four minutes, and then I want you to come with me to Beverly. My gut tells me that's where they will come ashore. In this fog they won't go any further than necessary."

"That could make sense, unless they had a back-up plan to go elsewhere."

"I don't think so. Fog wasn't in the forecast, so they must have planned based on clear weather. My hunch is that a lobster boat would have been too visible in Manchester harbor. Those gazillion dollar yacht owners use lobster boats for kindling. Beverly makes more sense."

"I'll call Beverly police now. You driving?"

"No, we'll take yours."

"Roger. I'll meet you in the lot down below."

10:28 PM, Day 4

Rocker slid the rowboat back in the slip where he had borrowed it less than an hour earlier. He couldn't tell if anyone had even noticed it was missing. Before climbing out, Rocker waited, listened, heard nothing, then crawled up onto the dock. He could still hear the music from across the water, although the lights on the point were now hard to see because of the fog. *Too damn bad we didn't know about the fog beforehand*, he thought. *Could've saved a bunch of time coming into Manchester instead of Beverly. Too late now, though.*

He debated trying to reach Valchon, thought better of the idea, unlocked the car that he had left behind the dumpster and headed out of the parking lot. It took him less than fifteen minutes to cross the Beverly-Salem Bridge and find the right turn onto a gravel road that wound down underneath the bridge to where Valchon said he would land.

10:29 PM, Day 4

Valchon had been watching the GPS reading, making minor corrections to stay on course. He had been concentrating so intently on the GPS that when he looked around to see how close he was, he was amazed to see nothing. Disoriented, he twisted in his seat and looked over the other shoulder. Still nothing. What the hell? Where were the lights from Gloucester harbor? Where was the lighthouse beacon? How could he have gotten so far off course?

Suddenly, the numbers on the GPS screen began to blink. He reached down to check the reading, and then looked up again. Blinking numbers meant dead on target. But why were there no lights? As he looked up and saw no stars either, he realized he was in fog, a white out, and with that felt the dinghy bump into something: a bright red buoy!

Excited, Valchon hooked the blade over the line attached to the buoy, pulling it towards him. He found the first life jacket and the plastic bag suspended below it. After cutting free the buoy, he lashed off the other end of the line to the ring bolted through the stern seat and brought the plastic bag inboard. He cut free the tape holding it closed and reached inside. It was too dark to see exactly, but it felt like stacks and stacks of bills. His heart was racing.

One by one, he removed the stacks and transferred them to a similar bag he had brought with him. Nearly at the bottom, he reached in again and touched something metallic. He pulled it out. He could see a tiny blinking indicator light. Bastards! Just as Rocker had suspected, a transmitter! He left it in place, finished emptying the money, and before throwing the bag back in the water; he tied it off with a piece of cord and went on to the second bag.

He found a second transmitter, left it in place also and repeated the process he had gone through with the first bag. When pulling in the remaining line to get to the last two bags, he saw a blinking light moving towards him in the water. His imagination on overdrive, Valchon thought it was a frogman coming for him and reached quickly for his pistol, nearly dropping the line. As he pointed his revolver at the light, Valchon was just about to pull the trigger when he realized that it was another transmitter that the cops had tied to the line. Clever bastards, he thought. But not clever enough

He kept pulling, found the third bag, and a third transmitter. Realizing this was taking longer than he anticipated, he hurried, finished transferring the stacks of bills, then slipped the last empty bag over the side without so much as a sound. Valchon didn't have much room in the dinghy. He hit the reciprocal button on the GPS, got the new compass heading and began to row for home. The whole process had taken nearly twenty minutes, but he was still pretty much on schedule.

10:45 PM, Day 4

From the car, Tony called Lewis. "Anything?" he asked.

"Nothing. Just this second spoke with both Jones and McGrath. Jones reported nothing on the radar and McGrath nothing visually."

"Where is McGrath?" Tony wanted to know.

"He and Andrews are holding position about 50 yards this side of the drop site."

"Can they see the buoys?"

"Not in this shit. They can barely see the blade at the end of the oar. Guess I should have said they have heard nothing."

"Shit. Can they close in any?"

"I'll see," Lewis said before ringing off.

Chapter 37

11:05 PM, Day 4

Tony called Lewis back. "What's happening now?" he asked.

"Not a damn thing. McGrath has closed to about 20 yards but hasn't heard a peep. Course in the fog, sound is nearly impossible to pinpoint."

"They've heard nothing?" Tony asked disbelievingly.

"You got it. Pretty frustrating! You think we've been had?"

"Don't know what to think. We never did hear back from them after their second call, but I can't believe they would walk from $800,000."

"Any chance they know we found the girl, smelled a trap, and just split?"

"Can't see how. We kept it off the air. No media yet. No, something else is happening. Listen, does McGrath have a weapon?" Tony asked.

"Both McGrath and Andrews do. What do you want?"

"Have them check both buoy lines. Then call me back."

"Roger; give me ten."

Actually, it didn't take ten minutes. McGrath had already approached on his own when he realized nothing was happening. Tony clicked on his phone before the first ring finished. "What did they find?" Tony snapped.

"You won't believe this. Line A is in place and intact. Line B, however, has been totally emptied."

"What? The bags are empty?"

"Totally empty . . . except for one transmitter in each bag."

Even in the tension, Lewis and Tony began to laugh. Line B had the fake stacks of paper. Line A had almost $900,000 still hanging from the life jackets.

Tony asked again: "Is McGrath certain?"

"Absolutely. They had cut one bag open just to make certain. They are more than a little chagrined that they didn't hear the loot being taken. I can imagine they won't live that down for a while."

"Probably not," Tony agreed. "Did Jones report anything?"

"Nothing there either."

"So how did Lot B get taken? Nothing on radar? Hard to believe there was no noise. Must have taken fifteen-twenty minutes to empty the bags, and they heard nothing?"

"Probably used a rubber dinghy. That would have no radar profile. No way someone swam out there. Not even Mark Spitz could pull that off."

So where did the dinghy go, Tony wondered.

"So what do you want from this end, Tony?" Lewis asked.

"Might as well get the money and bring in your men. Can Jones patrol the harbor entrance and see if he can pick up anything?"

"Sure, but if it's a dinghy, he will have to ram it to see it."

"I have a better idea. Have Jones hug the shoreline and run towards Beverly. Maybe we can luck out and find the bastards?"

"That makes more sense, but in this fog we won't be able to be in as close to shore as we could in clearer weather. Could miss the dinghy if it's in real shallow water."

"I know, but Valchon or Connors or whomever can't row forever. If they had a boat anchored somewhere nearby, you might pick that up."

"We'd get anything with an engine for sure. I'll keep in touch." Lewis rang off and issued some new orders. Jones acknowledged and left his position off the breakwater and slowly patrolled his way southeast along the coast. He posted two men as lookouts on the bow.

11:29 PM, Day 4

Muscles aching, energy nearly spent, Valchon saw the GPS blinking, signaling the turn off Misery Island back into the cove. He hit the reset button, pulled hard on his right oar to correct his direction, rowed for another few minutes until he nudged alongside his boat. He was exhausted, wanted a beer in the worse way. He threw the bags into the cockpit, grabbed the bowline and climbed up into the bigger boat.

He tried to haul the dinghy over the gunwale, but didn't have the strength left to muscle it in. *Screw it*, he thought; *who needs it*. After he tossed the line overboard into the dinghy, it disappeared into the fog, carried by the rising tide in towards shore.

Valchon opened the cooler, drew out a beer, drained it and opened another. He set the autopilot to the heading to Beverly harbor and went to check the bags. He turned on the lantern, pulled the first of the bags over, undid it and pulled out the first stack, taking another chug on the beer.

He spit out a spray of beer, reached for a second stack, and threw it against the engine cover. He tore through the first bag and went onto the second, found the same stacks of blank paper. No, dammit, no! He'd been had! But how had the police known to fake the drop? The only answer that made sense was that Rocker had squealed. Bastard had set him up. Why else would they have risked not using real money?

Valchon thought hard. Could Rocker also have told the cops where he was going to land? Could they be there waiting for him right now? But if Rocker squealed, why weren't the cops waiting at the drop site? Why wouldn't they have picked him up there? No reason to follow him if they knew he had fake money. Unless . . . maybe they thought he would lead them to Rocker.

But why would they want him to do that? Unless they thought Rocker had the drug money stashed. Now that was making more sense. If he found the bags were filled with paper instead of money, he wouldn't walk away from his share of the real pile, so they let him go.

He dialed the now familiar number. "So where is everyone stationed, he asked quickly?"

"They got all the marinas in Gloucester, Rockport and Manchester covered like a bad dream," Santinello lied. "I got to get in place myself, so where you going to be?"

"You settin' me up, Jimmy? You keep pushin' on me."

"Honest, no. Why would I do that? I set you up, I get nothing. Hard to pay medical bills with a ribbon on my chest. Believe me: I need the money."

Valchon made a quick decision. Meet me at the first restaurant south of the Salem Bridge. Should be there within thirty minutes."

"Thanks, Mike. Don't worry: I'll be there where the road blocks are."

His mind now focused on getting even with Rocker, Valchon was so involved with thoughts of revenge that he didn't notice the engine temp gauge in the red zone and the fuel reading near empty.

11:32 PM, Day 4

Tony's phone rang. It was Jones.

"We got something moving, Tony," he said. "We picked up a small craft leaving Misery heading directly towards Beverly harbor. The signal is not wavering at all; must be on autopilot."

"Can you tell what you're looking at?" Tony asked, feeling his pulse jump. "I mean size-wise?"

"We're getting a direct stern shot so I can't tell the length. Sonar says single engine making a bucket of noise. A cylinder must be out, as the signal sounds really rough. We're guessing 25-30 feet, tops, but from this angle it's too hard to tell yet."

"Valchon's lobster boat must be 15-20 years old. Looked in pretty rough shape to me, but I didn't see the engine."

"Course still steady for Beverly Harbor," Jones added.

"Tell me as soon as you get any change."

Tony immediately dialed the Beverly police station, told the desk sergeant what was happening and what he needed. Amero had overheard the conversation and was checking his revolver when Tony hung up. "Party time!" he said, flipping closed the cylinder, checking to make certain there was a round in the chamber. They were parked in the old MacDonald's lot on the Beverly side of the Beverly-Salem Bridge.

"Party time is right . . . if we guessed correctly and he doesn't turn off to Salem at the last minute."

"Have faith. You've guessed right so far," Peter said.

11:42 PM, Day 4

Santinello ran to his car and raced down 128 towards the Salem exit. *Damn! Too damn close*, he thought, looking at his watch.

11:45 PM, Day 4

Valchon had re-packed each of the moneybags, inserting a ten-dollar bill on the top of the last stack in each bag before resealing them. He was approaching the condos at the mouth of Beverly harbor and took the control off autopilot, manually turning the helm to starboard to follow the channel markers in.

11:46 PM, Day 4

"Fiori here" Tony said answering his cell.

"The boat has turned west into the harbor," Jones relayed. "He's passing the condominium project on the downtown side. He's about 500 yards from the bridge."

"Excellent. He'll have to moor in the harbor or come underneath the bridge. Either way, hold position just inside the harbor. If he turns and runs, I don't want him to get out."

"Roger that. We'll take over if he runs. Call if you need us to come in."

11:47 PM, Day 4

As soon as he flipped off the auto toggle, the engine started knocking, coughing like it wasn't getting fuel. Valchon looked down at the fuel gauge, was startled to see it read empty, and tapped the gauge with his finger. Just then he saw the engine temp needle maxed out on the danger line. *Shit, only a couple of hundred yards to go*, he thought, and then a stray spark ignited the gasoline that had been spraying on the battery cable, a fireball erupted—and he didn't think any more.

The force of the explosion was spectacular. Fiori felt the heat through the open window inside the car nearly two hundred yards away. The boat was completely engulfed in a flame that soared fifty feet into the air and lit the entire harbor. Debris rained down on the water for hundreds of feet around the boat, burning pieces of wood and lobster traps landing on nearby boats, starting small fires as the sparks hit sails that had been furled around their booms. Amero threw his arm across his face, ducked below the wheel and landed in Tony's lap.

"Holy shit!" they said nearly in unison, stunned by the suddenness of what had happened. Then Tony added: "Get the hell off my lap!"

11:48 PM, Day 4

As Santinello sped down Rantoul Street, he heard a massive explosion and automatically reached for his phone to call Valchon. No answer. He threw the phone down on the seat as he stopped at the light to turn up onto the Salem Bridge. *I can't miss this; but even if I get to Valchon, how am I going to get the money without Fiori seeing?*

11:49 PM, Day 4

Out of the corner of his eye, Tony saw movement under the bridge across the inlet. A car engine started, headlights flashed on and tires spun, throwing a rooster tail of debris and gravel as the car spun into action. Instinct told him the car had been waiting for the boat. Tony grabbed for the handset to alert the Salem police: "He's moving! He's moving up from the bridge. Block him!"

The two Salem patrol cars that had been waiting in the dry cleaner's lot sprinted forward, skidding into a "V" blocking the southbound lanes of Bridge Street. Two unmarked sedans came in behind them extending the "V" on both flanks, doors flung open as eight policemen with assault rifles knelt behind the inside fenders, their muzzles pointed with deadly certainty right at the center of the on-coming white line.

The Salem police chief skidded into position in the inside of the blockade, blue lights flashing, phone in hand. "Southbound is sealed; what can you see?"

By this time, a fifth patrol car that had been waiting on the east side of the bridge was joined by three Beverly police vehicles, which were just getting into position as the fleeing car bounced hard over the edge of the blacktop, A comet of sparks followed as it screeched over the bump, tires spinning, throwing rocks in a spray behind as they skidded in an out-of-control turn. Smoking trails of black rubber snaked across the pavement as the tires fought for traction.

Rocker saw the road to Salem was crammed with police cars, was tempted to run for the small opening on the outside of the leftmost squad car, but instead threw his wheel to the left, stomped on the footbrake, pulled up on the emergency handbrake and screamed into a four-point racing turn. Completing the 180-degree spin, he released everything, threw the wheel over to correct his spin and put all his thirty-seven years of anger smack down on the accelerator.

The car flew forward towards the bridge. Rocker cut down off the high side of the road and banked low to the inside of the curve, now in the left lane of the lazy s-bend. The speedometer needle jerked through seventy and was still climbing as Rocker brought the car through the curve, inches away from the cement Jersey barriers that lined the outside of the lane, back across the center line and down hard into the inside of the right hand curve. Speedometer now passing through 80, engine screaming as the car hurtled into the long rise of the bridge.

As he crested then began the descent onto the Beverly side of the bridge, Rocker gripped the wheel, every muscle tense, focused on escape. The accelerator was welded to the floor, speedometer needle now approaching 90 as he crested the hill and saw the four police cars about two hundred yards. Ahead.

"Fucking cops" Rocker yelled as he violently pumped the brakes, trying to split the slight opening between the two center cars. He had miscalculated; his right front tire caught the lower lip of the Jersey barrier, throwing the rear end out to left. Rocker corrected but nicked the barrier in the other lane and went into a counterclockwise spin broadside into the first cruiser.

The right front fender, quarter panel and wheel assembly of the lighter Honda telescoped inward and down, at once shearing the steel bolts that held the engine, dropping it off the frame and severing the drive shaft which caught in a pot hole, jackknifing the Honda up over the fender of the cruiser. The hurtling mass of now air-born steel rolled on its side. The severed drive train speared the hood of the cruiser, wrenched it completely out of its frame, pulling it along on its back like a whale breaching, before gravity took over, bringing what was left of the vehicle smashing down on the pavement, In one of those very brief moments when every cell in the body is so thoroughly focused that the eye and brain fuse into a recording device that captures unimaginable detail and provides such clarity of vision that even hundreds of instant replays, even if that were doable, could never fully display the scene that became imprinted, forever, in the film in Tony's brain.

Along the trail of mangled car parts lay strewn clear plastic bags, clear plastic bags that were green, clear plastic bags that were green because they were filled with more fifty and hundred dollar bills than Tony had ever seen. Tony had this fleeting image of a rich uncle Easter bunny dropping green eggs in some random pattern for kids to come along and scoop up and put in their baskets.

At the same time, he saw a liquid running out of the two cars that lay piled incestuously intertwined in some failed, back-breaking love-making position. The liquid splashed against the Easter eggs, spread, then merged again on the downhill side before engulfing another and then another and then another egg. He knew precisely what was going to happen. The Easter bunny giveth and now was taking. He yelled: TAKE COVER! EXPLOSION COMING!"

A small flame seemed to drip in very slow motion from the punctured fuel tank, over the undercarriage of the Honda, then onto the pavement where it spread over more meanderings than the Mississippi delta, before it exploded with a WOSH as the flames raced down the spreading gasoline, ate through the petroleum based plastic then devoured the green bills inside. The pavement was strewn like a Martian landscape with burning meteors as bag after bag was engulfed with flame. The ultimate irony: drug money burning in the veins of gasoline.

11:56 PM, Day 4

Santinello stepped out of his car, frozen in disbelief at what he had just seen. Numb with the reality that relief from worrying about his child's medical care had vanished right before his eyes, he got back in his car, too lost in his own thoughts to put the car into gear.

The annoying wailing of the sirens got louder. Fire trucks from Beverly and Salem converged on the bridge, ambulances from both towns just seconds behind, joined with the police cars already on site in the random pattern of an accident scene: red lights; blue lights; vehicles pointing this way and that; men running; instructions shouted; adrenalin pumping. And the smell. Always the smell: fuel, burnt rubber, blood, human waste.

Using foam, the firemen quickly smothered the flames, providing a safe passage to the two cars, or to what was left of them. The Honda rested upside down, leaning over the hood of the patrol car, teetering against the Jersey barrier, threatening to slide to the pavement with the slightest provocation. The growing crowd of police, firemen, medics seemed frozen, lit only by the red and blue lights of the flashing rescue vehicles, their positions changing slightly each time the beams went full circle. The rescuers approached the wreckage, then immediately stopped, backing as movement within the car started it rocking ever so slightly. Tony found himself holding his breath, wondering which way it would go. Then there was a moan. Ignoring the danger, two medics instinctively rushed the car.

Knowing the situation was still too dangerous, the Beverly Fire Chief reacted immediately and barked out orders through his battery-powered megaphone.

"Stand back! That car could go."

Then another groan. Was someone still alive inside the Honda? The fire Chief brought the megaphone to his mouth and shouted more orders. Two heavy-duty timbers were brought from the truck and propped against the front axel on each side of the car. As the hook and ladder truck backed in closer, a fireman crawled out over the extended ladder, reached down to hook a thick cable around the axel of the Honda, then signaled to have the tension winched in to hold the Honda from moving.

Now stabilized, the vehicle was safe to approach. Another fireman sprinted to the driver's side, knelt, then slid on his belly and pointed his flashlight through the broken window. No one was there. Another moan caused the fireman to look around when he spotted a body, somehow thrown clear of the vehicle behind the cement barrier. Blood was dripping from his arm and chin. Teeth were sticking through the man's cheek and his hand was at a very unusual angle.

He moaned again, and then mumbled something that sounded like "gedmethe fuckouda here", and passed out. The fireman shouted for the medics and reached to feel for a pulse on the man's neck.

Once the patient had been strapped securely into place, his neck and wrist stabilized they put him on the stretcher which was slid into the rear of the ambulance before it left with sirens blaring for the ER, just minutes away.

With the patient safely removed, the wooden blocking timbers were taken away, the cable slackened, and the car was allowed to slide to the ground, resting on its side. A second tow truck pulled in, another cable attached, and the car eased over upright onto its frame. As it rocked upright, bag after bag of money fell out of the trunk and spilled onto the road between the tow trucks.

"That's what I call cash on delivery!" the driver said, reaching for the nearest bag. Tony reached for the bag nearest him and as he picked it up, he noticed a smell. He handed the bag to Amero. "What's this smell like to you?" Tony asked.

"Fish, Amero answered without hesitation. "Yesterday's fish dinner."

Tony and Peter finished inventorying the bags, collected items of interest from the vehicle, including a revolver, police scanner, an old manual typewriter, and other items he sealed into evidence bags. Photographs were taken, forms signed and Tony released the car to the towing company.

"Let's swing over to the hospital and see if Connor is still alive. We need to get the Beverly cops to take formal custody while he's in the hospital."

"Don't think he's going anywhere in his current condition," Amero said.

"Rules, man; you know how it is.

"You rule, Tony. Nice job on this one."

But Tony was deep in thought and didn't answer as Amero drove towards Beverly Hospital.

12:16 AM, Day 5

Santinello looked in his rear view mirror to see the blinking red lights rapidly approaching. Instinctively, he pulled over to let the emergency vehicle pass, putting his finger in his ear to block out the wailing of the siren. As the ambulance sped by, he got a blurry view of a medic hanging an IV bag and another man leaning over the stretcher. *What? Wait! Maybe Connor is still alive. Maybe there's still a chance, Santinello* reached under the seat, found the blue strobe, which he leaned, out the window to put on the roof. Energized, Santinello took off after the ambulance.

12:18 AM, Day 5

Rocker kept his eyes closed as he listened to the medics talking over the intercom to the surgeon in the ER. His ribs hurt like hell, a little hard to take a deep breath, and his head pounded like someone was hitting his skull with an iron skillet. As he listened to their concern about possible spinal injury, he took an inventory of the pain: no numbness in either hand; fingers seemed to work; toes can wiggle; neck sore as hell but he realized he could still move his head ever so slightly against the air collar. *Maybe not as bad as they think?*

Chapter 38

11:56 PM, Day 4

It had taken nearly an hour for the pediatrician on call to get out of bed, drive into the hospital and finish his examination of the child. X-rays were all negative; cuts and scrapes all cleaned, one with a new Band-Aid; skin color healthy; color in her nails much improved from the IV drip. The child could be released to her parents and sent home to sleep. Just as he was signed the forms, the intercom to the ambulance burped with static and the in-coming notification of an imminent arrival of a car accident victim, possible spinal and neck injuries.

"How old?" the pediatrician asked over his shoulder to the attendant.

"Adult male," she answered; "you're good to go."

"My lucky night," he said. "Give the MacKenzey girl another few minutes of drip and send her home. I've dictated my notes for her own doctor, but if you need me, I'll be at home."

"Your lucky night, all right. I'm on till eight."

12:18 AM, Day 5

The piercing noise of the back-up beeper on the ambulance echoed under the cement overhang as the ambulance came to a full stop. The waiting technician yanked open the rear door and released the latch holding the gurney to the floor.

"Where do you want him?" the technician called over his shoulder as he backed into the

ER.

"Cubicle one is open; put him in there."

As Rocker was wheeled in behind the curtain, he caught a fleeting glimpse of the patient in the unit next to his. *Is that . . . ?*

"Mommy, can we go now? Please?"

The voice! The same? Yes, it definitely was! My lucky day, Rocker thought.

The nurse took his blood pressure and pulse, recorder their slight elevation, checked his IV and left to notify Radiology that they were about to have a visitor.

"Let me check with the nurse, sweetie," Laurie said as she pushed the curtain further aside. She came back quickly.

"OK, Carrie, but they want you to pee pee in this bottle before you go."

"Oh, Mommy: right here?" Carrie asked, embarrassment obvious in her voice.

"Yes, I'll close the curtain. You'll have privacy."

"I'm not going pee pee anywhere but the bathroom. I'll be right back," Carrie announced as she grabbed the bottle and went to find the bathroom.

Rocker over heard the exchange, made a snap decision and had already pulled his legs over the side of the gurney as Carrie marched past his cubicle. The pain behind his eyes made him dizzy, light headed as he reached to steady himself. He gained his balance as the little girl turned the corner down the hall. Peaking out of the edge of the curtain, he saw the nurses and technicians on the phone or otherwise occupied as he slipped out into the hall and down the corridor.

12:21 AM, Day 5

Tony approached the nurse's station. *Always the same,* he thought: *controlled mayhem, a*s he watched the understaffed overworked crew tend to too many patients and too many forms. He waited, checked his cell phone for messages, and was about to call into the station when Laurie MacKenzey poked her head out from the curtain.

“Laurie?” Tony asked, surprise in his voice. “Are you still here?”

“Hi Tony. Actually, we were just leaving. We had to wait for the pediatrician to come in from home, and, well, you know emergency rooms,” she added looking past Tony down the hall.

Tony saw her gaze and turned to look. “What?” he asked.

“They needed one more urine catch. As soon as Carrie gets back from the bathroom, we are out of here. That was nice of you to come to check on her.”

“Well, I didn’t expect to find you here. I came to check on Paul Connor; the ambulance brought him here a few minutes ago.”

They spoke for a few minutes before Laurie looked again at her watch. ““How long does it take to pee? I’ll be right back, “she said as she walked quickly down the hall.

Tony showed his badge to the admissions clerk and asked where Paul Connor was. He turned to walk towards the first cubicle just as a uniformed Beverly cop came through the outside door.

12:22 AM, Day 5

“If you are finished, I will take the bottle,” the male voice asked, knocking on the door.

Carrie unlocked the bathroom door and started to hand the bottle to the man when she looked up. Rocker pushed a towel over Carrie’s mouth and picked her up, wincing in pain as he held her against his ribs.

“Well, who have we here?” Rocker asked her. Carrie’s eyes were wide with terror; she struggled to free herself. Rocker answered his own question: “I’ll tell you what we’ve got here: your worst nightmare! That’s who, you little bitch.”

He carried her quickly to the stairwell, shutting the door quietly behind him. He ran down the stairs. Bursting through the door to the basement, he looked both ways, searching for an exit. The girl’s efforts to free herself were slowing him down. He winced in pain as her elbows kept thrashing into his ribs. He was too weak to hold her tightly but knew if he loosened his grip, she would cry out or escape.

The hallway was dark, lit only by an emergency bulb in the ceiling, and was littered with equipment, laundry carts, wheel chairs and old stretchers. Rocker had an idea. He kicked a stretcher against the wall as he threw Carrie onto it, lashing her down with two wide belts. He snapped the leather restraint cuffs around her wrists, found some tape in a supply cart, tore off a long strip and taped a double gauze pad over her mouth. Carrie started to cry. She was securely held in place, amazingly still holding her urine specimen.

Rocker frantically looked for more supplies and found a loaded linen cart just outside the laundry room, took what he needed, and wheeled the stretcher towards the elevator.

12:24 AM, Day 5

Laurie rounded the corner and knocked loudly on the bathroom door.

"Carrie? Carrie? Are you finished?"

No answer. She tried the door and pushed it open. No one. Now panicking, she pushed open the door to the handicap bathroom. No Carrie. No Carrie in the men's room either.

She ran back to the Emergency Room. "Tony," she yelled. "I can't find Carrie. She's not in the bathroom."

"Maybe she went further down the hall. Did you check?" Tony reached for the curtain to cubicle one and pulled it back. "Oh, shit," he said looking at the empty stretcher. "We may have a problem.

"Laurie, show me the bathroom, Tony commanded." Nurse! We may have an Amber Alert. Notify security and set up a lock-down right now. Sergeant: call your station; get every uniform you've got over here immediately. No one leaves this building period unless I personally give the OK. Got it?"

The cop was already talking into the mike on his collar as Tony ran down the hall, just steps behind Laurie MacKenzey.

12:26 AM, Day 5

Rocker had changed into green operating room scrubs, along with matching shoe-covers, cloth hair cap and mask. With the mask tied in place, only his eyes were visible, every- thing else covered, except for his limp. His breath was short, exertion and pain weakening him as he pushed the gurney into the elevator, then the button for the forth floor and surgery. As the elevator door closed, Carrie tilted her wrist just slightly and let some of the urine drip out of the bottle onto the floor. Rocker was too distracted to notice.

12:30 AM, Day 5

Once Tony and Laurie had checked every bathroom on the floor, they returned to the ER to find the sergeant issuing orders to the others who had arrived. All hospital doors were locked, an armed policeman on every exit with teams of two beginning to search every floor.

"He's not getting out of this building, Tony. The only problem is going to be locating him inside. We've got over 600 rooms and more than two miles of hallway. That's going to take some time."

"You're going to need more men. I'll call Gloucester. What about Salem and Danvers stations?"

"Already done," the sergeant said checking his watch. "Should be here within four minutes."

Tony turned to Laurie and held her by the shoulders. "We'll find her, Laurie. I promise. But you need to stay here. I can't be worrying about you and Carrie at the same time."

"I'm coming! She's my little girl," Laurie said through her sobs, trying to break free of Tony's grip.

"No, you're not, Laurie, if I have to tie you down, I will. You are staying right here.

That's final." Tony settled Laurie into a chair. "Nurse: this woman is not to leave this chair for anything short of a fire. Understand?"

Tony turned to the Beverly cop. "Sergeant: I'm going downstairs. Give me two men and the rest of you split up as you organized. Start with the stairs and elevators near the bathroom and spread out from there. Call me with anything. Anything! OK?"

Tony led the way. All three men had drawn their weapons by the time they entered the stairwell. “Which way, detective? Up or down?” the cop asked as he fanned his weapon in front of him.

“In his condition, down. I don’t think he has the strength to carry the girl and climb.”

Tony took the lead, taking the steps down two at a time. As he rounded the corner, he saw a towel on the floor. He picked it up, smelled it and threw it back down. “Smells fresh. No blood, fortunately.”

Just as they entered the basement hallway, a figure bent over a laundry cart emerged from a room down to the right.

“Halt! Police! Don’t move.”

The man froze. He put his hands over his head and started to pray out-loud.

“Who are?”? Tony lowered his gun. The man was black, obviously not Connor. “Have you seen a man down here with a little 6 year old girl?” Tony asked quickly.

“No, sah,” the man answered. “Seen no one but me.”

Tony’s eyes were adjusting to the darkness. He saw the carts and wheelchairs and noticed emptiness against the wall.

Tony asked: “What’s your name?”

“Buster,” the janitor replied, “but everyone calls me Bus.”

“Bus, it is. What all is down here?”

“Well, at this end are the laundry and all this storage in the hallway. Down the other end are the morgue, records room, and furnace room. Not much else. Most of the rooms just piled with boxes.”

“Any exits?”

“One emergency exit down there,” Buster said nodding with his chin, “but it has an alarm on it that ‘old wake my mother from her grave, God bless her. Oh, and the elevator.”

"Are these rooms interconnected?" Tony asked.

"No, sah. Keep most of them locked. Don't want no spirit tappin' on my shoulder when I ain't 'spectin' it. No sir-eee."

"OK, Bus, you come with me then. We're going to start at this end and search every room." Tony spoke to the patrolmen: "You two watch this hall. Stop anyone who moves." He turned towards Boster. "What was in this space, Bus?"

"Had an old stretcher there. Been known to rest my old bones on there, time to time. How 'd it get moved?"

With the two cops guarding the hallway, the search of the basement went quickly. When they reached the other end of the corridor, Tony stopped in front of the elevator and, by chance, saw the small puddle on the floor.

"Been cleaning down here, Bus?"

"No sah, my job's in the laundry."

Tony bent to look at the liquid and smelled urine. "When was the last time you saw the stretched, Bus?"

"Don't rightly remember. It was there when I got to the laundry this morning 'cuz I put my pillow on there. You know, just in case."

"Where's this elevator go to? Every floor?"

"No, sah. It goes to surgery and the patients' floors: four to six. Mostly we use it for laundry."

"Eddie, you stay here. Make sure no one comes down the stairs or this elevator. They do, call on your mike. NO ONE goes out that emergency door," Tony instructed. "Mac, you and me are taking the elevator. Let's move."

12:31 AM, Day 5

Rocker hugged the wall as the elevator door opened. He stuck his head out, saw nothing but a solitary night nurse at the station, and wheeled the stretcher out. As the stretcher turned, Carrie tilted her wrist once again. He pulled the mask higher and pushed the stretcher towards the nurse and the elevator bank at the other end of the corridor. He grabbed a patient's chart from a stretched waiting by the elevator. He had almost cleared the nurse's station when the woman looked up and asked: "Who've you got?"

Rocker thought quickly. "Emergency surgery. Where do you want her?" he asked.

Just then the phone rang. The nurse said: "Wait right there while I get this." She turned to the phone: "Surgery." When she turned back, the man was gone. Something didn't make sense. Why was the patient's head covered? She checked the chart on the foot of the stretcher. Blockage of the colon. Surgery pending as soon as the doctor arrived.

Damn orderly, the nurse thought. Leaving someone this sick unattended. As she put the chart back, the doors to the Surgical Suite swung opened and two attendants came for the stretcher. Carrie turned her wrist again as she was wheeled into the first operating room.

Running to the stairway, Rocker held his ribs, trying to catch his breath. *Need to find me some drugs for this pain before I get out of here.*

12:35 AM, Day 5

Santinello heard the all-hands call over his own scanner as he was pulling into the hospital. *Perfect cover, he thought. Now I just have to find Connor before anyone else.*

Joining the crowd of police uniforms at the entrance to the ER, Santinello grabbed the sleeve of the man in front of him.

"What's the drill? I just got here."

"They think that guy in the accident down on the bridge has kidnapped a little girl who was here and is hiding in the hospital somewhere. We're breaking into teams to search each floor."

"Thanks," Santinello said, as he pushed through the crowd to get inside. Once clear of the throng, he saw a stairway sign and raced for the door.

12:35 AM, Day 5

Tony came out of the elevator just as the nurse got off the phone. "See anyone in the last few minutes?" he asked as he rushed up to her.

"No. Wait; there was an orderly here just before the phone rang. He left a surgical emergency here and left," she answered.

"What did he look like?" Tony demanded, looking both ways down the hall.

"Couldn't really say. He was dressed in scrubs and mask. Never saw his face. Walked with a limp, though. I could see that."

"Where did he go?"

"The nurse shrugged. "He was gone when I got off the phone."

Tony instructed the policeman with him to call for reinforcements. "We're doing every room on this hall, every closet, every bathroom. Start at the far end down there. Nurse, where is the patient?"

"Surgery. Bowel blockage. Probably being prepped as we speak."

12:36 AM, Day 5

Santinello was on the third flight of stairs, his thighs burning, his breath coming in hard gasps. Pure adrenalin was driving him, desperate to find Connor and one more chance at the money.

In full stride, Rocker crashed directly into the cop running up the same stairs he was taking down. Both men fell, Rocker on his bad side, Santinello directly underneath. The cop had dropped his gun in the collision and was fighting for breath as he struggled to free himself. Rocker's mask had been pulled down as he fell. In the very brief second when both men recovered enough to see who the other was, time froze. Neither moved as the realization hit each man. It was then a question of whose desperation was going to prevail: Rocker's to escape or Santinello's to get money for his daughter.

Rocker recovered an instant before Santinello, grabbed the gun off the stair and slammed it down on the side of the cop's head. Santinello crumbled to the floor, blood oozing out of his ear. Rocker moved quickly; he wanted that uniform before it got bloody and before the man revived. He had found his perfect disguise. Minutes later, Rocker finished putting on the uniform. His head was pounding. He pulled the cap lower over his forehead as he mounted the stairs back to the fourth floor.

Rocker entered the corridor just as Fiori came out of the room nearest the nurse's station.

Rocker yelled: "I've got this end. Start at the other and we'll meet at the station. This stairway's covered. Hurry!"

Surprised at seeing another policeman, but glad for early reinforcements, Tony turned to comply with the instructions, then stopped dead in his tracks. The policeman was limping and the uniform was too tight. He dropped to the floor just as a bullet went where his head had been seconds earlier. As Tony rolled to free his gun hand, another shot rang out and plaster and shards of glass from the fire alarm fell on him. Raising his own gun, Tony's finger tightened on the trigger. But Rocker had already disappeared around the corner.

CHAPTER 39

12:40 AM, Day 5

With his good arm, Rocker pushed the bed against the door and tried to open the window.

It was locked. Grabbing a bedpan, he broke through the glass just as he heard the door opening and the bed casters squealing on the linoleum floor. Rocker used the bedpan to clear the glass shards away from the window frame then threw it at the figure coming through the door.

The throw went wide, missing Tony who had rolled in on his side, his weapon sweeping the room in front of him scanning for his target as he come up kneeling behind the bed.

The patrolman behind him sent a bullet into the window frame inches over Connor's head.

"Make another move and it's your last, Connor. Just give me an excuse to pull this trigger. Any excuse at all."

Connor hesitated, looked at the distance between the window and the fire escape next door, decided against a jump, and put his weapon on the windowsill. He pulled himself back through the window and as his foot hit the floor, the two men tackled him, Tony sweeping the gun from the sill onto the floor away from Connor as the patrolman put the plastic ties around Connor's wrists behind his back. Connor winced in pain as his arms were drawn up high towards his shoulder blades.

With Connor under control, the patrolman called in on his radio as Tony raced from the room. As he was approaching the nurse's station, he ran by the door to the OR, smelled urine, saw the puddle on the floor, realized what it might mean then burst through the doors clearly marked 'No Admission'.

He was challenged immediately by a scrub nurse coming out of the OR suite: "Get out of here," he called out: "This is a sterile area; you're not allowed."

"Where did the stretcher go?" Tony demanded. "The one with the little girl," he added flashing his detective's badge.

"In there," the nurse said nodding to the door behind him. "But don't even think about going in there. She's under anesthesia. Doctor is prepping her as we speak."

Tony pushed past the man and kicked open the swinging door to the OR and raised his gun.

"Don't anyone move!" he yelled.

The surgical team froze. The anesthesiologist took his hands off the dials, as the surgeon looked up, scalpel in mid air moving down towards the draped abdomen of the patient in front of him.

"What the hell?" demanded the doctor? "What the f . . . ."

Tony cut in. "Wrong patient. Charts were switched. That little girl is perfectly healthy.

Now stand back and get the goddamn anesthesia off of her. NOW?" he yelled again, thrusting his badge towards the group.

"Oh, my God," the surgeon said quickly looking from Tony to the girl to the anesthesiologist. "How the . . . Oh, my God. Bring her out," he instructed, laying the scalpel down on the tray and looking at his hands as if they belonged to someone else. "I almost . . . Oh, my God."

Realizing the team was responding to his command, Tony exhaled, put his gun away and leaned against the wall, rubbing his eyes and shaking is head in disbelief at how close they had come to removing a perfectly healthy bowel from a perfectly healthy child.

"Detective, you still are going to have to leave this room. Wait out in the hall and we will notify you when she is awake. Shouldn't be more than twenty minutes. Nurse, show him to the waiting room, please, while we clean up here."

1:12 AM, Day 5

Less than twenty minutes later, a pale but awake six-year old was wheeled out of recovery and into the arms of her mother, who kept sobbing: "Oh, my baby" as she rocked her daughter in her arms.

"Where is that bad man, mommy? I don't want him to hurt me ever again."

"Oh Carrie, he won't bother you ever. I promise," Laurie said through her tears. "I promise."

Tony tussled Carrie's hair. "Don't worry, sweetheart. We have him locked up good and tight this time."

"You better," Carrie stated.

Tony smiled. "You were pretty clever to drip us a trail to follow."

"I learned that from Mr. Pinto. He said he broke some branches so he could find me in the woods again."

"That reminds me. I'll be right back. I have one more thing to look into."

1:16 AM, Day 5

Tony found Santinello having his head bandaged out at the nurse's station.

"OK, Rick; you and I have some things to go over."

Santinello nodded and hung his head. "I know," he whispered. "I know."

And for the next ten minutes, Santinello spilled his guts, after which, Tony said, "Give me your badge and weapon, Rick. The chief is going to have to deal with this."

As Santinello handed over the things Tony demanded, he looked up. "How did you know?"

"The smell, Rick," Tony answered.

"Smell?"

"In your patrol car outside of Lumper's. Same fish smell as the bags of money in Connor's car."

Santinello shook his head. "Stupid, Tony. I was really stupid."

It was over. Four days. A little girl returned, reunited, rejoined in one sense, forever separated in another, missing some piece of her innocence and a larger piece of her trust, the realization of which not evident until . . . who knows? When she goes hiking in the woods? When she marries and her husband wants a child? When her own child wants to go camping? Perhaps a psychologist might know. Four days. Even longer four nights. Who would know?

Naomi might. She rang the doorbell and waited. She heard a little patter of bare feet running across the bare floor, watched the brass knob turn, then saw a smile that went from one ear to another.

"Naomi!" Carrie screamed, jumping up and down, clapping her little hands together and fumbling for the handle of the screen door.

"I brought you a little present," Naomi said, bending down to hug the little girl who had buried her face against Naomi's cheek, her arms around the woman's neck. At the news of a present, Carrie pushed away and started to clap her hands again.

"You brought me a present?" The smile was now bigger, the eyes wider in anticipation. She was bouncing up and down on her toes.

"Yes. Remember in the car you told me about your friend Mr. Chipmunk?"

"I spoke to Mr. Chipmunk a lot."

"Remember when?" Naomi asked, prodding the little girl. Carrie cocked her head to the side, hands on her hips.

"Sure, when I was lonely and scared and needed someone to be with. Mr. Chipmunk was my friend."

"Exactly. That's why I thought you might like this."

Naomi looked back as she walked part way down the front walk. Carrie was sitting on the porch in animated conversation with her new present, a stuffed chipmunk.